SCREAMING
WITH THE CANNIBALS

Vandalia Press publishes fiction and non-fiction of interest to the general reader concerning Appalachia and, more specifically, West Virginia. See our website at vandaliapress.com to learn of forthcoming titles.

SCREAMING
WITH THE CANNIBALS

by Lee Maynard

Vandalia Press

Morgantown 2003

Vandalia Press, Morgantown 26506
© 2003 by West Virginia University Press

Printed in the United States of America

10 09 08 07 06 05 04 03   10 9 8 7 6 5 4 3 2 1

ISBN 0-937058-81-5

Library of Congress Cataloging-in-Publication Data

Maynard, Lee 1936 -
    Screaming with the Cannibals/Lee Maynard
    000 p. 23 cm.

Library of Congress Control Number: 2003107277

Vandalia Press is an imprint of West Virginia University Press

Book design by Alcorn Publication Design
Printed in USA

To Helen
To Helen
To Helen

I can not say this often enough.

With most sincere thanks to
The National Endowment for the Arts
for support that made this novel possible

If you don't know where you are going,
any road will take you there.

M. N. Chatterjee

CONTENTS

FOREWORD

Crum, West Virginia
I used to live there.
But this is not about Crum, West Virginia.

The miserable little town sat on a flat valley floor at the edge of the Tug River, just upstream from the foot of Bull Mountain. No one I ever knew could tell me why the town was there, why it existed, why anyone would ever want to live there. For me, it was just another one of those places I had to get out of. Like Black Hawk Ridge and Turkey Creek.

The morning I left Crum there was no celebration. Maybe there would be when some of those kids knew I was gone. A celebration, I mean. But there sure as hell was nothing for me to celebrate.

I stood by the side of the road watching a small kid on a bicycle ride in circles on the pitted blacktop just across from me. He had been my best friend. Maybe still was. He just kept riding, around and around, and I think I saw tears making shiny lines down his sunken cheeks, but I'll never know for sure. His skinny legs just kept going up and down, driving the old bicycle endlessly around.

He was waiting to see if I would get a ride out of town, waiting to see the last of me. And he did.

I didn't even stick my thumb out, but an old '41 four-door Chevrolet stopped and I threw my cardboard suitcase into the back and climbed into the front and the thing started rolling down the twisting two-lane highway before my ass was even planted on the seat. Even so, the kid on the bicycle was gone. He rode away before the car door slammed and echoed across the river, bouncing off the hills of Kentucky. The sound died in the distance and my view of the kid died and I knew I died in his heart when the car door slammed, even if he wasn't there. He heard the door slam. The kid was rid of me.

But I would never be rid of him. I remember running with him through high fields of sugar cane down by the river and swinging on brittle vines tangled in the tops of trees and scrounging for black walnuts through the pungent, leaf-covered duff of the forest floor. I remembered him watching in awe as a small, just-right charge of dynamite sent the constable's outhouse into the sky. I remembered all that. And I always would. He was my friend, once, maybe the only friend in all my life I've ever really had.

I never saw him again.

But Crum served its purpose.

It was where I would learn there are worse places than Black Hawk Ridge, where I was born. Crum was where I would learn, real and true, that wherever I had been all my life, no matter where, I didn't belong there. And I had only been in West Virginia.

I belonged in some place far and away in the mists of distance and time, some place so high and bright and thin that I would have trouble just breathing the air . . . some place I had never seen, and could not name.

Where I would learn, perhaps, that I belonged no place, no place at all.

Crum will always be there. What happened there, what I did there, what I learned there — all of that is stuck in my head forever, a clutter of fading images piled high and dark against the back of my mind, teetering there, ready to topple at the slightest prod, or at the slightest intrusion of light.

I've already told you all that.

But what I've never told you is this . . .

Crum is everywhere.

There's a Crum buried deep inside most of us, pressed hard beneath some vital memory, burning quietly, waiting for the time it will leap before your eyes and show you, in one blinding flash, what you really are, where you really come from. It may be different for each of us, a place so painful, so vacuous, so truthful, so confining, so dark, so abrasive, so forming — so goddamn *forming* — there is only one thing you can think of to do.

Run.

PART I

West Virginia

Black Hawk Ridge

≈ One ≈

The night that lightning struck my great uncle, Long Neck Jesse, he had just come out of the hardwoods up on the high end of Black Hawk Ridge. He had taken the shortcut back to his cabin, down through the sodden graveyard, sloshing along through the blackness of the storm, the rain running in a hard stream from the brim of his floppy hat. He must have been picking his way carefully among the gravestones and the leaning wooden crosses, right next to the old slab-sided Baptist church. He was carrying a potato sack over his shoulder with fifteen quart jars of raw moonshine in it.

They tell me you could hear the explosion for miles.

Bits and pieces of tombstones, wooden fence parts and shards of Mason jars slammed into the church and sliced through the thick woods. The blast scorched the weeds and the early summer grass and ripped a gaping hole through the side of the church. They found a jagged piece of headstone with one word on it stabbed through the end of the pump organ. It said ". . . POSSUM"

But they never found Long Neck. Not a drop of blood, not a speck of flesh. They found one of his shoes, the leather burned and twisted, the thin rubber sole melted and bubbled. And a belt buckle. And a pocket knife. And that's all.

I got back to Black Hawk Ridge late the next day, mud sucking at my shoes as I walked the old rutted wagon road that twisted up from the holler, then through the trees and past the church. I had just come from Crum, down and away across the back end of the county, where I had been living with some cousins and going to Crum High School. I had graduated and hitchhiked out of town before the ink dried on my diploma. I left the diploma in Crum.

I had only come back to Black Hawk Ridge to say goodbye to Uncle Long Neck. And then I would be gone again.

I didn't know about the explosion.

It was still raining. Some of the Black Hawk men were standing in the graveyard, motionless, their hands stuffed into the pockets of their heavy, wet overalls, silent sentinels over the dead buried at their feet. When they saw me coming they looked away, or looked down, or looked anywhere except straight at me. And I knew something bad had happened.

My cousin Dorcas was standing there. "Howdy, Jesse," he said. "Saw you a-comin'. You ever git that rifle fixed?"

I had been gone three years. I had not set foot on the ridge in all that time, had not thought of the old rifle with the broken firing pin, not even once. But for Dorcas, it was only yesterday. Time, on Black Hawk Ridge, was a relative thing. And the son-of-a-bitch never said a word about Long Neck.

We all stood around in the graveyard in the misting rain, looking at the blasted earth and the hole in the side of the church. The breeze and the rain couldn't erase the smell of something scorched, something blackened, something hell-burned and vaporized there in the middle of the ridge against the close and hard side of the old Baptist church.

There had been some sort of explosion. I wondered, where was Uncle Long Neck? If any man up here on the ridge would know about explosions, it would be Uncle Long Neck.

And that is when I realized, without anyone telling me, that Uncle Long Neck *was* the explosion.

I had come back to Black Hawk Ridge from Crum to say goodbye to him one last time. And I missed it.

Long Neck Jesse was six-feet-four, as thin as a fence rail. When he walked, the various parts of his lanky body moved like links in a chain, each link jiggling and shaking, but connected to all the other links and eventually settling down to where they wanted to go. His shirt sleeves were always too short; his wrists and hands jangled out inches beyond the frayed cuffs. He had eyes the color of the sky at dusk and his voice rumbled up from his stomach like the sounds of a gathering storm, his Adam's apple bobbing high above his shirt collar.

I loved him. I could watch him for hours, be with him constantly. I was just a lump of a kid, barely out of the one-room school down on Turkey Creek, tagging around after the men, trying to find out what everything was all about, looking for lessons, waiting for words. I hung around Uncle Long Neck as much as I could, and what he taught will always be inside me. He was one of those men who could teach by doing. He could set examples just by living, just by going about his daily business, his big head bobbing at the end of his skinny neck, long-fingered hands stuffed into the side pockets of his faded overalls. The only clothing I ever saw him wear that was too big were those overalls. I never knew where he got them, those long yards of flapping denim with the brass buckles on the end of the straps that were always slipping off his shoulders. When he walked through patches of sunlight with the breeze behind him the overalls would billow out in the front and Uncle Long Neck would become a faded blue ship, gently setting its sails on a course to the moonshine still. The legs of the overalls were too long, even for him. But he never cut the legs off or had one of the women hem them up. When he got the overalls new he just wore them, the cuffs dragging on the ground until they simply wore off at exactly the right length.

I loved Uncle Long Neck like, maybe, no other man.

He made the best moonshine in three counties.

I only wish I had been there when the lightning struck.

❧ Two ❧

Jesse.

That's what they named me, those folks up there where I was born, on Black Hawk Ridge, at the head of Turkey Creek, in Wayne County, West Virginia; those folks who had lived on those ridges and in those hollers and on those creeks since just after the Revolutionary War, some of whom left that country only to fight in wars they didn't start and didn't understand and then came home to fight wars they *did* start, tight little wars of their very own. Others had never been out of the county, never been off the ridge, never knew where Turkey Creek came out or where it went when it did and would never go looking for the end of it.

But I would.

If you go far enough into any piece of woods, you come out the other side; eventually, there has to be an end to it. But not Turkey Creek. They used to say Turkey Creek was so far back into the mountains that there *was* no other side, that things just ended there, stopped, died. They said that Turkey Creek began as a trickle of sweet water coming out of a tiny spring at the foot of dark trees at the edge of the world and as long as it ran our people would be *there* and way down there in some other county where the creek ended up was no good place for any of us. We knew where we belonged.

And Black Hawk Ridge was farther back than Turkey Creek.

If you hiked a mile or so toward the far end of Black Hawk you could find the ridge's highest point. The holler below the ridge widened, gradually unfolding into a lush, shaded valley that stretched down and away, only to be lost again among the tangle of other hollers, other ridges that rolled far and forever across the Appalachians, a hopeless tangle of changing heights, dim shapes, knurled wood and broken stone that might have been dropped by God on a bad day during the creation of the world.

At the side of the high point a shelf of rock jutted out over the valley, one of the few places on the ridge where the view was not cut off by the thick stands of hardwood trees. The view went out in all directions, the heavy green ridges rolling up through the thin mists of the valleys and standing in the twisted formations of thousands of years, all the ridges exactly like the one I stood on. And all the ridges different.

On good days when I stood on the weathered rock I could see the bright green patches where the men of the ridge had cleared small hard fields to grow hay for the plow horses or corn to be stored in the cribs and fed, hard and dry, to the pigs that rooted continuously against the sides of hills. Now and then dancing plumes of smoke rose from the trees and twisted away across the valley, smoke that came from stone chimneys leaning against the sides of cabins and small clapboard houses. Our houses. Our smoke. Everything on the ridge was ours. We were all a family there, one way or another.

But even then, even on Black Hawk Ridge, I knew there was something beyond those ridges, something that waited out there, something that pulled me. Somewhere, the ridges stopped. I was sure.

Just below the weathered rock is where Long Neck hid his moonshine still. I used to follow him up there, high on the ridge, hiding in the bushes and peeking through the dense thickets, all the time trying to find out what Long Neck did there. I always hid in the same spot, watching silently. He always knew I was there. He never chased me away, but he never let me come near the moonshine still. The still was his, only his, and I never got near it. Not really.

He would sit and tend his still and read the tattered books that he always seemed to produce from the deep pockets of his overalls. And then one day I found one of the books in my hiding place, lying there on a small stump. I turned the book over in my hands, trying to figure out what Uncle Long Neck wanted, then realizing that all he wanted was for me to *read* the damn thing.

And for all the months of all the years when it was warm enough for me to hide out near the moonshine still, there were books. It would have looked strange, if anyone had known or seen, if anyone had ever found us, just sitting there, apart and yet together, the big man never acknowledging that I was there, me "hidden" in the brush nearby, both of us just sitting and reading. It would have looked strange, and they wouldn't have liked it, seeing us that way. The men weren't supposed to take the young'ens to the stills. So Uncle Long Neck would never let me near the coils and the vats and the fires, but he wouldn't chase me away from my hiding place. It was a good trade.

But no one ever saw us. No one ever knew.

Jesse.

They named me after Long Neck, they said. But that was no big honor, Long Neck said. They named a lot of people Jesse, both boys and girls. It was a name they liked, a name that went back into the far layers of the family, a name they strewed about as easily as they would dribble corn into the rows at planting time. They liked the name Jesse . . . and Amos and James and Mary and Minnie. And I had cousins named Elijah, Hester, Garfield, and Inis. And Dorcas.

But there were a *lot* of Jesses. To tell us apart, they gave most of us nicknames. Great Uncle Jesse was "Long Neck". My cousin Jesse, five-feet-five and two hundred fifty pounds, was "Stumpy". We even had "Black" Jesse — nobody would ever say how he got that name. And "Barkin'" Jesse, the best squirrel hunter on the ridge. Barkin' Jesse liked to tan squirrel hides and sell them, so he didn't like any holes in them. He would only hunt with his .22 rifle, and he wouldn't actually shoot the squirrel. He would shot the tree limb, just beneath the squirrel's head as it clung, frozen at the sight of him, to the tree. The concussion of the bullet and the explosion of tree bark up into the squirrel would usually knock it unconscious. "Barkin' a squirrel," they called it. Barkin' Jesse would just pick it up and knock its head against a rock.

And then there was "Hangin'" Jesse, a justice of the peace somewhere down in the lower end of the county. I don't think he ever actually hanged anybody. But then, in Wayne County, you never really knew for sure.

On the women's side there was "Red" Jesse, because of her hair; "Caner" Jesse, a stern and unforgiving woman who could lay a stick across your back so fast you wouldn't know it was coming until you hit the ground, the welts rising against your shirt. And there was my third cousin, "Slick" Jesse, who could suck the rust off a railroad spike. Slick Jesse, so the men said, would fuck any-body, anytime, and they called her "Slick" because that's the way the insides of her legs got when she was in the mood. Which was most of the time. So the men said. Of course, no one called her "Slick" to her face. Wouldn't have been polite.

It was Slick Jesse who first taught me what was up a woman's skirt, and how to get there.

We were sitting in the open door of the hayloft in Long Neck's barn, our feet dangling out into the near darkness, gently swinging over the ground below. All I had on was my overalls — not even a shirt — the ragged legs barely coming down to my ankles, the hot blue air feeling good against my skin. I watched her bare feet swinging next to mine, her full skirt shifting slightly. The skirt was old, worn often, and the thin material rounded out with the fullness of her legs. We had watched the sun go down behind the ridge and then the rise of an early moon, something we had never done before, something I didn't even know she liked to do. We were not touching, at least not at that time.

"Where does Long Neck keep his still?" She was some years older than me, and her voice was husky. I had never thought about taking anyone to Long Neck's still. I had never thought about women with husky voices.

"I never been there," I muttered. I told myself that that was true — I had never actually been to the still, only to the bushes just out to the side of it.

"I want to go to Long Neck's still. I ain't never seen a still."

"I can't take you. I never been there."

"Liar." She said it flatly, a statement of fact.

"I can't. I just can't. Long Neck would . . ."

And then she had her hand inside my pants. In a single swift motion she had unfastened the big brass button at the side of my overalls and slid her arm in all the way to her elbow. And like most of the kids on Black Hawk Ridge, I never wore any undershorts. She grabbed my dick.

I was so surprised I didn't know what to do. I just fell over backwards and lay flat on the hayloft floor, my legs still dangling outside. Please, God, I said to myself, don't let her take her hand away.

7

"I'll pay you. In advance." Her hand moved slightly.

"Huh . . . how . . . how . . ." It was the only word I could push out of my mouth.

"Well, it'll be better than you jist hidin' behind the barn, jackin' off," she said softly. Her hand moved again.

And then she had both hands up on my overall straps. She unfastened them and whipped my overalls down past my hips in one smooth motion, just like stripping the skin down off the ass-end of a dead rabbit. She snapped the overalls over my feet and flung them out into the night.

I don't remember moving. I just watched her rise above me and raise her skirt, her long legs glowing in the fresh moonlight. As the skirt got higher I could see the dark triangle at the top of her legs, and then her navel, and then I realized she wasn't going to stop. She peeled the dress over her head, sat on me, and drove me into her.

My legs were dangling out of the hayloft door and I couldn't brace my feet against anything so I could push up into her. But I didn't have to. She did it all.

Each time she drove against me my body slid just a little more through the open door until my hips were scraping over the edge, suspended above nothing but warm night air. Her ass was out there, too, stuck solidly to mine, and I thought about someone standing down there in the barnyard looking up at us, seeing one set of dangling legs and two asses sucking together, suspended in the near darkness. If one of my relatives were down there, I thought, they'd just stand there and wait to see what hit the ground first.

I tried to mutter something about falling out the door but every time I opened my mouth she leaned forward and put a breast in it. I spread my arms out wide, hoping to find something to grab, something to stop my slide. But there was nothing. My God, I thought, she's going to fuck us right out the hayloft door, right out into the night, right down into the barnyard. They'll find both of us there in the morning, stuck tight together, fucking dead.

And then the world turned blue and the moonlight turned liquid and somewhere in my mind some little lights went off against the back of my closed eyes and she was lying completely forward on me, her weight pinning me to the floor, holding me.

"Cousin Jesse," I whispered, "if you get up, I'm going to slide out the door. I'll probably die, down there in the cow shit, naked."

"If you don't promise to take me to the still, I am for sure going to get up, and right *now*. And you will look very bad, laying in your coffin, covered with cow shit." She shifted her weight and I slid a little more through the door.

"Goddamn, Jesse. Okay. I'll take you. Only don't move no more, okay?"

"I've got to move. At least just a little."

And she did. Moving and moving and moving.

Then she slid forward on me, raising herself so that I could pull my ass and legs back through the hayloft door. I rolled her over on her back.

I knew I wasn't going to fall out of the barn and die. Even so, it would have been worth it.

"And one more thing," she whispered. "When we're alone, you can call me Slick."

Later, we went out to the moonshine still. We didn't take our clothes.

We went out to the still a lot of times after that. I don't think Long Neck ever knew. But I'm not really sure.

Jesse.

I was the only one who was just plain Jesse. Nothing else. I was big for my age, strong from setting fence posts, blond hair tangling in the blackberry briars that grew at the edge of the fields. But I really just looked like a lot of the others in my family, nothing special, nothing odd. I had all my arms and legs and my eyes were in the right place and far apart and looked straight ahead when I wanted them to. So before they could figure out what to call me, before they could figure out what I would really be like — before they could decide much of anything about me — they sent me off to Crum to go to high school.

Going to Crum for education. Sort of like going into a coal mine to study daylight.

❧ Three ❧

Great Uncle Long Neck had gone up in a ball of fire in the cemetery and they wouldn't let me try to find any pieces of him. They told me to stay out of the graveyard but I sneaked out there in the middle of the night with a kerosene lantern that sputtered in the misting rain. I crawled through the mud around the fallen gravestones and the old wooden crosses trying to find Long Neck. Or some part of him. Or something left over. I crawled over the graves of relatives I had never known, men and women and little kids from other times on Black Hawk Ridge. My arms sank to the elbows in the softer parts of the graves and one of the heavy stones fell over right in front of me as I grubbed through the melted earth for pieces of Long Neck. The falling stone shot dark mud into my face and I had to sit for a while, my face turned to the black sky, letting the rain softly wash away the mud. I wanted something to keep, something of my own that was a part of Long Neck, something I could hold in my hand and feel in my pocket, something that would carry me back to when he read books to me in the fading light of late Sunday evenings and pointed out deer tracks in the light snows of early winter. Only there wasn't anything.

I wanted his pocket knife, or even the old belt buckle, but they were gone, buried by the Black Hawk men in some sopping hole at the far end of the graveyard. Unmarked. When God strikes a man dead, they said, it must be punishment for something he done terrible bad. They weren't going to make the pocket knife and belt buckle an easy target for another lightning strike.

And in a single night, the entire moonshine still disappeared.

Most of the summer was gone and Long Neck was gone and I knew it was time for me to go, too. They all knew it and I knew it. I had to go somewhere and learn more than I could by hanging around on Black Hawk Ridge, especially now that

Long Neck was gone. It was okay with them. They were sure that one day I would come back to Turkey Creek and climb the hill and work the rocky, thin-soiled ridge-top farm and cut the scrub trees to sell for mine timbers and try to keep the rambling rose chopped back from the side of the unpainted slab-sided house that I would build somewhere a little farther down in the holler out of the howl of the wind, a house maybe with its own kerosene-fired electric generator that would power the washing machine sitting out on a front porch made of rough planks with no paint on them.

Or so they all thought. And I never told them any differently. Long Neck was gone and it didn't make any difference what anyone else thought.

Long Neck was gone. I felt older, sadder. Felt like high school things and broken rifles and reading by the side of a moonshine still and grubbing through graveyard mud soaked in the heat of souls long gone and long forgotten . . . all those things were gone from me. I had changed.

So I got the hell out of there. One morning, I just walked away, back down the wagon road that twisted under the branches of the hickory trees and crossed the tiny mountain rivulets that fed into Turkey Creek. I was doing the thing I did best. I was leaving.

I got out of the far mountains and the twisted ridges that rolled away in all directions with their heads just above the mists that packed the hollers in the early mornings. I got out of the rutted graveyard and the busted Baptist church and the corn field where the corn never grew more than four feet high and off Black Hawk Ridge and down through the long and darkened holler that cupped Turkey Creek in the lower reaches of the ancient earth and I kept going until I came to dark country I had never seen before and people who looked like family but I knew were strangers and then I kept going some more down along the creek to where it fed into Twelve Pole Creek that ran past Doane and Wilsondale. I went off away from the creek and high onto some far ridges, across the hunched shoulders of Bull Mountain and off the other side and down among the thick weed growth until I slid over a sandy bank and there was the river, shallow, thick and brown, moving sluggishly in the heat beneath the glistening flight of dragonflies through a wilted, lacy overhang of willows.

I turned upstream and followed the bank as far as I could, walking slowly but steadily through rotting river-bottom cane fields and stands of tangled branches that hung out over the river, trying to reach the water. Finally, I moved away from the river, climbing up the soft banks and moving onto small fields until I came up to the railroad tracks and followed them until I came to some small town that I didn't know was there, and didn't really want to see.

I kept my head down and walked through the town as fast as I could.

It was the summer of 1954. I had graduated from Crum High School. I had been back to Black Hawk Ridge to pay my last respects. I had a cardboard suitcase with a few worn clothes in it, a sheath knife, a tattered copy of *The Mysterious Island* and thirteen dollars and thirty-seven cents.

And I had places to go.

Four

I don't know why he stopped and picked me up, that driver. He surely didn't seem happy about it. He was a lean and narrow sharp-faced man who didn't say a word for fifteen minutes after I got into the car. He stared straight before him through a cracked windshield as we rolled steadily beside the Tug River, the car's engine making little noises that I had never heard from a car before. The old Ford pulled hard to the left and the driver held tight to the steering wheel, the car constantly trying to run across and off the other side of the road, and I thought that maybe the tires on the front were different sizes. Uncle Long Neck would do that, would put any tires on his old truck that would fit the rims. He would let me drive the truck along the rutted, rocky dirt road that ran beside Turkey Creek. The hub-deep ruts would grab the wheels, twisting the ancient truck until the frame groaned, the truck a rusting mechanical beast under torture. Every time we were together in the truck on that road he would say, See, boy, you don't need for them tires to match. Makes no never mind on this road, and hit's the best dirt road in the county. And, besides, we ain't really goin' nowheres anyway.

But I *was* going somewhere. I didn't know where, but it really didn't matter.

A few miles later we clunked through Steptown, and somewhere between there and Kermit we crossed the Wayne County line into Mingo, only there was no sign along the side of the road and I didn't know exactly when we left the only county I knew anything about.

"Glad to be out of there." Trying to sound grown up, experienced.

"Out'a where?" he mumbled.

"Out'a Wayne County."

He glanced at me, his eyes flicking over my whole body. "I'd a heap rather be in Wayne County than in Logan County, boy. Got no niggers in Wayne County. I seed two or three of 'em in Logan just last month. Come in to take minin' jobs, I guess.

Taking them jobs away from honest white folks." He didn't say it with any feeling. He just said it, flatly, as a fact.

"Well, that don't bother me."

"It don't? You ever been up close to a nigger, boy?"

Nineteen-forty-six. I was 10-years-old, standing on the front porch of the general store in Dunlow, down out of Turkey Creek and across the wooden bridge that rumbled like thunder when Long Neck's old truck pounded across its timbers. I was listening to the old men talk about the war, talk about their sons in the war, as they leaned back in their chairs, chewed tobacco and waited in the stillness and the thick, damp summer heat for something, anything, to happen. Across the road Twelve Pole Creek hardly moved, dragonflies hanging suspended above the warm green water.

Now and then Long Neck would look my way to see what I was doing, but he never said anything. I think he was just satisfied that I would stand there, leaning against a post, picking out the good parts from what the old men were saying. Gathering words, Long Neck would say.

I heard it coming before I saw it. The faint rumbling grew in the distance, away and down the old, pitted two-lane highway, around a far heat-shimmered curve and out of sight. It wasn't much of a rumbling, but it was enough to stop the talk on the front porch of the general store. And to me it sounded like music.

I know now that it was a Harley, but I didn't know it then. All I knew then was that it was a glory machine, a freedom machine, a *motorcycle*. That much I was sure of. And when it swung around the curve and leaned into sight I knew that it was the most wonderful thing I had ever seen, or ever would see. I prayed silently for the bike to stop at the general store.

The Harley slowed, drew even with the general store, and then curved in to a graceful stop at the steps. My prayer had been answered and I was sure then that God liked motorcycles. The rider shut off the engine, put the sidestand down and then let a gloved hand rest on the handlebars for a moment before stepping off the machine. His movements were careful, calculated. He was not in a hurry.

He wore a leather helmet and aviator goggles, the kind with a little fringe of fur around the edges. His leather jacket was old and worn, but treated well, and had little things like bird wings sewn on the front, just below his left shoulder.

As he turned to check the bike, a long, white scarf floated along his back, reaching from his neck almost to his belt. His helmet, jacket and gloves were brown, and it was a moment or two before I realized that so was he. He took the helmet off and then stared calmly at the old men on the porch. They were stunned.

"My Gawd," one of them mumbled, "it's a Nigrah . . ."

A motorcycle and a black man. Not bad for one hot day on a lost little road in West Virginia.

He walked inside the store. All the old men stared after him, but none of them followed. I wanted to follow, to see more of this black man, but the lure of the motorcycle held me. I jumped off the porch and walked around the machine, smelling its heat. It seemed alive. Tiny noises came from somewhere inside it, little crackling sounds that could have been heartbeats. I reached out and touched it, knowing that I should not. There were more crackling sounds. I stepped back.

He came out of the store in less than two minutes, carrying two quarts of cold milk in glass bottles, cool drops of moisture already beginning to form on their sides. He didn't stop to drink them, just walked to the motorcycle and slipped them inside the black leather saddlebags. Casually, he pulled the leather helmet on and swung a leg over the bike. With his toe he flicked a metal bar, some sort of lever, out from the motorcycle and put his foot on the top of it. Then his body rose above the bike, his weight floating above the lever in a brief and elegant dance as he drove his leg down — and the motorcycle came to life and the engine music started again. He was going to leave, this black man and his glory machine. He was going to leave and I would still be there, wondering at the freedom such a machine could bring.

I stood next to the motorcycle, staring, my eyes round and full with the sight of it, my ears aching from the awesome sound of a Harley poised for full flight. He released the right grip and dug his gloved fingers into his jacket pocket.

With slow, deliberate movement he extended his arm to me, something held loosely in his fingers. Whatever it was, I was afraid to take it. And I was afraid not to. I held out my hand and into it he dropped a battered harmonica.

And then he rode away. I watched until he was gone from sight, until the rumbling of the engine was lost in the trees and the hollers and the heat. But I have never forgotten.

Behind me, I heard one of the old men say softly, "They don't feel no pain, you know, them Nigrahs. That's how they kin ride them motorsickles all thet way . . ."

Long Neck didn't say anything.

On a steaming Sunday morning a few days later we sat in the stifling little Baptist church up on the ridge and someone told about the motorcycle, and about the black man who bought milk in a white general store. And that was enough for the preacher. He blasted the motorcycle and the black man in his next three sermons, blasted the machine and the sound of it, blasted the black man who had had the nerve to walk right inside the general store and buy something, walked right inside, just like a white man. And I wondered if the black man ever knew, ever felt, that he had been condemned from the pulpit of a white Baptist church for the dual sins of being black and riding a devil machine. I listened, feeling the harmonica in my pocket, not really understanding.

Being black just didn't mean anything to me.

". . . well let me tell you I have, I have been up close to a nigger. Scared the white starch right out'a my shirt!"

I tried to picture what he would have looked like, with the starch running out of his shirt. I didn't believe he had ever worn a starched shirt.

"Saw one on a motorsickle, once," I said.

"You shittin' me, boy. I know you shittin' me. They can't none of them ride a motorsickle."

≈ Five ≈

I had never been out of West Virginia.

Behind me, back there in Crum, I knew tattered curtains had been drawn together and yellowed blinds pulled down from the tops of drafty windows. Books had been given away and junk thrown out of the shed I used to sleep in. I had already been closed off. I had always made it plain that I didn't want to be there, and now I wasn't. And the fact that I was gone would not change the price of a pound of nails at the general store or alter the schedule of the coal trains that hammered through the center of the narrow town, shaking a hard black rain of tiny cinders out of the sky with each passing.

Crum was over and my time in it was over and it was just another step along the way. There was nothing now but a cardboard suitcase and a meager handful of dollar bills and a pitted, twisting road in front of me heading somewhere to the south and east. And the only reason I was heading that way was because that's the side of the road I was standing on when the sharp-faced guy in the '41 Chevy stopped for me. I could just as easily have been standing on the other side.

But I had never been out of West Virginia.

Well, once I had been, when I waded naked across the Tug River in the sticky heat of dog days in August, a burlap bag held in both hands above my head. I had my clothes, a blanket, some food and my sheath knife in the bag and I was going over into Kentucky to spend the night and fight cannibals.

There was no town across the river from Crum, in Kentucky. No town, no houses. Nothing. Not even a road. But now and then, when a bunch of us Crum boys were down at the river digging a clubhouse into the riverbank, swimming out near the big rock, or rolling with the girls in the soft, sandy earth in the middle of the cane field, trying to shove our hands high up into their crotches until we could feel that warm place where . . . now and then we would see someone across the river, half hidden in the thick brush, watching.

Cannibals. The grown-ups in Crum told us not to go into the river. If we got too close to the Kentucky side those pig fuckers would catch us. Them folks over there ate their own kind, the grown-ups said. Don't never get in that river. Don't never go over there.

So, of course, some of us did.

But you had to go alone, and you had to spend the night. And you had to piss on a big rock high up on the Kentucky bank that we could see through the trees from our side of the river. Those were the rules. Anyone who did that was a man and the other kids would question you for days about what it was like.

None of the girls ever went, although I tried many times to talk some of them into it. The thought of wading naked across the river with a naked girl wading with me was about all I could handle on a warm night alone in my cot. I dreamed about the color of their flesh in the moonlight, the water swirling around their soft thighs, and, now and then when they stepped into a deeper place, rushing up to their breasts, their nipples as hard as country match-heads.

But I could never get them into the river, in the dark.

I stayed awake all night, trying to hear the cannibals creeping through the brush. But they never came. In the gray early light of the only morning I ever saw in Kentucky I pissed on the rock and went back to the river, wading in up to my waist, the burlap bag over my head, the knife in my hand.

Behind me I heard a twig snap, the sharp, crisp sound that's caused when you don't care who hears the twig snap. I never looked back. I swung the bag out and away from me, held the knife up in front, and plowed through the nickeled water in a dark panic against the growing light of day. I got to the West Virginia side and dove head-first into a matted tangle of brush, then lay still for a while, waiting.

There was no one there. At least, no one I saw. And the bag was gone. Somewhere in the river I had dropped it. I had to go home naked, creeping along the narrow lanes of Crum with my bare ass glowing in the dawn, holding the knife down in front of my dick.

Over time, a bunch of the boys went. And no one ever got eaten.

And that was the only time I had been out of West Virginia, but I thought it didn't really count.

Just before Williamson an old man in a rusted pickup truck offered me a ride south into Kentucky, across the bridge at Nolan, but I wouldn't get into the truck. I didn't want to go to Kentucky. Not ever again. I had already pissed on the rock.

I walked into town. I don't remember much about it, except the coal dust. There was coal dust on the road and on the trees, coal dust on the houses and in the eyes of the men I passed and I remembered my older cousin Oscar, back in Crum, trying to wash the grime from his eyes each night before supper, standing by the wash basin at the back of the house and scrubbing with his knuckles until his eyes were red and aching. But the coal dust in his eyes never completely went away.

A few cars passed and I stuck my thumb out but they never stopped, never even slowed, figuring, Damn, that boy's already *in* town, what the hell's he need a ride for?

Off to my right I could see a football field. I had played football at Crum, but never played in Williamson. Williamson wouldn't play a team, a town, like Crum. I was in no hurry so I crossed a road and went between a couple of buildings and came to the field. A high wire fence surrounded it but there were some ragged holes in it and I shoved through one and walked out on the field, walking between the goal posts. I set my cardboard suitcase on the goal line and shuffled out onto the field.

Funny, what I remembered about football. I remembered specific hits, specific plays. But I couldn't remember a single full game. The actual games didn't mean anything to me. It was the game inside the game that always kept my blood boiling on the front of the stove. Just me, and the guy across the line; just me, and the guy running toward me. Hell, half the time I didn't even know the score of the game. If I was winning *my* game, that was all that mattered.

And I remembered the weird things that happened, now and then, when two tiny schools buried deep in Appalachia came out of the dark and into the weak lights of raw-boned fields hacked out of the hard packed dirt of the river bottoms and played football. Sometimes it was ghost-like. Like the Friday night we played in Seth, a town almost as small as Crum. The field had a sharp slant to it, the lower end stopping just short of a creek. There were no bleachers — a sort of human fence of folks stood around the sidelines. I remember . . . we scored a touchdown and got lined up to kick the extra point. That was rare. We didn't score that many touchdowns. For once, our kicker got his foot into the ball, really into it. The ball sailed through the uprights and faded against the edge of the light, and then out into the night, heading for the creek. The folks around the sidelines went silent. The ball hit the creek and floated away on the dark water, a bunch of little kids trying to reach it, one of them poking at it with a long stick.

And then we got a standing ovation. That was easy. The crowd was already standing.

We never did get the ball back. Seems it was the only new ball either team had, so we finished the game with a practice ball that had tape on one of the seams.

Now, I stood on Williamson's football field and looked at the rocks, rocks everywhere, even more rocks than on the field at Crum. I wondered how the hell anyone could play football on a field this rocky, and then I remembered hearing that, before each game in Williamson, both teams would line up, walk down the field, and try to throw off most of the big rocks. But each week, every Friday night, there would be more rocks on the field. Somebody in Williamson loved rocks.

The rocks made good pretend-footballs. I picked one up and flung it at the goal posts, then leaped aside, grabbed another one and fired it off to the side. Another rock got faked as a hand-off to my tailback and then thrown to the corner of the end zone, but the receiver dropped the ball. Full of confidence, I went back to the huddle and called my own number. I picked up a rock, faked to the fullback, faded back to my left, then darted off the left end and across the goal line.

"Touchdown!" I screamed. "I scored! I scored!"

I dropped the ball casually and listened to the roar of the crowd. And for the first time in my life I knew what it was like to be the object of mad cheering. Because at Crum, in three years of playing football, I had never scored, never carried the ball, never thrown a pass. I was a lineman. A fucking tackling dummy.

But now I could hear the cheering . . . only it began to sound like laughter. And another football, a rock, landed just beside my foot. I turned and looked up-field. There, standing spread across the ragged grass, was a football team, out for late summer practice. They wore their full equipment, their torn jerseys showing the edges of leather pads, tape wrapped around anything that flapped where it wasn't supposed to. And they were all laughing.

The suitcase stood silently, waiting. I picked it up and backed toward the hole in the fence, pushing through and out the other side, heading for the road. Behind me the laughing kept coming, beating against my red face. But only one more rock came sailing across the fence and no one chased me. The rock missed me by a mile. A couple of minutes later I was gone.

It didn't take long to walk through town.

I never saw any niggers in Williamson.

And I never touched another football.

⇚ Six ⇛

The car had been patched together so many times with so many different parts, I couldn't tell what it was. Most of the car was green, some of it was rust, and it had one yellow fender. But it was running, some old guy was driving, and he picked me up out on the edge of Williamson. I never thought to ask him where he was going.

He smelled like beer and I could hear bottles rattling on the floor behind the seat. As he drove he would look at me out of the corner of his eye, peeking out over a puffy, pock-marked cheek, a little drop of spit gathered at the corner of his mouth. He drove in silence until we came in sight of the narrow, two-lane bridge across the Tug River. On the other end of the bridge was Kentucky. My God, Kentucky, the land of nose pickers and pig fuckers. The land of cannibals. I didn't want to go there, not at all.

"You can let me out here."

"You ain't going to Cain-Tuck?"

"No, sir, not me. I been to Kentucky, and I don't really aim to go back." I thought about telling him about wading across the Tug in hot darkness and hiding in the bushes, waiting for the cannibals to find me. But I knew he wouldn't understand.

"I be happy to take you on across, boy. No trouble to hit a-tall." He kept driving, his dirty, gnarled hands gripping the wheel so hard his knuckles were paling under the pressure. We were almost to the bridge and I began to panic.

"I said, let me out here. Sir." I said it as loud as I could, without actually shouting, but I tried to keep my voice low, growly sounding. I probably didn't make it.

But it worked.

"Well, shit, boy, whatever you want to do. I'll stop 'er right here."

He rolled the old car to a stop at the end of the bridge, not even bothering to pull off the road. I thanked him, grabbed my cardboard suitcase and backed out of the car, never taking my eyes off him. He was rolling away across the bridge even before the door was shut. I watched him go, over the narrow bridge and off into Kentucky.

And then it occurred to me that I couldn't remember ever having actually walked on a bridge. Not on a bridge made of steel, a bridge for cars. I had walked across railroad bridges, of course, and I had ridden in cars over bridges, and I had walked across the wooden bridge across Turkey Creek on the way to Doane, but I had never walked on a steel car bridge. I stared across the bridge. Okay, I thought, I would walk out to the middle, just to center, just so I could say, if I ever wanted to, that I could have walked to Kentucky. There really wasn't room for people to walk on the bridge, but I did it anyway. I shuffled slowly out onto the rusting metal of the bridge.

Before I got ten feet, the car with the yellow fender came back.

He was on the narrow bridge before I knew it, drifting a little into the center. Looking directly at me.

I pressed back against the railing. As he went by he stared at me out the window, his eyes not wavering. But the car didn't slow down, and in a few seconds he was gone, off the bridge and back into West Virginia, down the road and around a turn in the near distance and out of sight. I listened for the sound of his motor, but it was gone. There were no other cars. I was alone.

I went out to what I thought was the very center of the bridge, put down the suitcase and stood leaning over the heavy pipe that was the railing. The railing was low to the road, designed to keep cars, not people, from falling into the river. Down below, the sluggish water oozed past the bridge, making sucking sounds around the concrete and stone pilings that held the bridge.

That water was going somewhere. Once, when I had been hiding out in the tiny room that Crum High School called its library, I found an old book of maps. I found West Virginia, and then Crum, and then the Tug River and some other rivers and for the first time in my life I figured out that there were some things that actually *went* somewhere, even if they didn't know where. The Tug went to the Big Sandy, which went to the Ohio, which went to the Misi . . . Misspi . . . hell, I never learned how to spell it but it was a dammed big river. And here I was, standing over the water, the water I saw on the map. If I had a boat, I could go . . .

A car came by. The driver blew the horn and I jumped, startled, just as he knew I would. He laughed, waved and kept going.

And right behind him came the car with the yellow fender, drifting into the center of the road, a little closer this time, a little slower. He was past me before I could figure out what to do. So I did nothing, just watched him slide by. He drove out of sight, back on the Kentucky side.

I thought about picking up the suitcase and running. But before I did that I thought about something else. I untied the strap around the suitcase, snapped open the cheap brass latches and took out my knife. It was an old World War II bayonet that I had found stuck into a rafter in Long Neck's barn on Black Hawk Ridge. The tip was broken off, but I had taken one of Long Neck's files and worked it down, ending up with a heavy knife with one good, sharp edge and a blade that was almost perfect for throwing. I would practice throwing it at trees and if you threw it right the weight of the steel and the thick handle would drive the blade so deep through the bark and into the hard flesh of the tree that I had to use both hands to pull it out.

The knife was in a sheath I had made from some leather scrap that Long Neck gave me, and I took it out of the suitcase and stuck it down inside the back of my pants.

Again. Here the son-of-a-bitch came again. As I closed the suitcase and picked it up, the car with the yellow fender came out onto the bridge. This time, the sun glinted from the windshield and I couldn't see his face but I knew that he was staring at me, the eyes set deep in the pock-marked forehead. The car drifted toward the center again and I wondered when he would actually try to run me down. And I wondered why the hell I hadn't just run off the bridge the first time.

The noise the horn made was the dumbest sound I had ever heard. It didn't sound like a truck horn, but it didn't sound like anything else, either. It came screeching at me from behind, one long continuous scream that, for a split second, took my mind off the yellow-fendered car. And I knew there was another car on the bridge.

Only it wasn't a car. I glanced behind me and saw a truck coming hard in my lane, a sort of stake-bed with the stakes sticking out at odd angles, some almost raking the railing of the bridge, the driver laying on the horn. Back in front of me the car tried to jerk back into its own lane, close enough now for me to see the frozen features of the driver. He stared wide-eyed at the truck, hands locked to the wheel, foot still on the accelerator. If he didn't do something, *something*, there was no way he could miss the truck.

And then I remembered where I was, standing there above the Tug River, my back to the railing, waiting patiently for two pieces of motorized junk to come together and smack the life out of me in a thunderclap of metal, gristle and flying shit.

There was nothing else I could do. I rolled backwards over the railing and let go of the suitcase, my body slowly turning, the suitcase floating beside me in the fall, with all the time in the world for us to reach the water.

❧ Seven ❧

My nose and mouth were full of water and it tasted vaguely like shit. At least, it tasted like what I thought shit would taste like.

In Crum, we would spend hours on hot afternoons messing around on the riverbank. We sucked on the sugar cane that grew on the flats, smoked corn silk and tried to hide from the heat by digging holes in the soft banks and curling up in the damp sand.

The water in the river flowed so softly and slowly that we could hear insects buzzing over on the Kentucky side. We talked about where the water went, flowing out of our sight down and around the far bend in the river. Where it went and what we would do if we could go with it. We spent hours talking about that.

We found an old bicycle, half buried in the sand almost at the water's edge. It must have been there for years. The sprocket chain was so welded together with rust we thought it would never bend and the rubber of the tires cracked like thin tree bark, large chunks of it coming off with each creaking turn as we forced the wheels around.

We cleaned it up as well as we could, stripped off the broken tires and rotted innertubes, got some used motor oil from Yvonne Staley's brother and soaked every part that was supposed to move. Eventually, they did.

There were no tires to put on it so we kept it down at the river bank where the rims would cut into the sand and bury halfway to the hubs. We made a mound of hard packed sand just below a steep part of the riverbank and took turns shooting down the hill and over the jump, to land in the softer sand below, always crashing. After everyone had a turn, the winner was the guy who wasn't bleeding.

And then somebody got the idea to put the jump next to the river.

The idea was simple. Ride the bike down the steep riverbank, fly over the jump, and stop in the deep sand before you hit the water. If you could turn sideways, slam on the brakes, and spray sand into the water, you scored a lot of points. If you got the bike's wheels wet, you won.

I dragged the old bike higher up the bank than anybody, far up, where it was so steep that I had to turn the thing sideways just to get on before it slid down the bank under its own weight, its rear brake locked tight. So I got on, and pointed the front wheel down the bank.

I got the bike's wheels wet. In fact, I got the whole bike wet. The damn thing shot down the bank and over the jump, flying, free in the air and the sunlight. I was sailing in an empty space, a spectator, watching as the jump dropped away below me and the riverbank faded from my vision. Water appeared under the bike and I wondered what the hell it was doing there. I would have to hit the sand soon, I knew, if I were going to stop where I wanted, but the sand seemed suddenly out of reach. For some reason, the bike tilted forward, no longer really under me, but trailing slightly behind, my hands still locked to the handlebars, my ass rising from the seat. I couldn't understand why the water was rushing up to meet my face.

The water was only about two feet deep. I slammed into it nose-first, the bike following close behind. As I hit the water my forward motion slowed and the heavy bike slammed into me, the frame driving up between my legs. My face and head plowed through the shallow water and into the mucky bottom of the river. My mouth popped open and the muck drove in, plugging my nose and throat. At the same time, the pain between my legs made me try to puke. The muck going down met the puke coming up. I thought my chest would explode from the collision.

Shit. The whole thing tasted like shit.

My face hurt and my chest hurt and my balls hurt. But what really hurt was — somebody had hold of my hair and was dragging me out of the river. I managed to clear my eyes and spit out the muck and puke and twist around to see what was going on. Two of my buddies were dragging my aching body up on the riverbank. They were laughing. They were all laughing.

"You win," they said, still laughing.

Somebody had hold of my hair and was dragging me up and out of the river. He was laughing.

He grabbed hold of my wrist and flipped me over, leaving me face-down against the dried mud at the edge of the water. I thought that when I got the water out of my mouth and nose, when I could see clearly, when I could stand up, that I would kick the shit out of whatever sort of bastard would pull me out of the river by my hair and laugh about it.

But I changed my mind.

When I rolled over and looked up at him, he blocked out the sun. He was wearing a sleeveless undershirt and a pair of denim pants, both with holes in odd places, almost as though he had put them there. His chest and shoulders seemed to be formed from a single tree trunk, rolling down and spreading into a stomach that looked like a small blimp trapped under a tent. He had no hips to speak of, no huge ass. His thick legs just flowed down from his stomach, not seeming to taper as they reached his feet, huge stumps of legs boring straight into the ground.

He weighed, near as I cold tell, three hundred pounds.

PART II

Kentucky

Screaming With the Cannibals

❧ Eight ❧

He said his name was Lard and that he could drive cars trucks, tractors and any manner of other farm machinery that had ever been invented and the son-of-a-bitch pulled me out of the water on the *Kentucky* side of the river.

I still had my knife; it was still stuck down inside the back of my pants. But that's all I had. By the time Lard pulled me out of the water and I could talk and think straight again my suitcase was gone into the lower murks of the Tug River. The brittle old cardboard probably came apart before it got a hundred yards downstream. I didn't really care about the suitcase and the few clothes that were in it, but somewhere down there in that crap-tainted water the best book I had read in my whole life was soaking apart in liquid shit.

I wasn't exactly a small guy, but that didn't seem to matter to Lard. He reached down, pulled me up out of the sucking mud and stood me on my feet. His arms were as big as my legs and he slipped one of them around me, snaked the knife out of the back of my pants and shoved it into his back pocket. Then he half carried, half dragged my filthy, dripping ass up to the road where he had parked his truck. It was an early 'forties model Chevrolet with a stake bed and Lard said it belonged to Eli Rumson, a farmer who lived in Bean Camp, off west in Kentucky at the edge of the mountains. Said he'd delivered a load of Eli's farm produce to Huntington, back in West Virginia. And Eli had a room to spare and needed a farm hand and did I want the job? Was the least he could do, Lard said, for brushing me off into the river.

I was headed somewhere, anywhere, but I sure as hell didn't want it to be Kentucky. But there I stood, dripping muddy water onto the side of the road, and the only things I owned in the world were the old sheath knife and the few sodden dollars I still had in my pocket. Eli had a room, Lard said. And Eli would feed me.

The big fat bastard. He never told me Eli's spare room was in the barn and that I had to share it with a rat as big as a full-growed dog.

And he never told me about Ruth Ella.

I took off my clothes, hung them out the window of the truck, and we left the river behind, left West Virginia hulking darkly in the cracked glass of the rear window. I sat twisted in the seat, watching the far ridges pull away behind us, knowing that I was leaving West Virginia exactly as I had entered. Naked, and wet.

There was a pulling sensation in my gut, or maybe in my mind. Hard to tell. Like some sort of wire attached to a place inside me that I hadn't known about, a wire that kept growing longer as we drove away from the river, a wire that is with me yet. Always attached to West Virginia. As time went by messages would come over this wire, bits of images, fragments of sound. In the middle of a steaming night on a wooden sleeping platform at the edge of the jungle in Honduras I came staring-eyed awake, seeing the barn on Long Neck's farm and hearing the grinding squeal of the rusted hinges as the doors moved in the breeze. Once, stuck on the side of a mountain in Canada, I heard clearly the rush of wind through hardwood trees in autumn, the brittle leaves rustling like the soft rattle of dried gourds. I was five hundred feet above tree line at the time.

The wire. Over the years, I would try to cut this wire. It couldn't be done. Instead, I grew to wonder when others would know that it was there, wonder when I would be found out, when it would be known to anyone who cared to look that I was for damn sure a West Virginian, that I was born to the mountains and the ridges and the hollers, that the world would simply swallow me if I tried to escape. When would they know? When would they throw me back?

And somewhere, along in there, it became a matter of pride.

At first, Kentucky was just like West Virginia, only worse. The ridges ran together tightly, trapping the tiny towns in the dark grip of the hollers. Coal mines ripped into the bowels of the mountains, great wounds dripping into the towns and directly into the lives of the miners, discoloring their hearts, fading the forests, draining the people. Just like home.

It was *too* much like home, and I didn't like home.

Lard seemed in no hurry and the old truck never got above twenty miles an hour on the twisting, pitted roads. But just when I thought about telling him to let me the hell out of the truck so I could hitchhike in some other direction, the land began to flatten out, just a little. The ridges got shorter and lighter and the hollers opened out into brighter, rolling land that looked green and peaceful in the late summer sun. And farms. Real farms, not like those on Black Hawk Ridge, but farms where actual tractors were used to cut the hay, and small orchards grew, the trees in rows so straight you could drive a wagon right down them and never make a turn.

Lard hung both arms over the top of the steering wheel, like two sides of beef dangling from a rack, his belly pushing against the wheel. Now and then, on a straight stretch of road, he would take his arms away and his belly would hold the truck steady for a short stretch, Lard shifting his belly back and forth, trying to steer. We cruised slowly among the farms, the truck drifting back and forth across the road.

"I call this belly drivin' kid," he said, laughing. "Got near to five miles, once't, 'fore I had to touch the wheel with my hands."

His voice was a sort of wheeze, a high pitched blowing of air and sound that worked its way out of his throat with effort. He noticed that I noticed.

"Don't pay no never mind to my talking, kid. Sounds like a broke church organ, don't it? Got my neck caught in some baling wire once't. Come near to cutting my head off."

He put his hand to his neck and pushed a couple of folds of fat back up toward his chin. A thin, reddish line ran across his neck, a glowing scar with tiny jagged places that didn't look healed and probably never would. I looked at the scar, and then at Lard. His voice sounded pretty good after that.

It felt odd, him calling me kid. He couldn't have been much older than I was. He had never lived anywhere but Jubal County, Kentucky, which was where we were heading. Never been anything but a farmer. Owned his own little farm with a small white house, a porch that ran across the front, and no barn, just a big shed where he parked his huge, red Farmall tractor. Mostly worked for other folks in the county. Didn't finish school, didn't get married, didn't owe anything to anybody. Liked to read a little. Still had a couple of books somewhere around his house, he said. Said he liked to eat, and drive his Farmall, in that order. Liked women, but couldn't seem to find one who would put up with his size. He liked fucking if he could arrange it, he said, but he didn't want to go out of his way. Said mostly the women were afraid to screw him, afraid he might roll over on them, or something.

"But don't worry 'bout screwin', kid," Lard said. "There ain't enough single women in this county to make you get your pecker up. You live on Eli's farm, you ain't never gonna get none."

After a couple of hours on the road we came to a small slab-sided diner, shoved back from the road at the edge of a patch of oil-stained gravel. There were a couple of cars parked on the gravel, their paint faded, the fenders rusting. Lard twisted the old truck onto the gravel and killed the engine.

"Let's eat, boy," he wheezed. "It's near three o'clock."

"Three o'clock? You always eat at three o'clock?"

"Hell, no, kid. But this here diner's the only one between here and Bean Camp, and if we don't eat here, won't get no diner food at all. Diner food's good, boy. Lots of grease and shit.

"Besides," he said, "we can always eat again when we get home."

I opened the door to get out, and that's when I found out that my pants had blown out the window.

Lard had an extra pair of pants in a gunnysack behind the seat. I put them on and tied them with some twine. I looked like a mouse wearing elephant pants.

The diner was one long room with a counter at the back. A man in a dark work shirt leaned on the counter, reading a magazine. He didn't look up when we came in. Just over his head, a big fan hung from a wire rack, trying to blow the hot air away from the customers. A bunch of small tables were scattered across the front and two men sat at one of them, playing cards. The chairs at the tables didn't match, a collection of sticks and wicker and glue. Some of the tables still had leftover food on them.

"Look at them good leftovers," Lard whispered. "Jist what I was countin' on."

I headed for the counter but Lard pulled me back, tugging me across the room. As he passed the first table he scooped up part of a hamburger and a bottle of ketchup. Still moving toward the far end of the room he soaked the hamburger in ketchup and finished it in two bites.

He caught me looking at him.

"Don't go giving me that shit-eatin' look, boy. If you and me was sitting here with some ole boy eating hamburgers, and he didn't want to finish his, and you was still hungry, and he offered the rest of it to you, you'd damn well take it. And you'd damn well eat it. Well," — he pulled air into his huge chest — "that's what I just did."

Somehow, it made a sort of warped sense.

There was a pile of crackers at the next table and he got them all in one pass of his huge hand. The crackers and the ketchup were still with us when we got to our table, as far across the room as we could go.

We sat dipping crackers in the ketchup and eating them as fast as we could. Lard looked around the room, scouting for other food. On the next table there was a bowl with a chip out of the rim. Lard leaned over and checked it out. It still had some soup beans in it and Lard drained the soup into a coffee cup and put the bowl down between us. He dumped more ketchup on the beans, gathered up some more crackers, and we dipped up the red, dripping beans, a cracker-full at a time. Then Lard drank the soup.

The guy from the counter started to shuffle over toward us, and I pulled out my money and carefully counted it.

"Forget it, boy. This'ns on me. Least I can do for Eli's newest farm hand." He chuckled his wheezing chuckle.

We ordered fried baloney sandwiches and bowls of beans and while we were waiting Lard found two whole slices of bread at another table. He offered me one, but I turned it down. He ate them both, with ketchup.

About halfway through our sandwiches, a big family came in, two or three grown-ups and a bunch of kids. Their clothes didn't have any holes in them and the kids had haircuts so I guess they had money enough to feed the whole bunch. They pulled three tables together and gathered around them like doctors at an operating table. The counter guy seemed to know them and he got there quickly, knowing it would be a big order. As we finished eating, the counter guy was bringing their food.

He brought a lot of food. They had hamburgers and fried egg sandwiches, bowls of beans and one big bowl of mashed potatoes. The kids scooped the mashed potatoes out on their plates, poured beans on top and ate with their spoons. No one at the table used a fork.

I noticed Lard watching, like a scavenger, waiting.

A few minutes later, Lard got up and headed for the back door, to the customers' outhouse, out back. On his way, he nodded to the folks with all the food, said "howdy," and then strolled on toward the door, picking up a spoonful of fried potatoes from an empty table as he went.

In a minute or two he was back. This time he stopped at the table where the kids were still eating their beans and mashed potatoes. I couldn't hear what he was saying, but he seemed to know those people. He just stood there, talking to one, and then another, verbally working his way around the table. The next thing I knew, he had pulled up a chair and had joined the group.

He never looked my way, so I just sat where I was. The counter guy was in no hurry to do anything, so I guessed I could sit as long as I wanted. But I didn't have to wait long. In a couple of minutes the people at Lard's table began to get up and stretch themselves. Lard shook a couple of hands, the kids ran out of the restaurant, and one man went to the counter to pay the bill. As the last one went out through the door, Lard finally looked my way and motioned me over to the table.

"Look at all this good stuff," he said, almost giggling.

The table was a disaster, but there was a lot of food still lying around. A whole fried egg sandwich lay in a sheen of grease on a cracked plate. There was at least a cup full of mashed potatoes still in the bowl, some beans hid in a cup at the end of the table, one full cup of coffee still steamed — all waiting for the passing hand of Lard to scoop them up. And he did.

A few miles down the road, I said, "Was awful nice of them folks to leave that food for you . . . for us. You know them a long time?"

"Hell, kid, I never saw them folks before in my life."

We had been back on the road for another five miles or so before I realized that no one had said a word about my pants.

❧ Nine ❧

Sometimes I woke up and realized that the only thing I had moved was my mind. Everything else was stillness, silence. My eyes were closed, motionless in their darkness. Not even my heartbeat broke the faint buzzing in my ears that I have always taken for true silence, the absolute lack of sound that fluttered in my ears. Only my mind seemed to be moving, free to race through my body and limbs with a speed and clarity that full wakefulness would not allow. It was a curious feeling, one that I had often sought in those seconds just after awakening. It was the way I felt now, almost. Almost, because now I could hear the rat.

I could hear a small sound, a tiny scratching, a scurrying along the wooden floor, a sound that was almost a whispering. I tried to concentrate on the whispering, but it came and went, quick little shuffling sounds.

I lay on the cot in my small room high in the hayloft of Eli's barn, feeling the dampness seep through the old blankets and into my skin. The room seemed thick with moisture and I thought it was going to rain soon, or maybe already had. I shivered. It was the moisture, I told myself, the wetness that makes everything cold. But maybe it was the rat.

Gradually I opened my eyes. As they began to focus I could see the wall on the other side of the room. The faded planks picked up a faint glow from the one small window above my cot, the early morning light made weak by the layer of dust that coated the inside of the glass. The dull light gave the cell-like room a closeness that was even more intense than usual. There was nothing bright in the room, no welcoming spark to cheer a mind struggling up from sleep. The walls and floor were bare wooden planks and the ceiling was tin. The tin was also the roof of the barn, one layer of metal between me and the rain, or me and the sun, or me and the cold. Earlier in the summer I had cut apart some cardboard boxes and tacked the stiff panels to the rafters of the ceiling. Helped to keep out the heat. Some.

The room measured approximately four paces by four paces. For furniture, I had a cot, a straight-back cane-bottom chair and an apple crate. In the top of the apple crate were an extra pair of jeans and a clean shirt, things I had been able to buy since coming to work for Eli Rumson, the biggest farmer in Jubal County, Kentucky. In the bottom half of the crate was a worn copy of *For Whom the Bell Tolls*. It was a strange book. I had found it at Lard's house and he had given it to me and I had read it all in one weekend. And then I read the last chapter again. And again. Over the years I read it, and each time I was put in another place, my body so packed with strange feelings that I couldn't breathe. That last chapter. I always tried to read it only when I was alone. Alone, like Robert Jordan.

On top of the crate I kept some food, a small store of things to eat when I didn't feel like going to the house — some crackers, a small jar of peanut butter, part of a loaf of bread.

Awakening, I began to work at seeing things in my room, but I could see only shadows. I explored them as best I could, straining my eyes for better views without turning my head. Across from my cot, at the base of the wall, one of the shadows moved a few inches, stopped, then moved again, making its way carefully toward the apple crate. I knew the moving shadow was the rat, a rat nearly as thick as my forearm and easily as long.

The rat and I had been playing a game for nearly two weeks. The rat would come into the room through a hole near the door and make a try for the food on the crate. If I were there when the rat came in, I would freeze, motionless, not even blinking my eyes, letting the rat get closer, letting him commit himself to the final few feet to the apple crate.

My job was to try to kill him. The rat's job was to try to escape. So far, the rat had won.

When I was not in the room, any food I left in the crate was fair game for the rat. It seemed to be a contest we both understood.

Gradually, so the sagging springs of the cot did not make their grating noises, I slipped my arm toward the wall behind me. I had my knife there, stuck lightly in a two-by-four where it would be handy. The knife was one of the rules: I could try to kill the rat only with the knife.

It took me a long time to get my hand on the handle and the rat got closer to the food, closer than I had ever seen him. He was down in the far corner now, across from my feet. I was reaching for the knife with my left hand and realized that I would have to throw with that hand. Not exactly my best shot, but possible. I had been practicing.

The rat was concentrating on the food now, his head looking up at the corner of the crate, his body flat against the floor.

I eased the blade out of the wall. I had to hurry now or the rat would be inside the crate and I didn't want to throw the heavy bayonet anywhere near my book. The blade felt cool against my fingers. I was hunting. It seemed as though I had been hunting forever, hunting for something, anything, that would prevent my hunger, keep me warm, make me happy: hunting for a way out, for a way in, for a way up, for a right time and a right place, looking for the top when I was at the bottom, looking for a bright place when I didn't know where the light was. I was hunting, intent on the killing now, raising my arm as carefully as I could in a controlled race against the disappearance of the rat.

I threw.

The rat was playing the game well. As I released the bayonet the rat whirled around, pointing his nose directly at the hole by the door. The bayonet crunched into the floor behind him, spearing into the wood, thudding into the silence of the room. The left-handed throw had been awkward. In a blur of dark shadow the rat was gone, not pausing at the hole, making only the tiniest sounds on the boards. Then, silence.

I sat up and leaned against the wall, staring at the apple crate. The springs of the cot sagged and grated. It was shivering cold in the room but now I didn't seem to notice, even though I was wearing nothing. My heart was beating rapidly and I was charged with the excitement of the hunt. I stood up, pulled the string that turned on the single, naked light bulb in the middle of the ceiling and stepped over to the crate. As I stooped to pull the bayonet I noticed a small, blackish, shiny thing on the floor. It was less than four inches long, lying next to the blade of the bayonet. I had cut off most of the rat's tail.

The game soured in my mind and I frowned against the thought of it. I left the room and walked naked along the upper floor. At the back of the barn I found a rusted tin can. I took the can and went back to the room. The can fit almost perfectly into the hole the rat used and I jammed it hard in there, kicking it tight with my foot. I put the bread and crackers outside the door, by the can, and went back into the room.

It began to rain lightly. The small drops made a muffled drumming on the tin roof of the barn, a steady sound, as though it had always been there. I went to the window and scraped my hand across the dusty glass. Still not able to see through clearly I opened the window and stood in the rush of even damper air that came into the room. I couldn't help but smile to myself. There would be no work today, I thought. I can read, or I can go over and see Lard. Or I can work on the bike. I can do anything I want. Rainy days are mine.

The drops came steadily and bounced off the windowsill, splashing on my chest. The rain carried a chill, one of those early winter rains that wished it were snow and made promises that it would be. It fell straight down from a flat, gray sky, making no announcements, no claps of thunder, no wind. It just came, half rain, half mist, from clouds so low you could taste them. And even when you were not out in it you could feel the rain everywhere.

I closed the window and put on my clothes, putting on the extra shirt and an old, floppy hat. Downstairs, on the main floor of the barn, I found a ragged piece of tarpaulin that I had used before as a rain poncho. I knew where I was going. I was going to walk down the dirt road past Ruth Ella's house. I had to. It was Sunday.

≈ Ten ≈

Lard had dropped me off at Eli's farm a couple of months ago and now it was hard into a boiling summer.

It hadn't been hard to get a job. Eli needed a farm hand; his last hand had left suddenly in the middle of last summer. Some said it had to do with Ruth Ella, a woman who lived down the road. Some said the farm hand couldn't stay away from her house and her husband had run him off with a shotgun, and the guy had just kept on running.

Don't pay no attention to that kind of stuff, Lard said. You know how people talk. Why, he said, Luther and Ruth Ella are the salt of the earth. But he had kind of an odd grin on his face when he said it.

Eli was a serious man, tall and stringy, with a sharp face and hands made strong from his early days, before he owned a tractor, of walking behind a mule as he plowed countless furrows in the black Kentucky earth. His wife, Geneva, was as short as Eli was tall, a plump woman with a kind face who sometimes sang hymns in the kitchen as she broke string beans or peeled potatoes. She had a big garden behind the house and a coop with more chickens than I had ever seen penned up in any one place. Eli and Geneva didn't seem to have any kids, at least none that I ever saw or Lard ever mentioned. But the two of them were a family, as surely as any family I had known on Black Hawk Ridge.

Eli's farm sat tucked into the southern edge of the county, two hundred acres of hay and apple orchards, Geneva's garden, elm trees the size of Lard's appetite, a large two-story white house where Geneva cooked — the first house I ever spent any time in that had an actual dining room.

And the barn. Bigger than Long Neck's barn, bigger than Eli's house, bigger than any house I had ever seen, the barn rose out of the field fifty yards from the house, a place of wonder and silence, coolness, and the smells of honest work. A long open shed ran along the far side, where the larger pieces of farm machinery sat. There was equipment stored there and inside the barn that hadn't been used in years, wondrous machines and parts of machines, wire, bolts, and mystery. There was a repair shop on the ground floor, the tools, hundreds of them, hanging from nails on the wall. Upstairs, the huge loft held enough hay for an entire winter of feeding Eli's stock, with enough space in the front corner for the room I slept in.

There was electricity in the barn, but no plumbing. The field hand, me, used an outdoor toilet and I drank and washed at a cistern at the corner of the barn, the water brought up by a hand pump, cold and clear.

So I went to work for Eli and Geneva and he showed me the room in the loft of the barn and the shop and the wondrous machines and said I could fool around with anything I wanted.

And there, in the back, under a rotting tarpaulin, was a motorcycle, or part of a motorcycle, or maybe almost all of a motorcycle, or maybe just a pile of motorcycle junk. It didn't matter. I couldn't take my eyes away from it.

"Don't even know where the feller is who owned it," Eli said. "Feller from New York. Worked for me for a while, some years back. Then just up and left. Motorsickle wouldn't run even then, I reckon, so he just left it here. You want to, go ahead and try to get her running. You get it running, you can have it."

Go ahead and get it running.

And so I worked for them and they fed me and let me sleep in the barn and work on the motorcycle and they even talked to me like I was a grown man. It got so I had to be careful. I began to feel a little like family, and I knew I wasn't.

When Lard brought me to the house, Eli asked if I could drive a tractor and before I could answer Lard told Eli he would teach me and for days on end we took Eli's old John Deere out into the hay fields and I mowed hay and raked hay and tedded hay and then Lard would bring his Farmall and his baler and we would bale hay. I had never done this sort of work before and it all seemed so easy, because of the tractors. Eli paid me fifty cents an hour. It was the easiest money I ever made.

The days went by and the hay was baled and I thought that was the end of it. I was wrong.

The heavy bales lay strewn over the fields like huge building blocks scattered from some other time, the leftover remnants of pyramids. Lard and some other men would come by and get me and we would go out into the fields again. We would get there in early morning, just enough light to see, the bales heavy with dew. Lard would drive his Farmall with its lights on, pulling a low flatbed trailer, and we would walk beside it, stumbling through the stubble, picking up the bales as we came to them and throwing them on the trailer, one man and one bale, sinking a baling hook into the hay and grabbing the wire, the wire cutting through our gloves, lifting one end of the bale off the ground and slamming a knee under it, using the knee and leg, throwing the bales as high as we could, stacking them higher with each pass around the field, straining as the pile on the trailer grew and the sun rose and burned our necks and hands. Until we couldn't throw them on top any more. And then one of the men would climb up on the pile and keep stacking until the trailer tipped back and forth from the weight, all the time the grit and bits of hay raining down on our heads, carried by running sweat into our shirts and the tops of our pants. The sun baked us and the grit made tiny wounds in a thousand places on our hides and sweat ran in dripping streams into our eyes and when we wiped our faces with our shirts and hands the sweat seeped in through the cuts in our gloves and burned into the red-stripe gashes in our fingers. We would work until all the bales were in the barn. It didn't matter if it got dark.

Eli paid me fifty cents an hour. It was the hardest money I ever made.

The work hardened me. Before first light, when I heard the big Farmall pounding down the dirt road toward the barn, I would roll off the cot and pull on my sweat-crusted clothes, almost without opening my eyes. I would ride to the fields lying on the empty hay trailer, my mind in some sort of sluggish space between sleep and wakefulness — far enough into sleep that I could lie there, bouncing on the hard boards of the trailer, and not care where I was; far enough awake that I didn't fall off. And then we would be in the fields and time and sweat and pain would compress into a single thought: *get through the day*.

It wasn't like Black Hawk Ridge. Back there, I was a kid, and they treated me like a kid. In the hay fields, I wasn't a kid, but I wasn't a man. Yet.

But one thing I knew for sure — this wasn't high school anymore.

Nobody cared. Not about me, not about high school. All I had to do was pick up the bales, pick up the bales, in the endless hay fields in the oven of endless summer.

There was other work, mostly in the orchards. We picked apples and sorted them in the sheds, gathered them in baskets for the market. I built fences for Eli and hoed Geneva's garden and repaired the chicken coop. Eli hired out his John Deere to other farmers and sometimes he hired me out with it and I would get to work other farms, see other people, usually with Lard if the job were big enough. And Eli always paid me fifty cents an hour, no matter what.

But there were no girls on those other farms. Or, if there were, the farmers kept them away from hired hands. Like me.

Whatever my working life lacked in money, Eli and Geneva made up in food. Feeding me was part of my pay and they paid me well.

Eli told me once that I ate as much as any man he knew in Jubal County, except Lard. Lard ate for the sheer joy of it. When Lard and I were working together, I always wanted to eat lunch with him, just to see the show. When lunch rolled around, Lard would always park his tractor crossways to the sun and we would sit on the shady side, tucked hard back against the huge wheel, eating our lunch and talking about anything that came to our minds.

Lard had lived in Jubal County his whole life and probably worked on every farm and he knew about everything that ever went on there. He liked to talk, but he didn't like to tell you everything he knew. Like the time I complained that there wasn't much to do in Jubal County.

"Jis wait 'till spring, boy," he said, his mouth full of meatloaf sandwich. "You'll see some livin'-up then, for sure."

"What happens then? The ice melt and we can watch the water drip off the barns?"

He didn't think I was funny. "Just you wait. We get our-selves a revival goin' here in the spring. Preacher Hitch from over in Sulphur County, he's been comin' over and puttin' the revival on us for some years now. Shovels out the hell fire and brimstone. Gets 'em all up to the front of the church and runs 'em through the baptismal tank. It's the baptisin' part that's fun. The good Reverend Hitch has got a bad arm and leg, and a bad eye, too, for that matter, and he puts on a good show, now and then, just handling them bodies in the water."

I remembered some of the revival services back in Crum. I didn't like them. I had no intention of going to a revival ser-vice in Kentucky. But I was curious about Reverend Hitch. "So what do you mean by 'good show'?"

"Well, now, the good reverend, he has a lot of trouble with that bad arm and leg and he has to grab people funny when he lowers 'em down into the water, up there in the bap-tismal tank. Can't hardly hold onto 'em, especially them big ones. Drops one every now and then, just lets 'em plop back-wards into the water and then pretends that nothin' happened, nothin' a'tall. There's this big splash and water slops over the front of the tank and drips down on those chairs up there be-hind the pulpit. I hear tell he had to stop baptizin' people in creeks because he'd drop one every now and then and they'd just float away!" Lard laughed, his huge stomach rolling up and down over his belt.

"Well, he ain't goin' to drop me, because I ain't goin' to be there."

"You don't know Abel Hitch, boy. You don't know what kind of power he has over these here people. Take my word for it, hillbilly, if you be here in Jubal County come spring, you will be at a revival service, one way or another. The good Rev-erend Hitch will sure see to that."

Bullshit, I thought.

In spite of what Lard wanted you to think, he was smart, a lot smarter than any other guy I had ever known. The kids back in Crum, some of them were smart, but you would never know it by talking to them. Seemed like, if you were smart, you couldn't let on. Nobody I knew in Crum, no guy, wanted the other guys to think he was smart. Only girls were allowed to be smart.

Like Yvonne. She was smart. And I wondered if she still hated me.

There was a large wooden box that was bolted underneath the seat of Lard's tractor. Lard had built the box himself, lining it with some kind of insulation that he had found in the barn and carefully fitting the top so it was as tight as possible. The box held Lard's lunches, if you could call them that. Each morning he would put a small block of ice in the box and then put his lunch in beside it. During the day you could see the cold water from the ice drip from the box, and at noon his lunch would be chilled and fresh in the humid, searing air of mid-day in a hay field. The box held enough lunch for three or four men, but for Lard it was barely enough.

When I worked with him, he would make my lunch at his house and put it in the box with his. Today, for instance, he brought me a cold meatloaf sandwich and a can of tomato juice. For himself, he had brought a ham sandwich, and one of meatloaf, and one of cold chicken. There was a Mason jar full of potato salad and a large piece of cheese wrapped in butcher paper. A small crock of baked beans was in the box, and a quart of milk and two bottles of beer. Last, placed carefully on the top of the other stuff, was half an apple pie, wrapped neatly in waxed paper and tied with string. Lard held the lid up and stared into the box. "Damn," he mumbled, "I didn't bring anything for a snack this morning."

I grinned. It was Lard. I knew he wasn't kidding.

One day Lard gave me one of the bottles of beer to drink with my lunch. It tasted like goat piss and I could only sip at it. But he kept giving me a bottle now and then and before long it began to taste pretty good. Pretty soon, Lard was packing an extra bottle for me in his lunch every day.

Eli would watch Lard eating and just shake his head, grinning. Eli was different. Sometimes I thought Eli only ate because it helped him do work — I thought if he didn't need food to work, he wouldn't eat. I was sure of it. On those autumn Sundays with other farmers at the house, I never really saw Eli doing much in the way of eating. Mostly, he just talked with the other men as they sat around the heavy table, their plates so loaded they had to eat around the edges to keep the food from falling off.

But it was different during the week. Then, Eli ate, and I ate with him. When we weren't out in the fields, too far away to come to the house, we ate four meals each day.

Each morning, when I got to the kitchen, Geneva would already be there. I don't know when she got up in the morning, but the kitchen light was already on and things were already cooking, no matter when I showed up. I would sit down at a narrow table against the wall near the stove and Geneva would feed me. Early breakfast, she called it. It wasn't much, really. She would have some kind of cooked cereal, bread, milk, home canned preserves, and coffee. Eli would be there, of course, and we would eat in silence, me enjoying the first food of the day, Eli just stoking his furnace for the work ahead. During the fall and winter I spent at his farm, I don't think I heard him say five whole sentences during early breakfast.

When we finished, we would head out to do the early chores. It would still be dark.

By nine o'clock in the morning, we would have put in more than three hours of farm work, milking cows, feeding the live stock, fixing the tractors, balers, and other equipment, getting ready for the real work of the day. And by that time, we were ready for breakfast, real breakfast. Back at the house Geneva would have loaded the table — biscuits, gravy, eggs, fried pork side meat, fried potatoes, apple butter, coffee. This was breakfast. Work breakfast, Geneva called it.

And after work breakfast we did just that — went back to work. We cleaned the orchards and fixed fences; painted every barn in two counties; plowed.

And in the middle of the day, there was dinner. Geneva didn't call it lunch. No one called it lunch, no one I knew in West Virginia, no one I knew in Kentucky. Lunch was something other people ate, people who didn't work too hard, people who had to figure out what to call things when they didn't know what else to do. In the middle of the day we didn't eat lunch on Black Hawk ridge. We didn't eat lunch in Bean Camp. We ate dinner.

And it was heaven. Geneva would make fried chicken, mashed potatoes, cole slaw, and green beans cooked with thick slabs of bacon. There was always a pitcher of cold buttermilk. And there was always apple pie for desert.

Dinner would get us through the rest of the day. And then in the evening we would have supper. Geneva got to rest a little at supper. Mainly, she served all those things that didn't get eaten at the other three meals of the day, plus some "greens" that she either cooked or served as a small salad. Had to have some greens each day, she said. Good for the digestion.

But not on Sundays. Sundays belonged only to the people who lived there, in Jubal County.

❧ Eleven ❧

I never ate at the house on Sundays.

I never knew why.

Eli never worked on Sundays and sometimes he would have company at the house. They would arrive in shiny cars and pickup trucks. They would park on the wide gravel turn in front of the barn and I could lie on my bunk and hear the slamming of the car doors as the men and women got out, could even hear the crunching of their stiff shoes on the gravel as they walked off toward the house.

I could see the back of the house from the window in my room and sometimes I would see picnics in the back yard, the men wearing coats and looking somehow uncomfortable in white shirts that were too large for their necks, the women in high-necked flowered dresses that hung almost to their ankles. There were large bowls of food spread out on a massive plank table that sat under a huge elm tree. The table was at least twelve feet long and I never saw it moved and I never saw it used for anything but picnics. Chairs of many types and shapes were brought from the barn and the house and men and women sat in the shade of the elm tree and talked and drank lemonade, anticipating a true Kentucky picnic.

But I was never asked to any of those picnics. I wanted badly to scrub myself under the hose that hung from the shed beside the barn, to put on my cleanest pants and my one good shirt and go down to the house on Sunday. I wanted to join the picnic and talk and laugh. I wanted to hear the voices of ladies who never got dirty and listen to the men talk of hay, corn and the price of tractors. I wanted to turn the crank on the ice cream maker and drink hot coffee after apple pie. But I never did. I was a hired hand. I never ate at the house on Sundays.

So I would watch through the window, watch the pitchers of iced tea being passed around, watch the platters of fried chicken and the bowls of mashed potatoes travel around the table, chased by pans of corn bread, mounds of sliced tomatoes, and jars of homemade pickles. Sometimes I would stand silently beside the open window and try to hear what they were saying, try to imagine what they were talking about, try to imagine what I would say if I were down there. But I was too far away to hear. I just imagined what they were saying as they passed the bowls and pitchers back and forth. It made me hungry. In my heart.

Fuck that, I thought.

I went downstairs to the shop and switched on the lights, staring for a few minutes at the bike. I thought it was beautiful, an old Triumph. I had dragged it to the shop, its flat tires crumbling as I shoved, taken it almost completely apart, piece by piece, and inspected, cleaned and washed each chunk of steel, each bolt, each tiny rust-covered part, even the New York license plate. The carcass of the bike stood in the middle of the shop, held upright by planks. I thought of the day when all the pieces would fit together again, when they would meld and hum and run and pump oil and burn gasoline. I thought of the day when they would carry me to some place I had never been, when the wind would scream past my ears and the tears would come just from the thrill of it. Going somewhere, anywhere . . .

This time I would go somewhere.

The concrete culvert stuck out of the railroad bed and was big enough for me to crawl into. I hid there, curled into the dark and dampness, my breath coming in rasping gusts and echoing through the yellowing pipe. I had made it just ahead of the freight train and I could hear it coming around the bend, pounding slowly up a slight grade, the weight and power of it shaking the earth and the culvert.

And then it was there, above me. The culvert became a huge drum with me inside and my ears went dead, refusing to hear any more of a noise large enough to fill the Earth. The train was empty, long, the cars rattling and loose, a string of black metal boxes coming from downstream, heading up through Crum and then on to the coal fields. I knew most of the train would be empty coal cars, but usually there were some freight cars in the string somewhere, their doors sagging open, square empty eyes staring at the passing ridges and small open fields of stunted corn and sugar cane.

The bend was a long one, the train penned between the mountains on one side and river on the other, and I knew the engineer couldn't see me, once the engine had gotten well past. All I had to do was find an empty freight car, its door open, before the caboose came into view. Nothing to it.

I jumped from the culvert and scrambled up beside the moving train. The railroad bed was wide in front of me and I waited for a freight car, knowing that I would have to time my run at the car just right. I had never done this before. The drumming in my ears got louder and I realized it was my heart. I was going to hop a freight train and ride away from Crum.

The open door was directly above my head before I realized it. I started to run with the train, keeping one eye on the track and one on the open door, my old high-top basketball sneakers sliding sometimes in the loose cinders and gravel. It was easy. Almost loafing, I caught the car and pulled even with the open door, then in a burst of speed I gained the middle of the door and ran beside the car, trying to look inside. I could see nothing. The roadbed was narrowing and seemed to drop away from the car and the open door rose slowly above me, sneaking gradually out of my reach. I aimed my hands at the corner of the door and jumped.

My fingers locked on the edge and I swung upward, legs flailing behind me, the wind screaming past my ears and the tears coming just from the thrill of it. I was going to make it. I was going to some place I had never been, going somewhere, anywhere.

Somehow, I had done it wrong.

I had watched some guys in Crum jump the trains and I thought I knew how to do it but this was one of those times in my life when I learned that watching and thinking did not make up for doing, and sure as hell I had done it wrong. My own speed and the movement of the train did not join in the effort and I dangled from the edge of the car, my feet dragging in the cinders of the road bed, my body flailing at the side of the car like a heavy sack being dumped in the wind.

There was no way to get into the car. I pulled my legs up under me and let go, trying to turn and hit the cinders running. And that didn't work, either. One foot hit the ground and I never knew what happed to the other foot but it wasn't there and then the front of my shirt was gone and cinders and railroad gravel were scraping the skin off my chest, working down to my belt buckle. My face augured down into the gravel and my mouth opened, a large mistake in the general scheme of things. Somehow, before my mouth filled completely from the forced infusion of cinders and gravel, I stopped sliding.

I wasn't in pain yet, but I knew it was coming.

All my parts seemed to work and I jumped up, gagging and spitting, watching the freight car pull away from me. Behind me, more cars kept coming, but none of them were freight cars. I panicked. If I were going to jump this train, I would have to catch the one car I had missed. I started running again, the tattered shirt flying behind me, a beaten battle flag.

In less than a hundred yards, I caught the car again. I leaped for the door, got my arms inside, pulled hard and ended up in a heap on the floor. I was in, but I didn't really know how I had done it. Gasping, I rolled over on my back and folded my hands across my chest, staring out the door at the moving wall of ridges across the river in Kentucky and trying to calm my breathing. My hands felt slick and I moved them across my skin. Blood oozed from a thousand cuts, ran down my sides and disappeared under my back. And that's when the pain started.

When I sat up, I realized the train was picking up speed, heading through a straight stretch that would take it through Crum. We would go past the bus stop and the high school, then the old clapboard church and the tiny post office, and then slide by the general store. And that was all there was. We would be out the other side of Crum and I would be on the way to anywhere else.

The pain was making me a little crazy, but I knew I should get to the side of the freight car door, out of sight, especially when we went past the general store. The men who sat on the porch every day looking at the passing trains would see me, and I didn't want that. Not that anyone would really care whether I left town or not. I just didn't want anyone to know I had actually gone, or in what direction.

As I slid toward the edge of the door my hands moved through an inch-thick layer of something on the floor, something as black as coal dust, only it wasn't. It was slicker and lighter, rising in the air with each movement I made, coating every inch of my body. As the train gained speed the hot air rushed through the old car and the bumps of the wheels on the worn rails grew sharper and the stuff on the floor rose into the air all by itself and hung there, whirling, a black and lingering fog. I peeled off what was left of my shirt and wrapped it around my mouth and nose, pulling the stink of my sweat deep into my lungs. The general store slid by in the white sunlight outside the car and I knew I was out of Crum, bleeding, covered with blackness, with no idea where I was going. With no idea about anything.

The train stopped. I didn't know how long I had been riding or where we were, but the damn thing just stopped. Since we left Crum I had been sitting just to the side of the door, my eyes closed, my arms wrapped around my gut. The ooze of the blood had stopped but the heat in the wounds hadn't and all I was trying to do was block out the fire.

The freight car was on a narrow trestle, thirty feet above a small river. I didn't know what river. I scooted around and dangled my feet out the door and looked down at the dark green water moving like a great flat snake off and into the coolness of shade in the near distance. In the light of the doorway I looked worse than I had imagined. I was covered with a mixture of blood, black dust and sweat, a thickening plaster of darkness that clung to my body and blackened my mind. I fought for control of the pain. I couldn't stand it. When I realized what I had to do, I just did it. With no hesitation, without even a second's thought, I jumped. And I was in the air. Free.

Seems it took about an hour to hit the water. The rushing air softened the pain in the cuts and blew through the sweat and then the water caught my feet and shoved my legs up hard before the dimpled surface split and swallowed me in a blinding flash of light and wet. I never touched the bottom. When I knew I wasn't sinking anymore I just hung on to my mind and let myself float up. The dark green water turned pale and I was on the surface in the warmth of a noon sun, floating gently away from the train, the trestle standing crosshatched and black against the mountains behind it.

As the thrill of the jump wore down, a thousand stinging needles came alive. The water seeped through the black covering of my wounds and made the cuts fresh again, each nerve-ending screaming from the soaking. A sandbar humped golden out of the water a few yards downstream and I stroked toward it. The water shallowed and I touched the bottom. I crawled out on the sand and took off my clothes, what was left of them. Blood was oozing out of me again, and I thought maybe I should get rid of as much of the black coating as I could. At the edge of the river I scrubbed myself, as lightly as I could, with river water, mud and sand. I only screamed once.

Afterwards, I lay on the warm sand and let my pants and shoes dry until the shade edged out and covered me. I didn't know what I was going to do, or where I was going to do it. All I knew was, I was out of Crum.

But it wasn't going to work. I knew that. Not this time. I had no money, no shirt, no direction, no heart. I just couldn't do it. As the day faded into the heavy trees I pulled on my pants and shoes and started walking gingerly toward where I thought the road might be. I didn't know where I was going, so it didn't matter what direction I walked.

It took me two days to get back to Crum.

The rat wasn't dead but I knew I probably would never play that game again. It was Sunday and I would work on the old bike. Maybe read another book, wondering at the words and how they were put together. Wondering if I could use words like that, talk like that.

I would do that. But not right now. First, I would take a walk down the road, in the rain. Even though I knew I shouldn't.

❧ Twelve ❧

The dirt road led away from Eli's farm and off through the edge of the apple orchard, twisting gently through a couple of open fence gates and then past the back of the house of Luther Pritchard and his wife, Ruth Ella. The road was a shortcut to the paved county road and we used it often, moving the tractors, mowers and other equipment back and forth among the farms. The road was hard packed and even in the rain it gave some solid feel to my feet, a kind of wet grit that let me keep going, didn't give me an excuse to turn back.

I was going to do what Lard said all the other farm hands did. I was going to walk past Luther's house, in hope of seeing Ruth Ella.

The house sat about ten yards from the road, facing away from me, back at the edge of a ragged lawn. The house had once been white but now it was gray and there was not a single decoration to be seen anywhere on or around it. There was no painted trim around the doors, no railing on the small back porch. The windows looked out on the road like square, vacant eyes and I couldn't see curtains or window shades in any of them. There were no signs of flowers having been planted by the wooden steps that went up to the back porch; there were no flower boxes. The house had been reduced to its elemental purposes. It kept out the weather, and it was a dry place to eat and sleep. And in no way did it compete with the greater glory of God.

In some ways Luther Pritchard reminded me of my Great Uncle Long Neck. He was probably fifty-five, maybe even sixty. It was hard to tell, like looking at a weathered piece of wood, tangled among ancient rocks. He was as tall as Long Neck, thin as a split rail and probably as hard. And he wore bib overalls, even to church. But that's where it ended, the comparison to Long Neck. Luther had a hawk face — he was ugly, and he had no particular personality that anyone had ever seen. He was always solemn, tense, never at ease with himself or with the world in general. He was a man without humor and when his neighbors tried to interest him in social things like picnics he turned them down with curt shakes of his head. From the few times I had seen Luther when Lard and I had worked with him in the fields, from the one single time I had gone to church since I had been working for Eli, and from what Lard told me, I knew Luther was a man totally bound up in the service of his God, and in nothing else.

He should have been a preacher. He should have been a revival preacher, an evangelist, one of those raving screamers. But Luther didn't have the voice to be a preacher. Or if he did, no one ever really heard it. He didn't even sing hymns, Lard said, just looked down at the hymnal, his head nodding now and then.

Lard said Luther went to church four or five times each week, arriving early and staying late, his wife, Ruth Ella, sitting silently beside him.

Lard went to church regular-like, just to have something to do. Said it was nice to go and sit with all those folks, especially the women, even though he knew some of those folks didn't want to be there. Lard would play a game during the service; would try to pick out which of the women might fuck him if he just walked up and asked them. But he was careful to play this game only in his mind even though he knew some of them would. Fuck him, that is. And Lard said, in all the times he had been to church and watched Luther and Ruth Ella, he has never seen Luther touch her. In fact, he had never seen Luther touch anybody. And, even though Luther was Eli's closest neighbor, he never came to the Sunday picnics at Eli's house.

All Luther did was work. And go to church. Nobody knew if he did anything with Ruth Ella.

In the fields, at lunch time, Luther would pray for fifteen minutes before he began to eat, mumbling long into the hot air until the other men would carefully, silently move away from him. He was a plain man doing plain work in a plain world whose only source of light was his faith, and he practiced the rituals of that faith at every opportunity. He was a man who was easy to understand. It was easy to figure out what drove him, and what his reaction would be to any particular situation. Luther was the servant of his God.

There was only one thing about Luther that no one could understand. And that was how, as old as he was and as plain as he was and as flat as he was . . . how did he ever get a wife as young and as pretty as Ruth Ella.

They were a strange pair. Mismatched, the women said. Ruth Ella couldn't have been more than twenty-five, they said, and her married to that scrawny old man, and her with them breasts that stood straight out and they just knew that sometimes she didn't wear nothin' underneath that thin cotton dress that she always had on. Just outrageous, the women said, although they couldn't really explain what they meant by that.

Probably the only dress Luther ever bought her, the men said. The farmhands talked, especially farm hands who had put in ten hours in the steaming hay fields and had another four or five hours to go. They talked a lot about Ruth Ella Pritchard. Some said Luther bought her, went back into the far hills — some said it was in West Virginia — and just paid her family so he could take her away. Some said she was crazy, or near crazy, and that Luther had taken her out of the state asylum, or off the Poor Farm, or from whatever place they kept crazy people in Kentucky. Some of the men thought that was the most likely story — that Ruth Ella was crazy, especially since she was never seen off the farm except with Luther. Couldn't afford to let her go sashayin' around by herself, they said. Might do something nuts and get people all riled up.

In any case, the men said, she was too much woman for him. Old boy probably needs some help, now and again. But the men only said that when their women weren't around.

In spite of all the talk, there was only one thing that was known for sure. The guy who had worked for Eli before me had walked down this dirt road past Luther's house one-too-many times. And he had met Luther, and Luther's shotgun. And that guy wasn't in Jubal County any more.

I strolled past the house, in the rain, my hands shoved into my pockets, trying to look out from beneath the dripping brim of my big hat, trying to see through the walls of the house, imagining what might be happening in there, between Luther and Ruth Ella Pritchard. I thought I saw a movement, deep inside the kitchen window, but I couldn't be sure.

≈ Thirteen ≈

There should be more to tell about Kentucky, at least the time when I wintered there, but there isn't. Mostly, it was like West Virginia, just a little flatter. The people I met there weren't cannibals. They weren't even pig fuckers, like we used to yell across the river back in Crum. Mostly, they were like the people back on Black Hawk Ridge, families wound tight at the stem, sweating out the long summer days on the farms and trying to survive the cold, heavy days that marched across the winter in silent, gray, suffocating procession.

There just isn't anything to tell. I did very little that winter, my first winter out of West Virginia, except the kind of work that fades in memory like old photographs left in the sun. Mostly, we did whatever work we could to get ready for spring, and the planting, and the plowing and the haymaking when grass stood thick in the rolling fields.

And every chance I got, I walked the road past Luther's house, or drove the tractor by, shoving on the hand accelerator to make the old John Deere buck and snort as I drove slowly past the kitchen window in the distance. Once when I drove by Ruth Ella was on the back porch. She stood silently, her arms crossed in front of her, watching me without turning her head. I rolled past, embarrassed to gun the engine, and I knew her eyes followed me. They followed me until I was gone, through some apple trees and off into a field on the far side. But she never turned her head.

What I remember most was the way her arms were folded. They were under her breasts. I could swear she was pushing her breasts up and I never realized until then how big they were.

And then I drove by the house three times in a row and didn't see Ruth Ella at all. The windows were blank spaces in the wall and the kitchen light wasn't on and the porch was black under the tilting roof. Three times, and Ruth Ella nowhere in sight.

The fourth time I drove by it was the same, the house dark and cold in the early steely light of a gray day. I pulled out the hand clutch on the John Deere and sat on the vibrating old tractor, just watching. And then Luther stepped out from the corner of the house. He had a long, double-barreled shotgun cradled in his left arm. He wasn't looking at me, but he wasn't exactly looking away, either. Like he was looking behind me, trying to shove me on, get me out of there, make me move.

Whatever he was trying to do, I didn't want to ask him about it. I shoved in the clutch and the tractor lurched forward, sputtering. My hands were sweating on the wheel and I could feel Luther's eyes on my back and I couldn't help but grab a quick look behind me, just to make sure he had stayed where he was.

He hadn't. He had moved out into the yard, both hands on the shotgun now, shuffling slowly in the general direction of the John Deere. I shoved in the throttle, trying to do it casually, trying not to seem panicked. The old tractor belched and picked up speed and just when I thought I could slide through the whole thing without having to look Luther in the eye, the shotgun went off.

I was driving a tractor, an old tractor, a tractor with a muffler system standing on top of the engine just in front of me, rusted through and through and dropping tiny bits of red soft rotten metal each time the engine belched. The rhythmic pounding of the engine escaped easily through the useless muffler, a noise that drove into me each long day in the fields. And in spite of the noise of the tractor, the thunderclap of the shotgun moved me hard against the steering wheel . . .

We used the old flat-bottomed boat as a diving platform, leaping over the side and plunging down to the bottom of the shallow river to find pieces of coal rubbed shiny and dustless by the water and the sand. The coal was pretty — you could pick it up in your hands without your fingers turning black. We were going to sell the coal to the women of Crum to put in baskets in their living rooms during the winter. We were going to be rich.

My buddies, Mule and Nip, were in the boat with me. We were in the Tug River, just downstream from Crum. We kept edging closer to the Kentucky side where there was more coal.

And that's when we got into a shouting match with a couple of Kentucky pig fuckers who thought the coal belonged to them, just because it was closer to their side of the river. They wanted us to quit gathering it up. They stood on the Kentucky bank and we hollered back and forth for a while, stuff like "Cornholers!" and "Pig Fuckers!" Stuff like that. Nothing serious.

And then they started throwing rocks and we had to move the boat out of range, about six feet beyond their best throw.

Mule and Nip wanted to quit the coal business and go home but the Kentucky boys had made me mad. I didn't want to give it up. The Kentucky boys threw some more rocks, but didn't even come close. So we stayed there for a while, yelling insults back and forth, showing them the pieces of shiny coal we had. All of a sudden, we couldn't see them. It was a strange sort of business, and after they were gone we sat there feeling the letdown that sometimes comes after an exciting string of events. For a long while we didn't say a word, using long poles to hold the boat against the easy current, feeling the sun and listening to the water suck against the bottom of the boat.

It was a calm day, the sun ballooning its way toward the tops of the trees, the air silent and quiet, our backs drying in the heat. We contemplated the shiny pieces of coal in the bottom of the boat and tried to estimate the size of our fortune. In the midst of trying to figure out all the money we would make a shot crashed across the river and shotgun pellets sprayed water into the boat.

For an instant no one moved. We just looked at the bank, trying to see what the noise was and where it came from. We knew it was a shotgun but we just couldn't believe that someone was shooting at us because of a few pieces of coal. The next shot hit the water, the boat, my right arm and Mule's chest and there was no use pretending any longer. We dropped the poles and the three of us hit the water at the same time. I swam underwater downstream for as long as I could, trying to angle in toward the West Virginia side. When I came up for air, I chanced a look at the boat. It was closer to me than I thought, then I remembered that we had no anchor and the boat was floating free. We would lose it. It was headed for Kenova and the Ohio River and Cincinnati with our fortune aboard, and another shotgun blast reminded me that to try and stop it would only bring more lead flying my way. I went under again and headed for shore, pulling myself out of the water and in among slimy tree roots. I felt that I was safe, and I crawled up the bank and into the weeds, lying quietly. The shotgun couldn't reach me there, but I wanted to take no chances.

I was wet and I was cold. I began to crawl farther away from the bank. I could hear some thrashing around in the weeds to my right and I crawled toward the sound, found Mule, holding his chest, rolling around in the weeds and moaning into the mud under his face as he rolled over and over. There was lots of blood and I figured that he was going to die and I wondered if I would ever get the chance to get even with those pig fuckers who were probably still sitting on that other bank laughing and pissing into the water.

Nip crawled up and we turned Mule over. He had six small holes in his chest with little black pellets sticking in them. When I saw the tops of the pellets, I knew Mule wasn't going to die, after all. A trickle of blood came from each tiny hole. Nip calmly took one of the pellets between his fingers and squeezed underneath it until it popped out. Jesus, I just don't think I could have done that. When he was finished with Mule, Nip took my arm and squeezed out the pellets. All the tiny holes bled more, but at least the pellets weren't in there.

I whirled in the tractor seat, letting go of the wheel, grabbing at my back, a scream clawing solidly into the bottom of my throat, sure that, any second now, the first numb shock of the blast against my back would wear off and I would feel the deep sting of the lead shot.

My shirt was in one piece. There was no blood. I hadn't been hit at all. In the road a few yards behind the tractor a ragged dog lay dying, bits and parts of it scattered to the side, some ribs exposed where raging shot had stripped the thin hair and stringy meat.

I held the wheel with one hand, half twisting in the seat so I could keep one eye on Luther. I turned the tractor off the lane and across a bald-cropped hay field. All the while Luther just stood there, the shotgun gripped and held high, one barrel still loaded, staring after me. He never looked at the dog.

Sometimes I would go down to Fletcher's Beer Garden, a couple of miles down the road toward the tiny town of Bean Camp. I guess I looked older than I was because they never asked me any questions about my age in Fletcher's. I would sit in a corner and drink cheap beer and not talk to anyone, mostly because no one would talk to me. I never knew why. I guessed it was because they knew I was just a field hand and that field hands came and went in Jubal County and there was just no use in wasting time talking with a hand who probably wouldn't last out the winter.

I wondered about that, about not being around long. I sort of liked it there in Bean Camp. The room up in the barn wasn't that bad and I had gotten used to scrubbing myself out by the cistern, even when the air was thick and heavy with snowflakes. Eli saw me out there once, scrubbing down in the snow. He just shook his head and walked away. That's what Long Neck would have done.

But, seems like something was missing. I was out of West Virginia, but, goddamn, I was in *Kentucky*. Seems like there should be more to it than this, I thought. This is too much like whatever it is that I'm trying to get away from. The air is the same and the people are the same and the dark places between the trees still stare at me in the fading evening and I know if I stare back long enough I'll see all of Black Hawk Ridge in there.

Mostly, I worked on the motorcycle. As the short days and long evenings drifted by, the motorcycle began to reform itself. I got parts cleaned and oiled and back where they belonged, for the most part, and one evening when I came in from helping Lard replace a broken part on his baler there were two new motorcycle tires leaning against the wall of the shop. I sat on the floor and hugged the tires and for some reason I had trouble seeing. Water pooled stinging in my eyes.

The next morning when I went to the house for breakfast Eli sat silently at the head of the table. We ate slowly, in no hurry, for once, to get out into the cold.

I couldn't seem to get any words out. "I, uh, I'm gettin' pretty far . . . uh, the motorcycle . . . might be able . . ."

Eli looked up and glanced at Geneva, taking biscuits out of the stove. His face reddened slightly and he put a finger gently to his lips. I shut up. Geneva came to the table.

"You still fooling with that old machine? You know it won't ever run. Been out there in the barn for as long as I can remember," she said, shaking her head.

Eli said nothing. I said nothing. We finished our breakfast and got out of there.

I wondered how someone made a decision to stay some place, or to leave some place. I mean, I never decided to leave Black Hawk Ridge, I just knew that I would. And Crum? Hell, I knew I wasn't staying in Crum from the day I walked over the top of Bull Mountain on the way down into town and felt my bowels cramp. But I got to wondering about Bean Camp. How would I know if I was supposed to stay? I would catch myself wondering about that as I turned wrenches on the motorcycle or wiped the grease from a fender.

I was still wondering about it late one night, with the bare bulb burning hotly in the shop, when I kicked the starter on the old bike and the Triumph coughed, farted, and came back from the dead.

Turns out, I didn't have to decide about whether to stay in Bean Camp, and it had nothing to do with the Triumph.

Decisions are easy, sometimes, when you don't have to make them yourself.

✒ Fourteen ✒

One day there was a different smell in the air and the rain tasted softer and a couple of green shoots shoved up through the mud and a bird that I had never seen before landed in the barn. And when Eli changed the oil in the tractor, I knew it was spring.

And that's when the Reverend Abel Hitch showed up.

Lard and I were in Eli's barn sharpening the blade on the mowing machine. A 1941 Chevrolet came up the road and made the turn toward Eli's house. The car was black but everything but the roof was coated with mud and the left front fender had nearly been torn off. The fender hung by a metal strap that had been bolted to the hood and the bumper.

Abel Hitch got out. I had never seen him before, but I knew who he was. His left leg seemed to hang in the air when he opened the door. It didn't hit the ground until he swung the other leg out, and then I saw his left arm. The arm and leg were short, crooked, hanging from his frame like Halloween decorations. When he stood up he tilted to one side and I thought he would fall over. But he moved toward Eli's front door with an almost graceful step, swinging his good leg forward and then rising on it, his body moving up and down like a man seen at a distance on a child's teeter-totter. And he moved with a purpose.

"What do you think he's doing here?"

Lard was staring after Abel Hitch. "Well, best guess is, it's time for revival meetin', and Abel knows that Eli can bring a lot of people to the church. Reckon he's here to set Eli up."

"How'd he get like that, anyway?"

Lard stared vacantly at the house, watching Abel Hitch disappear inside. "Story is, his pappy was a preacher, too. Self ordained — you know how that is. Preached in all them little churches out in the mountains, little churches what couldn't afford a regular preacher. Well, they say Abel Hitch was just a young'en, just a little kid who would go with his pappy when he preached. One Sunday, Abel got restless and sneaked out of church, out to the churchyard where the horses were tied and the wagons were hitched. He played out there for a while, then he got tired and sleepy — seems his pappy could preach for longer than the devil could keep up, could go into trances and speak in tongues and things like that. Sun was high and hot. Abel laid down under his pappy's wagon and went to sleep, just a little kid napping in the shade.

"The preaching finally stopped and the people come out. Some said his pappy was still in his preaching, still tuned into God. His pappy climbed in the wagon and started off, not even looking for Abel. Wagon wheel rolled over Abel's leg and then his arm and then clipped the side of his head. When Abel felt the wagon wheel crushing him, he screamed, screamed like no other scream has ever been screamed, some said. The horse jumped and bucked forward and then twisted. Slammed the wagon into a tree. Abel's pappy hit the tree headfirst. Broke his durn neck.

"Then all the people just stood around and looked at the dead preacher and the little kid with half his body rolled over. Devil's doin', they said. Served the little servant of Satan right. And they left him there."

And they left him there. And they left him there. Jesus, God. "That's a damn lie. You made that up."

Lard looked at me. He wasn't smiling. "Well," he said softly in his squeaky voice, "don't think I'd lie about no preacher. Specially one that's been preaching all his life, trying to make it all up to God."

We worked on the mower blade in silence.

Abel Hitch came out of the house, his bouncing gait seeming more pronounced. At the car, before he got in, he stared at the barn. I couldn't really see his eyes, but I was sure he could see mine. He drove away.

"How the hell does he drive that car, him with that short leg and all?"

"Don't rightly know. Been wondering about that myself. Don't nobody know. Nobody'll get in the car with him to find out."

"Don't matter. Don't like the looks of that 'un. Think I'll just stay from him. Church ain't my kind of thing, anyway, and revival sure as hell ain't, neither."

"Yeah. That's what I used to say. But I got to tell you something, boy. You could live here in Bean Camp for fifty years, and you ain't going to see no better show than Abel Hitch's revival service. No, sir, you ain't."

Lard was a prophet.

≈ Fifteen ≈

I still drove by the Pritchard farm, but I was a little more careful about it. I only went by when I was driving the big John Deere. I thought maybe it was fast enough to outrun Luther if he came bustin' out the back door of his house. I tried not to think about the shotgun.

You'd think I'd learn. But sometimes I never did.

I still saw Ruth Ella sometimes in the late evenings, if I was lucky enough to get out of the fields before full dark. As I brought the huge, clanking tractor home, its lights flickering along the trees that lined the road, I would catch sight of her on the porch, or moving slowly around the side of the house. And I knew that she watched me, too, sometimes, from her kitchen window. You could tell about those things. You really could. I liked the idea that she was watching.

I knew she was watching. I just knew.

And then I was coming back to Eli's barn in the dark again, the tractor loafing through the night on the road past Luther's house, and Ruth Ella was standing at the window in the kitchen, plain as day. This time, I was sure that she had been waiting for me to go by. She disappeared from the window and the next thing I knew she was standing on the back porch, just staring at me. I pulled the hand clutch and the John Deere rolled slowly to a halt. I shoved the fuel lever a couple of times, just a little, popping the engine. I sat there in the dark, a fool on a tractor looking at the silhouette of a woman standing in front of a lighted window, a woman looking out into the dark, neither of us moving.

I shoved the clutch in and the tractor crept forward, the big wheels hardly turning.

And Ruth Ella raised her hand there in the dim light, a soft and lonely wave into the darkness. I thought maybe she could not actually see who it was, out there in the dark, but she knew the sound of the tractor. And the wave made me feel lonely.

Two nights later, scared and excited, I stopped the tractor behind her house again, flicking the lights, pretending some sort of engine trouble. Almost instantly the light in the kitchen window went out. I sat on the tractor, not knowing what to do. And then the light went on again. I heard the screen door of the kitchen open and close and then Ruth Ella was walking across the grass toward the tractor, her long skirt casting a shadow from the light in the kitchen window. She walked to the rear of the tractor, put her foot on the drawbar and without hesitation swung herself up to the seat. In one swift motion her skirt was up and she was sitting on my lap, facing me, the tractor still running, its lights off. She pulled my head to her and kissed me. I had never been kissed like that before. Not even by Slick Jesse.

I was petrified. I didn't know what I was supposed to do, sitting on a tractor vibrating from the running engine, with the wife of a religious fanatic astride my lap, *grinding* her hips into mine, feeling for the back of my mouth with her silky tongue. For a few seconds I did nothing. Then, caught in the craziness of what was going on, I slid my hands along her bare legs until I felt the round softness of her buttocks and I cupped them, massaging her, working with her grinding motion until the pressure of her on my lap, shifting, wet, made my jeans chafe my legs like sandpaper. I was only mildly surprised that she wasn't wearing panties.

She was sucking the breath right out of me and my mind wasn't working properly. With an ease that I never knew was possible I was going with her, moving with her. We were an instant team, joined neatly together, welded tightly to each other and to the seat of the tractor, humming with the tractor's heavy vibrations as the engine ticked in rhythm with her grinding. She showed no signs of stopping. I wanted desperately to lift her, to get off the tractor and onto the soft grass but she pinned me to the seat, her legs wrapped tightly around the sides.

She gripped the narrow metal arms of the tractor seat and leaned backward, driving herself even harder against me. Her breasts pushed up against her high-necked blouse and I put my hands on them and squeezed and I could feel her stiffen at the pressure. The buttons on the blouse came open easily and I could feel a brassiere that was strong enough to hold rocks in a rainstorm, a bra designed never, ever, to let a soft fold of flesh creep out around the edges.

I pushed her blouse down off her shoulders and hooked my fingers under the shoulder straps of the bra and slid them down her arms. She was still leaning hard backwards and her breasts popped out of the bra and stood straight toward the sky, nipples hard. I squeezed them both, then slid my arms around her and pulled her tightly against me, burying my face between the most perfect breasts I had ever seen.

With a fumbling effort I pushed my hand down into my lap, forcing it between us and into her crotch, my knuckles running hard against her. She was slick and wet, wetter than I thought possible. My arm was covered with her juices halfway to my elbow. Her wetness caused me to gasp and my mouth popped away from her breasts.

"Unnnnhhhh", I grunted, the sound coming from deep within my stomach, and then she covered my mouth again with hers.

She pulled back on me, driving her hips harder into my lap. I lurched forward and extended my other arm for support. I hit the gas lever.

I had never heard a sound like it, the sound of a tractor, in neutral, revving at the top of its throttle. The old machine vibrated wildly, the engine trying to tear itself from the rusting mounts. I fumbled for the gas lever but couldn't find it and in the middle of wondering whether the engine would blow I forgot about the whole thing. I really didn't care. I had other things to think about.

I pulled my arm back and forced it under her, lifting her slightly. I forced my fingers to the buttons of my jeans, ripping them open. I fumbled for my dick but my jeans were too tight and she left me no room to work with, her hips still grinding into me. In a final effort before I burst I shoved up against her with my hand and forced a small space between us. In one swift motion my prick pushed free from my jeans and I turned my hand, aiming it, and popped it into her, deeply.

Instantly, her motions stopped. She sat stock-still, me driven into her farther than I ever thought possible, the tractor thundering beneath us.

And then she jerked backwards from me, sliding sideways from my lap. She stood, her feet planted on the metal platform beneath the seat, her breasts suspended above me, her skirt flowing back down around her legs. She stepped out on the rear axle of the tractor and in another long step was on the ground and walking back to the house. She walked not too fast, but not too slowly. It was a calculated walk. It was not a running away.

The top of her dress still hung down around her waist.

And neither of us had spoken a word.

I watched her fade into the darkness toward the house, now and then catching the movement of her against the yellow lights of the kitchen as the heavy crackling of the tractor engine beat against my ears. I pulled the gas lever toward me, quieting the engine. I wondered briefly if Luther had heard the heavy pounding of the old tractor, then thought maybe he wasn't even home. If he had been, he probably would have been out there behind the house, with his shotgun. And then I wondered if this is how it happened to the other guy, him thinking Luther wasn't home, or thinking Luther was already in bed, having turned in just shortly after dark, exhausted from the day's work, eyes made heavy from the dust of the fields and from his hour of reading the Bible before he turned out the light.

Maybe that's what the guy thought. And maybe he had been wrong.

My God, I thought, I have been in her, I have been in another man's wife. But what the hell happened here, anyway? Did I fuck her? I didn't even get to make a stroke.

I put the tractor in gear and drove away, my balls aching, my stomach so tense that I was almost sick, my dick still out, still slick from the wet of her, flapping in the warm night air. The tractor bounced over the dirt road and the movement worked inside me, up and down, jumping, slamming. I drove faster, trying to get to the barn before the aching and the bouncing combined to finish me, to make me throw up there on a dirt road in the back side of a county that was too much like I remembered and never wanted to see again in the summer blackness of my nightmares.

> It wasn't my fault.
> She started it.
> I just happened to be there.
> Luther didn't deserve her.
> She needed it. She really needed it.
> I just helped out.
> I couldn't get away from her.
> She held me in the seat.
> She wanted it.
> I was just driving by.
> If her old man wasn't such a Jesus freak . . .

I tried to sell myself all those things, all those reasons why it wasn't my fault.

Bullshit. I did it, it was my fault, and I knew it.

The cold of the workshop floor came up through my jeans as I sat cross-legged at the side of the motorcycle, turning bolts and making adjustments and trying to convince myself that it wasn't my fault. Nothing that two people do together is all the fault of one, Long Neck used to say. Maybe so. But what if one of them is crazy? And who decides which one is the crazy one?

I spent days wandering around the farm thinking about Ruth Ella. When I went out on the tractor I drove the long way, out to the highway and across the backside of the valley, just to avoid going by her house. I *wanted* to go by her house, I wanted to see her standing there, I wanted to come back in the dark and stop the tractor on the road near her kitchen window. I wanted to finish what I started.

Somehow the air seemed charged with Ruth Ella. She was the first thing I thought about in the morning, the last thing I thought about at night. For two weeks I walked around in a fog, seeing Ruth Ella ghosting through the mist and walking in graceful steps across the blackened grass of night. The days drug by slowly, the dampness of spring creeping into my jacket as I hauled deadwood from the orchard. My thin blanket seemed to strangle me as I lay in my cot in the loft, half charged with fear, half with ache, my mind full of Ruth Ella. I had to stop thinking about her. She didn't belong to me, not even in my dreams. But something had started that had to be resolved. It couldn't just stay this way. Something had to happen.

What happened was, Lard talked me into going to the last night of the revival service. I had forgotten about revival service, and Abel Hitch, and all the people who would be crammed into the little brick church. But Lard made me remember. He made me remember that Luther would be there, at the revival service, with Ruth Ella sitting beside him.

Lard made me remember. I would never forget revival service again, not as long as I lived.

☙ Sixteen ❧

The voice had the power, the glory in it. It came storming out of the pulpit, driving through the hot, thick air inside the old brick church, blowing through the open windows and out into the dark, deserted churchyard and off down through the trees. I thought it probably caused ripples on the creek.

The people sat on the hard wooden pews, row upon row of sweating faces and bodies, transfixed. The voice slammed into their minds, making their heads seem heavy, their necks hunched into their shoulders.

I wanted to get out of there but there was no way I could break loose from where I was sitting without the whole church seeing me. Without Ruth Ella seeing me.

And besides, there was the voice. It was the most God-awful, beautiful, wonderful voice I had ever heard. It lashed the Word of God from wall to wall inside the church, whipped the Word across the shoulders and down the backs of the people, cracked it over their heads, a punishment and a burden made heavier by the terrible timbre of the voice. Its sheer force jolted some of them to their feet, drove them out into the aisle and stampeded them, joining them with mindless trampling to the front of the church, there to be rescued from eternal hell, to be pulled back from the very brink of everlasting roasting above the fires of the black universe. To be saved.

As the voice went on it grew slightly higher in pitch, now and then wavering a bit, allowing the subtle underpinnings of hysteria to creep through the strength of the performance. The voice flew and dived, sometimes cracked, quivered on the edge of dissolution only to come back with even more power. It roared and purred in the same breath, the same sentence, as it spewed from the mouth of the stumpy, warped, little man with the barrel chest who stomped and strutted back and forth behind the pulpit, his crooked leg and withered left arm flailing, his left eye astray. As he stood on the raised platform he would stare intently at the far side of the church, his face squarely in that direction. But his wandering eye, the left one, would flick across the faces on the other side of the aisle in an eerie, frightening and detached search for unbelievers.

His bad leg and the curl of his arm made him walk with a pronounced stoop that brought him even closer to the floor, a fierce gnome clumping back and forth across the wooden platform, dust from the ancient floorboards floating in a thin cloud about his legs. He waved his good arm, keeping his withered one against his chest, using the contrast of the two limbs for maximum effect.

But the thing I noticed most about him — besides his voice — was his chest. In spite of his abnormalities, the man's chest was perfect, so large that it, too, was almost an abnormality. The chest was far too large for a man of his size, a chest that swelled and filled his dripping white shirt and pressed against the little narrow black tie he wore. For some reason I kept noticing that tie. It was longer than any tie I had ever seen, hanging down below his belt, dangling in front of his fly, almost to his crotch. I had never worn a tie. I had seen some, of course, but I had never seen one that long. It must have been made special, just so it could get down over that chest. The preacher wore no coat and that long tie cracked back and forth like the whip of the very devil as he snapped himself across the platform.

Abel Hitch enjoyed his work and the sound of his own voice. He pulled the voice from deep inside his enormous chest and the chest sweated. The thin white shirt passed the sweat through to the outside very quickly, giving the people in the first rows a whiff, now and then, of hard-working preacher, undiluted, undistilled.

The old platform shook and the pulpit quivered from the stomping of his feet. Behind him, along a low plank wall that stood about chest high, were several straight-backed cane-bottomed chairs. No one sat in them. Heavy drapes, the color of old blood, hung behind the low wall. The drapes were closed over the baptistery, an alcove above and behind the pulpit. The baptistery housed an oblong tank full of water, a converted stock tank, originally used to water cattle. Now, installed in the alcove beneath a heavy plank cover, the tank was used to baptize sinners who wanted to be cleansed.

The drapes were closed. The tank was full of water. Ready. "Always ready to baptize," the church said on its signboard out next to the road.

The whole thing should have been ludicrous, but it wasn't. To me, it was real and frightening, a vivid reenactment of scenes I remembered as I stood on a rotting stump outside the window of the little wooden church on Black Hawk Ridge, hidden deep in the forest, watching the people shout and weave and make strange sounds in their throats. Religion had been a little heavy for me then, weighing on my chest and sagging into my stomach; a dead weight, cumbersome, dragging at me. Now, here in other hills and among other people, it was still the same. And it was still too heavy.

I had not moved a muscle for several minutes, trying not to draw attention to myself. The revival services had been going on for five consecutive nights and this was Sunday, the last night of revival, and my first night there. I had heard the preacher had a way of picking out the newcomers, calling the attention of the congregation to the fact that a new member of the unfaithful was now among them.

There must have been four hundred people jammed into the church, some of them trying to be there but be invisible, trying not to be picked out as the preacher searched for a glint of lipstick or shoes with heels too high. Both mortal sins. At fifty feet his good eye could see the bulge of a pack of cigarettes in a shirt pocket, smoking being a sin next to murder itself. The eye flicked over every woman in the congregation, trying to find just the hint of a knee showing below a skirt, a transgression second only to prostitution. I could never figure out what his bad eye was seeing.

Revival time.

A Sunday night when the early spring had turned hot and the old church reeled with the impact of the heat, the press of the people and the voice of the preacher, the preacher brought in to stir the souls afresh, to drive His Word and His power more deeply into the hearts of sinners than the regular preacher ever could. He was not afraid of the congregation. He already had been paid and the deacons could not fire him. When this revival was over he would go back to Sulphur County, leaving the regular preacher to pick up the pieces as best he could. He had a reputation, this evangelist. He worked hard at living up to it. It was said in Sulphur County that he lived alone and that he was never seen in the company of anyone else except when we was in a church.

I had never breathed thicker air. Others were shouting but I thought that if I tried to speak that nothing would get beyond my lips, that the sounds would die in the thickness at the edge of my tongue, would stagnate in my mouth.

The voice crept higher, the roar became a scream and the purring became scratched and hard as the sermon went on. The people sat tightly packed, swaying, sweating, clapping hands, murmuring low Amens! and Yesses! and Praise Jesuses! Their legs and shoulders pressed against those of the people next to them and the swaying rhythm was led on, encouraged, by the cadence of the sermon.

And then I realized that it wasn't really a sermon, that long ago any attempt at a coherent message — except one — had vanished from the preacher's words. Only the main point was driven home, again and again. Come forward and be saved! Come forward and be washed free of sin! Come forward!

Come forward and raise the head count, I thought.

I sat as still as I could. My heart was beating quickly and I could feel the effect of the hypnotic words pouring over the pews and down around my feet, creeping in waves up my legs and into my stomach. I had a vaguely familiar feeling oozing through me, a feeling that I seemed to recognize, seemed to know. I felt the deep stirrings but the familiar feeling was coming from an unfamiliar direction and I couldn't identify it. I became preoccupied with the feeling, pushing it around in my mind. It disturbed me. It wasn't fear. It was something far different. To fight it off I carefully turned my head and tried to look at others in the packed congregation. They were mesmerized, caught, staring hard at the preacher, eyes wide, tears streaming, some blinking, mouths moving in spasmodic jerks, spitting out their low murmurs and words in fits of energy as the preacher led them on. The preacher's voice had caught me so fully that only when I turned to look did I realize there were other distinct sounds in the room, low rumblings that became sharp, glittering sounds that I was not used to hearing. People began shouting, opening their mouths to loud AMENS! and HALLELUJAHS!, the spittle flying from their lips and spraying through the thick air to settle on the people in the rows in front of them.

Sometimes when they shouted they would leap to their feet in mid-shout, coats flying open, skirts bouncing, only to flop down again, hard against the shiny wooden benches, butts mashing into butts, ass to ass contact between people who believed that dancing was a sin. I was totally caught by the people, by their almost complete abandon. I could not take my eyes from them, from the puppet dance of the jumpers and the shouters, from the jack-in-the-box gyrations of the believers, of the confessed sinners.

Far to the rear of the church and high up there was a small balcony. A woman hung over the railing, arms stretched toward the preacher, full breasts being pushed hard against the top of her dress as the railing shoved up and into her stomach. She was shouting in spasmodic bursts at the preacher, flinging her arms forward as though flicking water from her fingertips, keeping time with a shouter down below, a man who alternated his deeper voice with her high pitch to produce a rhythmic staccato of religious fervor, spittle flying from the balcony, spittle flying from the pews.

≈ Seventeen ≈

Lard had dragged me to a seat near the aisle, only a few rows back from the pulpit, and then the big bastard had disappeared, laughing, leaving me there within sweat-smelling range of the preacher. My neck began to ache from being twisted far to the left as I watched the people. As I tried to find Ruth Ella.

Suddenly, the woman sitting just to my right leaped to her feet, her face rigid, her arms clamped against her sides. I turned to look at her as she stared at the preacher, trembling in anticipation of something she did not understand. She was a plain woman, tall, her hair pulled back in a tight knot at the back of her head. She looked to be about thirty-five or so and standing there with sweat running down her face and arms she was a basic human animal, focused on something that was compelling. There was sweat running down the insides of her legs, too, I thought. There were others standing in the church, many others, but this one was standing right next to me, swaying, building herself for some final plunge. Her shoulders were back and her nipples were standing hard against her dress. My God, I thought, if she's like all the other women here, she's wearing a bra that could hold a sack of nails without showing through, and yet her nipples are making little bumps on her dress; nipples like hard-boiled bird eggs. She spread her legs, jamming a leg against me. I could feel the trembling in it, the anticipation of something to come.

I didn't want to, I told myself. I tried to control it, but in spite of myself I felt the creeping hardness begin in my crotch. I was getting a hard-on.

The woman moved a little, edging forward, then began to make her way past me, heading for the aisle. As she stepped in front of me she momentarily lost her balance and flopped down onto my lap, awkwardly pumping her legs to try to regain her feet. In reflex my hands shot up and clamped to her ass, each hand cupping the outside of a hard cheek, squeezing. I suddenly realized that I was sitting in a frenzied crowd with my hands jammed against a firm farm ass and that I was pulling that ass harder against me. But no one seemed to notice that I had a woman sitting on my lap. I fought the urge to hunch upwards into her as I felt myself grow harder, as the woman ground her hips into me. The vision of her nipples flashed through my mind and I thought I could see them clearly, even though my nose was pressed flat against her back.

Suddenly she was on her feet again, moving into the aisle, then rushing quickly toward the front of the church. She never looked back. The preacher watched her come, his eyes shining in the dim light, sweat pouring down his face. He watched her come but he never lost the rhythm of his sermon, never lost the flow of his voice, never lost control.

It was one of the most sexual things I had ever been a part of.

I was stunned. I suddenly recognized the vaguely familiar feeling running around in my guts. It was lust, pure and simple lust, a basic drive to couple hard and fast with the first woman who crossed my path. I felt myself being drawn into it, into some ritual which I knew had nothing to do with God or religion or worship or goodness or sin, into some ritual which existed for its own sake, for the power and drama of its own personal being, a ritual that rose and fell in great waves of light and blackness. I was held. My mind darted back and forth, trying to understand, trying to cope.

A few years later I would think back on it and would say to myself that the ritual, this thing called a revival, was an outlet for people whose lives did not provide such outlets, an outlet for people who slept in heavy nightclothes, who undressed and dressed for bed while standing in the darkness of their closets, who wore no makeup, who did not dance, who went to church five or six times a week, who lived hard, Spartan lives of incredible pain and dullness, and who were told all their lives that they were sinners. The ritual, I thought then, was necessary. It probably kept them from going crazy. I would state this opinion while standing in the bright sun of a cool Oregon forest. I would be talking to a lumberjack, a man of huge size and strength who kept a baseball-size wad of chewing tobacco pounded into his cheek. And the lumberjack would hit me, the mallet-fist smashing into my mouth, splitting the skin and neatly removing a tooth. But the fist would not change my mind.

In the frenzy of the church I found Ruth Ella. I had been looking too far away — she was just across the aisle, tucked into the pew on the far side of Luther, rocking back and forth, caught in the rhythm of the preacher. Even at a distance I could see there was sweat on her upper lip and on her temples, the small drops running down her face like tears. I knew the taste of that sweat, knew how it felt to rub my face against it, knew the warmth and slickness of it under my hands. Her jet-black hair was pulled tightly back, caught there with a long black ribbon that bobbed as she nervously twitched her head.

Luther stared straight forward, motionless. Amazingly, he looked bored. His face was turned down in a slight frown as he stared hard at the preacher, not giving away for a second anything that might be going on inside him. I had heard that Luther's religious fervor could be a terrible thing to see, but for some reason Luther seemed to be holding it in check. He sat tense and motionless, trying hard to follow the preacher's words. His long arms and wide, thin shoulders hardly moved, even though Ruth Ella fidgeted in her seat beside him.

I kept staring at Ruth Ella. Cautiously, she turned her head in my direction, a fraction of an inch at a time, carefully, afraid both of Luther and the preacher. She flicked her eyes toward me. I could tell that she was caught up in the ritual, the revival, pulled into the flow of words, shouts, the stamping of feet, the thump of asses on the hard benches. Flashes of pain and confusion snapped across her face, glimpses of near-hysteria, and I thought she might actually run down the aisle and throw herself at the feet of the evangelist. She could do crazy things; I had learned that for myself. Oh, God, I thought, if she runs down that aisle and blurts out her sins to the preacher, mine will be the first name she calls. And Luther will kill me in the name of God. His friends and neighbors will trap me right here in the church. Jesus Christ! I might become a sacrifice!

Suddenly, the eruption stopped. The torrent of words from the front of the church was cut off. A few shouters in the congregation kept it up for a few seconds, then they, too, stopped, but still moved their mouths in silent frustration as the words still struggled to come out. In spite of myself, I pulled my gaze from Ruth Ella and looked toward the front of the church. For a moment, I thought maybe the preacher had died, maybe from the sheer weight of his righteousness.

The preacher was at the pulpit, gripping the wood with his hands, his knuckles white with the effort of it, his clothing soaked with sweat, the stains running underneath his belt and down into the top of his pants. His face bulged and shone with a redness that I had never seen before in any other man, the veins standing out in his neck, his thin and stringy hair falling down over his face.

It was then that I noticed the front of the church was crowded with people, people standing in rows, jammed together in the space between the very first row and the raised platform on which stood the pulpit. They were packed together, swaying back and forth, pressed, rubbing. There didn't seem to be room for more, but the preacher wasn't satisfied. He stood there in silence, glaring down at the crowd. He seemed about to explode.

He was preparing for his final onslaught against the devil.

≈ Eighteen ≈

"There are SMOKERS among you!" the preacher screamed, seeming to reach his full volume instantly from a standing start. The words whipped out across the tense congregation and slammed against the back wall of the church, trapped and echoing underneath the balcony.

"SMOKERS! There are SMOKERS, I say, and ye must be cleansed! Ye must confess your sin and be washed free! Ye must rid thyself of the devil weed!" The preacher's voice had not lost its pitch — he had no intention of allowing anyone to back up from the edge of the frenzy he had created.

"Now, listen to my word! Listen to the word of God! All of you, ANY of you who smokes, who inhales the devil's weed, I want you to stand up and face the rear of this church! Any of YOU! Stand up, sinners, stand UP and face the rear of God's house!"

Christ, I thought, I've never seen this before.

The last AMEN! died a strangled death in the back of the church as the shouters suddenly lost their enthusiasm. A nervous twitching crept through the crowd and people glanced quickly at each other. But, hell, they thought — I could see it in their faces — it couldn't be all that bad. Smoking wasn't that hard a thing to confess to. And, besides, they were trapped. They had willingly joined the ritual, the madness, and now they had to take the last step. Since every mortal sinned every day — so they had been told each day, all their lives — they had to confess to *something*, so why not confess to smoking? Probably, most of the men in the congregation smoked, and they and all their friends knew it, friends who were also in the congregation and who also smoked. Why the hell not stand up and show the people that you could confess your sins?

Luther was the first in the congregation to get to his feet. For a second or so he stared at the preacher, stared at the crowd of sinners waiting to be saved, swaying, a little more easily now, at the foot of the pulpit. Tension knotted through the room. Then Luther turned sharply and faced the rear of the church, his face ablaze with the enormity of his confession. He was a smoker. And he would be damned.

I turned my head until my neck hurt, trying at the same time to watch Ruth Ella and to look at the back of the church, half expecting to see God Himself back there waiting with clenched fists and an ashtray to smite Luther.

It was then that the people in the church learned a very simple thing. When a sinner stands up and faces the rear of the church, he is looking directly into the faces of his friends and neighbors. They are staring right up his nose, the whole church-full of them. The preacher had chosen his tactic well. Luther's eyes rolled and he wobbled a bit, his legs going soft under him. He grabbed the back of the pew to keep from falling.

Around the church, following Luther's cue, other people got to their feet and turned toward the back of the church. They were mostly men. Some rose and turned slowly, driven by the hot voice of the preacher as their bodies twisted in a sticky dance of confession. Some leaped up and snapped around, trying to get it over with as quickly as possible. But no one looked directly into the eyes of those still facing the front of the church, those non-smokers — or those liars. Everyone standing looked *over* the other people in the congregation, looked *over* those staring eyes and those hot nostrils. Everyone standing stared hard at the blank wall of the rear of the church, under the narrow balcony, where the silent bricks did not stare back at them.

"Before this service is over I want all of you sinners up here, in the front of God's house, joining with the others already here, good people who have come forth to cleanse themselves!" The voice screamed its message in the shrill tones of damnation, sending chills stabbing behind the eyes of the congregation, skywriting its dictum across air grown even thicker with sweat and the stench of fear.

The preacher raved on for a while, then ordered the sinners to sit. Instantly, all the confessed smokers turned and sat. There was a mass thump as asses hit wood, accompanied by a clearly audible sigh as the smokers were, for the moment, relieved of their place in the spotlight. But they were still trapped. The preacher knew who they were.

I was beginning to feel a little panicky. Something bigger, something worse, was coming and I could smell the fear of it rising from the floor of the church. I wanted to get out of there but I couldn't think of any way to do it. I wasn't anywhere near a door and, besides, there was no hope of just sneaking out. I could feel the panic rising higher in my mind. I wasn't a smoker — well, maybe one cigarette now and then, or some corn silk — so I didn't stand up. Hell, I wouldn't have stood up if I smoked a carton a day.

But I knew the preacher wouldn't leave it alone. I knew there was something else coming down.

I looked at Ruth Ella. She was crying, huge tears sliding down her cheeks and actually splashing onto her blouse. Her head nodded up and down with her sobs and the bun of her hair snapped back and forth with her movements.

"LIARS! There are LIARS among you! Stand up and be cleansed, you LIARS, as your neighbors have been cleansed of their smoking!"

Jesus Christ! I was right! The sins were going to get harder and harder to confess to.

"Any of you, ANY of you who have ever told a lie and not been washed clean by the forgiveness of God, stand and be washed! A lie of any kind, even the smallest, must be cleansed!" he screamed.

Lies. I had told my share. I had lied to keep from going to school, I had lied to keep from not going to school. I had lied to keep from getting my ass kicked. I had lied to Ruby, back there in Crum, when I told her I didn't care what she did.

I had never lied to Yvonne.

But I was not about to stand up and face the rear of that church.

The preacher was getting to the real sins now, and I began to wonder when he would get to a sin that I couldn't avoid, a sin that someone else in the congregation knew I had committed.

Actually, the whole thing was getting pretty interesting. I was scared to death, but I couldn't wait to see what was coming next. And besides, I thought, I'm only an itinerant farmhand, just hanging around here for as long as the work holds out. Then I'll move on. No one knows me. Not really. They don't know if I'm a liar — I've never lied to them. I sleep in a room in Eli's barn, I drive his tractors, I rake his hay, I pick his apples, I fix his fences and sometimes I get to eat at his table, but I have never lied to him.

I'm safe, I thought.

Ruth Ella, I thought.

Oh, shit.

I sat still, my head heavy with the thought of escape, of running from the church. I thought it was serious, but somehow I couldn't completely accept it as so. What was the power here, anyway? Was it God? Was it the crippled little preacher? What was holding all these people? And suddenly I could feel it creeping up inside me, forcing its way into my consciousness and into the back of my throat. The uncontrollable urge to laugh.

Some of the liars stood and faced the back of the church. A white lie, they must have thought, is not so hard to confess to. It looked like a long night and a body had to confess to something to get out of the church with a whole skin. Better to confess now, because bigger sins were on the menu.

The liars were ordered to sit down.

"The demon RUM has washed your throats! Ye have fallen to the idol of alcohol, ALCOHOL!"

Oh, shit, I thought, choking the laugh down deep in my throat, remembering the times I left my room in the barn long after dark to walk down to Fletcher's Beer Garden to sit in a booth and sip cheap beer from long-neck bottles and to listen to the hillbilly music that never seemed to stop coming from the jukebox. I felt the panic rushing up into my chest again, pushing aside the urge to laugh. Was any of the Fletcher's crowd here? Not likely. But the thought didn't seem to help much. I shifted to the edge of my seat but I didn't stand up. My God, I thought, what if I don't stand up for anything? The damn preacher knows he's going to get everybody on something. So if I don't stand up, what the hell will he do then?

The preacher was at a fever pitch, punishing the drinkers with a volley of short, hard words that left no doubt in the drinker's minds about their eternal futures. They were doomed to hell. A dry hell.

❧ Nineteen ❧

I couldn't take any more. I began to feel giddy with tension, with the compression of the place. I was coiled to do something, anything, except sit there and wait for the preacher to get to me. I knew that my body was going to make a move, with or without my mind going along with it, was going to jolt itself upright, some sort of spasm. But I was not going to the front of the church and I damn well was not going to stand up and confess to a sin, any sin. But I thought I knew what was coming next . . . and if I didn't get out of there . . . and if Ruth Ella confessed . . . and if Luther went crazy . . . shit!

I stole another look at Ruth Ella. She was looking directly at me and her mouth was open, working, words dripping out in some wavering flow that I could not hear over the din of the congregation. But I didn't have to hear. I knew my time had come.

"HALLELUJAH, BROTHER! IT'S WONDERFUL! OH, GOD, IT'S WONDERFUL! THE WHOLE THING IS WONDERFUL! I BELIEVE, I BELIEVE, I BELIEVE I HAVE HAD THE COURSE! HALLELUJAH! HALLELUJAH!"

The screaming voice shattered me and it was a split second before I realized that the voice was mine, half shouting, half laughing, screaming nonsense out into the confusion of the church, joining the other shouters in their wildest moments. My own voice, driving against the best of them. I leaped to my feet and began to make my way toward the aisle, trying not to look in Ruth Ella's direction.

A man in the row behind me grabbed my arm as I went by and said "God bless you, brother! God be with you . . ." and I pulled away hard, afraid that he would hold me there.

I stepped over the last two people in my row and popped out into the aisle. The preacher had just ordered the drinkers to sit down and was stoking his furnace for the biggest and hottest blast of all and I could hear the voice cutting over my own, in competition, in dreadful contest.

Yes, oh yes, I knew what was coming.

I was only one of a number of shouters and movers, but my energy had been stored. I was fresh, and I was scared all the way down to my bowels. My voice was louder, harder. It carried like a rifle shot, ringing against the sides of the church, daring to challenge the preacher in volume. The preacher began to stare directly at me, but did not slow down his delivery. He could not afford to slow down, could not afford to have the momentum taken away from him. He had to continue, just as I continued. Still screaming at the top of my lungs, I leaped forward a step or two in the aisle. Flinging my arms at the ceiling I dragged up more "HALLELUJAHS!" and "AMENS!", using them to punctuate jumbles of meaningless sounds that I forced up out of my lungs. As my voice rose, the preacher worked harder. Others began to join in the competition.

"HALLELUJAH! BITE IT OFF! HA HA HA!" I screamed.

". . . and all of you know what I mean!" the preacher was shouting. "You are not free from the sins of the body!"

Yeah, here it comes, I thought. Right on schedule. He was finally going to get right to the screwing.

"AMEN!" I shouted, waving my arms frantically. "JUMP RIGHT ON IT!"

". . . yes, that's right, I want all of you who have COVETED THY NEIGHBOR'S WIFE . . ." The preacher's words shot down into the congregation.

Covet? Hell, I didn't *covet*. I had actually *fucked* her.

"Oh, God, it's wonderful, WONDERFUL!" I shouted, my throat hurting from the effort of it.

And then I saw Luther staring straight at me.

It was now or never; it was now, or end up in the front of the church with a weeping Ruth Ella and with Luther charging across the aisle at me to twist my head off my aching neck as easily as he would wring the neck of a chicken. I spun around, looking toward the back of the church. The aisle was littered with people, but there was still a chance. I charged.

Straight into Ruth Ella.

She was in the aisle, arms reaching for me, eyes brimming with tears, her face a total contortion of craziness. I can see her face now, know its every line, the color of her eyes, the smell of her hair, the glistening of her wet lips as she worked her mouth in wordless sound. Her expression is carved into the far wall of my mind, but, to this day, I don't know what it means.

I dodged around her, knocked an old man down into his seat, screamed another lung-full of meaningless tripe into the crowd and leaped over a young girl who was kneeling, weeping, tearing at her blouse, her teeth sunk into her own arm.

Jesus Christ, it was true. They *were* cannibals.

A huge farmer in bib overalls threw his arms open and high, his eyes rolling up, showing their reddened whites. He was ecstatic, deep in the orgasm of his own salvation. And he was blocking the aisle.

I lowered my shoulder and slammed into him about belt high. He didn't budge, didn't even shudder. His stomach was like a mattress, absorbing my weight without flinching. I bounced back, then dug in and tried to drive him backwards but I couldn't move him. The man was rooted to his place by the very power of his salvation. I thought I might be trapped and a taste of panic bubbled up into the back of my throat. Or maybe it was bile. I threw my weight to the side and pulled the farmer off balance and we twisted to the floor in a slow ballet of heavy, moving bodies. The farmer's arms clamped around me, bending my ribs. In desperation I brought my knee up into the crotch of the bib overalls and the farmer's arms flew open magically.

"HALLELUJAH! PLAY BALL! IT'S WONDERFUL! STRIKE THREE!" I shouted, leaping to my feet. I whirled and faced the pulpit, still screaming, trying to see if Ruth Ella was still behind me. I thought I could see her, but I wasn't sure. I could make no sense from the scene back there, the people massed in the aisle, the noise, the jerking bodies.

I stepped backwards and my feet tangled with the farmer. I fell heavily, directly into a woman who was coming up the aisle on her way to the front of the church. The farmer on the floor made gagging sounds and his stomach heaved and he vomited under a pew. The woman caught me as I fell and we both went down, mashing backwards into the crowd behind us. For a moment we wrestled on the floor, the woman clinging to me, her fingernails biting into my neck, both of us gasping for breath. My face was pressed against hers and suddenly she opened her mouth wide and covered my mouth, her tongue washing my lips in long sweeps. I rolled my eyes toward the ceiling, trying to see a way out, struggling with the woman but liking the feel of her mouth. No one else in the aisle seemed to notice, all of them busy making their own sort of noise, their own movement, pressing and rubbing.

Somehow, I broke loose. The aisle was even more crowded now and it was not a time for subtlety. I leaped up, lowered my head and charged toward the back of the church. A hand grabbed me by the shirt and I shot a stiff-arm in the direction of the grabber, connecting with soft flesh. I was only mildly surprised to see a fat woman in a flowered dress tumble backwards into the pew, flattening three of her fellow worshipers.

I shoved and pushed, goaded by the sounds behind me, driving in panic toward the doors at the back of the church.

Suddenly, I was free.

I hit the doors in full stride and burst through them, out into the hot Kentucky night, across the dark-filled space that I knew was grass, toward the massive trees that stood on either side of the gate that led to the narrow road. Even running at full stride the silence of my feet on the soft grass let the preacher's words slice through the open doors and across the darkness, catching me. The words sounded strangely alone and I realized that the church had gone suddenly quiet. Silent, except for the preacher.

". . . yea, let you who have LAIN with thy neighbor's wife stand and face . . . !"

I ran harder.

≈ Twenty ≈

I ran all the way back to Eli's farm, the hot night air pushing against my face and singing in my ears. At any moment I expected to hear the sounds of other running feet or of car engines cranking into motion, a posse coming to get the sinner who had lain with his neighbor's wife.

My legs seemed hampered by my jeans and I had difficulty getting up to full stride. I was a good runner, my hard legs carrying me easily, my thick chest and wide shoulders slightly forward, pressing, as my arms drove back and forth to the rhythm of my legs.

Sweat began to streak across my forehead. I ran my hand through my short hair and it came away wet. I was warming to the run, my body gearing itself to the task, heating itself into that smooth, liquid state that could sustain work and motion for hours.

As I ran I began to feel a sort of exhilaration, a feeling of tremendous strength and well-being. I felt as though I were safe as long as I could run, that somehow there was security in the very act of running and I felt as though I could run forever.

I left the narrow paved road as soon as I could and turned down one of the dirt farm roads that strung together the fields and orchards of the countryside. The earth was soft on the road, and springy, the roads not used often enough to keep them hard packed. I ran smoothly, flowing along the ground in even strides, pumping the earth away beneath me.

As I neared Eli's farm I could see the silhouette of the barn against the night sky. There were no lights burning anywhere but I slowed my pace, then walked, then stood motionless for a few minutes, letting my breathing calm down so I could hear something else besides the rush of blood in my own ears. I stared at the barn and listened carefully, but there was no movement or sound. If there were someone waiting for me they were being very, very careful. I circled the barn to its darkest side, then eased up against the wall.

There was no one there. I felt a rush of relief in my chest, but not enough to make me careless. I did not turn on any lights, groping my way to the stairs at the back of the main floor, then up to the loft, then along the wall to my room.

I pulled my old knife out of the beam and slipped the sheath on my belt.

And then I heard the squeak of rusty hinges as a door was slowly pulled open down at the far end of the barn.

I knew I was trapped if I stayed in the room, but I couldn't go back out the way I came in.

The single window above my cot was open and I shoved against the hinged window screen, hearing it swing back against the side of the barn. On the floor was a long, heavy rope, one end held securely by a large bolt in the wall below the window, an emergency fire escape that Eli had installed years ago when he had used the room as a repair shop. I picked up a blanket from the cot and threw it out the window, then threw the loose coils of the rope out after it. I swung my legs through the window and slid down the rope, panic tightening my hands. I grabbed the blanket and headed out across the back pasture toward the orchard, running again.

The apple trees stood in ordered rows and sheltered the grass beneath them, creating a carpet, a bed of velvet softness. I had slept in the orchard often, smelling the fragrance of the trees and the pungent odor of soil fed by old fruit. I listened to the faint night sounds, looking up through the limbs at the stars. I had never told anyone I slept there.

I went to the far edge of the orchard and folded myself against the trunk of a thick tree. I lay there, but I couldn't sleep. I began wondering if they really were looking for me, wondering if Ruth Ella had stood up and confessed, wondering if I should leave, now, in the dark. Wondering if I had really heard the door opening.

Gradually I began to get the old feeling again, the uncomfortable feeling, the feeling that had followed me ever since I could remember, a feeling I had on Black Hawk Ridge, a feeling I had in Crum, so strong in Crum that my stomach ached, a feeling I must have been born with. I felt trapped, closed in, surrounded, caught in a place I didn't want to be. Always in a place I didn't want to be.

I felt as though I were some sort of prisoner, wasting away behind bars of words set into the muck by some screaming preacher and a crazy nympho farm wife to whom I had not even spoken a single word, not one. But I had been inside her.

It had seemed like a game. And I had played. And now I was lying in an orchard, waiting for the daylight. Trapped.

I damn well deserved whatever I got. But they would have to catch me first.

Somehow, before that moment, the idea that I was not free had not occurred to me. It seemed normal that I should crawl through the long days of labor and the nights of mangled sleep, normal that I should go into the fields and orchards at daybreak and not return until dark, normal that I should be paid fifty cents an hour for the effort. It seemed normal that my eyes should burn from the dust of the hay fields, that the wires and strings of the bales should cut through my thin gloves and into my fingers, leaving scars that I would not notice until, once, some years later, when I had caressed the face of a beautiful woman and she had flinched from the roughness of my hands.

What am I doing here, I wondered, sleeping in an orchard, wondering if I'm going to be arrested or run out of the county in the morning. Or if Luther is going to shoot me. How smart is that?

It just never occurred to me that I was not free.

And I never slept at all.

Thin morning light dripped down through the tangled branches of the apple trees. A ragged mist lay close to the ground, dampening my blanket. Clouds had moved in during the night and I could smell the rain coming. I sat up and leaned back against the tree.

I had to get out of here, I thought. Sooner or later they'll come for me. Luther will come for me. And he'll bring some of the other men with him. They probably hang fornicators in this part of the country. Or maybe just beat the hell out of them, leave 'em broken and bleeding by the side of a dirt road. Sooner or later Luther will think to look for me here in the orchard. He'll check the room in the barn and see that I'm not there and he'll come for me here.

I was driving myself nuts.

There was only one thing to do. I'd go back to the barn, get the few things I actually owned, see if I could start that goddamned Triumph, and just ride the hell away.

I stood up, and it started to rain. Not a good sign.

The rope was still dangling out the window of the barn. I lay in the dripping weeds staring at it, soaked, water running under my chest. It was raining steadily, one of those patient Appalachian rains that seem to settle in for days.

Fucking brilliant, I thought. I make a sneaky escape from the room, and I leave the rope hanging there like that. And while I was looking at it, it began to move, being drawn slowly and steadily back up through the window.

They were in there, waiting. I couldn't go back to the room, at least not now. And I couldn't stay out here in the woods. Not in this rain. And it might rain forever.

There was only one place I could go, one place to protect me from the rain, one place that would be warm and quiet, one place I could be sure they wouldn't look.

I went back to the church.

⇜ Twenty-One ⇝

Somehow, when all those sweating, moaning people had been stuffed into the fragile little building, it had seemed larger. Now, in the rain-filtered light that managed to get through the grimy windows, the church seemed to have shrunk, to have squeezed itself down to some below-normal size, a size it lived with when the Reverend Abel Hitch's voice was not blowing out the walls.

The shadows were lifting quickly. I was tired and all I wanted to do was hide. I looked up at the small balcony at the back of the church, the one the woman had been hanging over, her breasts about to pop free and dangle above the heads of the congregation. The front of the balcony was a solid wooden panel with a railing on top. I could climb up there and lie down behind the panel. I couldn't be seen from the floor of the church.

He was mumbling something almost under his breath and it was a while before I realized he was praying. He kept it up, a steady stream of grunted words that tumbled out of his mouth and bounced gently toward the back of the church. Toward me. As my head cleared and I came more awake I could hear every one of the words, as clearly as if he were whispering in my ear.

He was praying for a miracle.

I had fallen asleep, lying behind the panel in the balcony, safe, hoping they wouldn't think of looking for me there. There were some baptismal robes hanging on a nail at the back of the church and I had taken a couple to the balcony, using one for a pillow and the other as a blanket. I was snug and I slept soundly. When the praying woke me the light had begun to fade in the windows.

I eased up and slowly stuck my head over the edge of the railing.

It was the Reverend Abel Hitch.

"They can't do this to me, Lord," he muttered, his voice low and in control, respectful, almost pleading, not the voice of his terrible sermons, not the language of his preaching.

"They can't turn me loose like this, can't tell me not to come back, not until my great and good work is finished. They're sinners, Lord, sinners, and they must be cleansed, cleansed, I tell Ye."

He was standing at the front of the church, facing the empty pews. As he talked, he started down the aisle, his withered arm tucked hard against his chest, his bad leg dragging along the scarred wooden floor.

"They are wrong to do this, Lord. Yea, *wrong*, and will suffer for their actions. I am the one who saved their souls, Lord, the one who made them come forward and confess their sins, the one who made them make public witness to their transgressions."

He was almost under the balcony and I could hear his breath rattle as he dragged himself around the back of the pews and started up the other aisle. His voice was even more pleading, almost whining. It was an incredible voice in its own way, the exact opposite of the voice he used in his revival service the night before. It was the voice he used privately, with his God.

"They can't tell me to leave this here church, to give up my work. They ain't got no right, Lord. But I know why they done it, Lord! I know why they done it! It's 'cause of *this*!" And Abel Hitch flung his withered arm up as high as he could, a withered, trembling hook reaching into the darkness.

I heard his voice catch. He was crying. He dragged his bad leg toward the front of the church.

I couldn't figure out what he was talking about. I didn't know anything about the operations of a church, who was responsible for what, and who told them what to do. All I knew was that Abel Hitch was in some sort of agony, and, as long as he never found out I was up here in the balcony, I was very happy about that.

"My name is fated to be spoken in all the churches of the land," he whimpered. He had reached the front of the church again, standing at the foot of the short flight of stairs that led to the baptismal tank, nestled up there in a small alcove. He started up the stairs.

"I am *The Baptist*!" he said, more strongly now.

By the time he reached the top of the stairs he was speaking clearly, the words stronger, the cadence easy. He seemed to be calmer now, more steady in his delivery, more like the Abel Hitch of the night before, the Abel Hitch who, with just his voice, had put me to flight out of a crowded church in the middle of a revival service, shot me out into the night in a blur of flailing legs.

"God will save ye!" he said, his voice coming from a deeper place now. "God will make ye free! I am the messenger of God, I am the One, I shall command ye to come forth and ye shall come!"

He broke off quickly, the hard words like canon firing in an empty room, echoing from the back of the church and slamming around inside the small balcony. Maybe he had never heard that sound before, I thought, the sound of his own voice in an empty church, with only God to listen.

He was at the top of the stairs, standing at the edge of the baptismal tank, its heavy cover a cross-hatch of thick planks nailed together.

The light was almost gone and Abel reached out with his good arm and felt along the wall. I heard the click of a switch and then the tank was lit with a soft, golden glow, a floodlight that filled the alcove with a light as soft as honey. It was the light of Christ, a light of spiritual quality that may have flowed from His presence.

Actually, Lard had told me, it was a light that cost $14.95 and had been ordered special from Lexington.

He was talking again.

"I will be sittin' here," he said, in a near normal tone of voice, as though talking to himself, "just sittin' here in this golden light as they come through the door . . .

"No, maybe I'll wait in the water. I will raise my arms and they will know, they will *believe*, and then I'll climb out of the water and speak to them, walk among them on my legs and hug them with my arms."

He stopped, and then looked directly at me. I froze — I had been frozen in place ever since I first heard his voice and I wasn't about to move now.

But whatever it was he was looking at, whatever he was seeing, it wasn't me.

He turned and grabbed the brass handle on the edge of the tank cover. He heaved awkwardly at the cover and it rose slightly. I wondered if he had ever tried to raise the cover by himself, with his bad arm and his crippled leg.

He dropped it.

The heavy cover slammed into the top of the tank with a noise that sounded like a bass drum from hell. I could feel the vibrations all the way up where I was, my eyes frozen on the warped body of Abel Hitch. He stood there in shock as the massive booming noise pounded the walls of the church. As the sound died, I could hear him talking.

"You know what it is, Lord, you know what has to be done. You told me to come here, Lord, you told me to do this, so let me open the cover, I ask you, Lord, I ask you IN THE NAME OF YOUR SON, JESUS CHRIST!"

He bent again and heaved at the cover, working only with his good arm and leg. He dropped it again.

Abel Hitch stood looking at the ponderous cover, stained from the ecstatic splashings of a thousand baptizings. I didn't know why he wanted the cover up, but I could tell, just by looking at him there in the golden warmth of the floodlight, that it was the most important thing in the world to him. He bent and grabbed the handle again.

He spoke almost quietly. "All right, Lord. This is the time." I thought his body seemed to glow.

The cover came up to his shoulder and he slid under the edge of it, almost gracefully. I heard him grunt, his body straining against the weight, his good leg close to the edge of the baptismal tank, balanced there, motionless.

"Oh, God, You are going to do it! You are going to open the door to bring the miracle! You are going to open the door to the salvation of souls in this devil land!"

The cover came upright. He spun and put his back against the wood, keeping it pinned against the wall. A minute or so went by before I realized he was crying again. It took several minutes more for him to calm himself, to get his tears under control, to check his heaving chest. When his hands were steadier he found the dangling hook on the wall and pushed it through the thick ring at the edge of the tank cover. As he released the cover it seemed to balance, the mass of it held in place by some divine power.

Abel Hitch stood sweating at the edge of the tank. And then he began to take off his clothes.

Abel Hitch had two bodies. On his right side, the arm and leg were full and powerful, layered with muscle developed from carrying the whole of him through the years of his pounding the pulpits that rose in front of the sinners. On the other side, he was shrunken and shriveled, the leg short and twisted, the arm nothing more than a pale stick of thin bone and parchment skin.

But I can say this for Abel Hitch — he had the biggest dick I had ever seen. It hung, pendulum-like, dangling almost halfway to his knee. It was the penis of a god. Abel Hitch could have flailed wheat with his cock.

The cock disappeared behind the rim of the tank as he stepped over the edge and lowered himself clumsily into the water. He turned to face the light and stood there for long moments, seeming not to know what to do next. Motionless. The silence of the small church amplified every little sound and I thought I could hear him breathing, but I knew I couldn't.

But I could hear him as he began to pray. It was a low-volume prayer, personal, the type of prayer a man might utter when he was on the verge of being caught at something, and didn't want to be. The words dribbled off the edges of his lips, barely audible. The only word I heard clearly was "miracle". I thought his eyes were closed, but I couldn't be sure.

He wobbled in the water, almost losing his balance, flailing with his good arm.

"I know you want me in the water, Lord! I know you want me to re-dedicate myself before the miracle! Of course! Of course You do! I'm sorry it took me so long to figure that out! But I know now, Lord, I know now! You want me to *baptize* myself! Of course, Lord, who else could baptize ME? Who else could have the power, the strength, Lord, but ME?" And he dropped like a stone into the water, shaking the old tank.

He blew upward through the surface of the water, spray flying, his good arm shoved above him in victory.

"I am here, God, I am here! I have re-dedicated myself to Thee and Thy service! I have done Thy will and Thy work, God, and I am ready for THE MIRACLE!"

He was spinning in the water, thrashing, screaming, the voice once again the weapon he used in slaying congregations of sinners. Water flew out over the pulpit below and into the first of the empty pews.

"Bring the miracle now, Lord! Bring the miracle NOW! Oh, Lord, I have served you for so long! Waited for so long! Envied others for so long! And I confess to that envy, Lord! Yes, envy! I just couldn't help it, Lord! Please! PLEASE, BRING THE MIRACLE NOW!"

He was crying again, his words punctuated by sobs that worked up from his stomach and into his mouth. He continued to twist violently in the water, looking at himself, examining his short, misshapen body.

He stopped. The water calmed.

"What is it, Lord? What is it You want? I'll do it, Lord, I'll do it! Just show me the way . . .

"Oh, Lord, I know what it is! You want me to do it again! Yes! Do it again! Well, I will, Lord, I will! I'll be the only preacher BAPTIZED TWO TIMES IN THE SAME NIGHT! I WILL, LORD! I WILL!"

And Abel Hitch baptized himself again, flinging himself sideways with an effort that shot water almost to the wall. He clawed to the surface, grabbing at his contorted body, searching, holding his shriveled arm in front of him.

"They're still here, Lord! I still got 'em!" He waved his bad arm. "Make 'em well, God! YOU ARE SUPPOSED TO MAKE THEM WELL!

"I want to lift my people up with TWO GOOD ARMS, God! I want to carry them on TWO GOOD LEGS!

"I want the miracle you promised, Lord! FIX MY BODY!"

He was in constant motion now, a continuing state of agitation, jerking back and forth, water flying everywhere.

"YOU WANT ANOTHER ONE!? OKAY, I'LL GIVE YOU ANOTHER ONE, YOU SON-OF-A-BITCH!"

Abel Hitch flung himself under the water again.

When he popped up over the edge of the tank, his stringy hair covered the front of his face. He waved his bad arm wildly, then pressed it hard against his face, as though looking at it.

"I'VE STILL GOT 'EM, GOD! I'VE STILL GOT 'EM, YOU BASTARD! I'VE STILL GOT 'EM!"

He dumped himself into the water again, straight down, and again, slamming up and down in a rhythmic frenzy, the water rolling back and forth in the tank, pounding against the sides. He couldn't seem to stop himself. He couldn't stop the leaping, the dunking, the shouting. Up and down he went, up and down.

"YOU LYING SON-OF-A-BITCH! YOU PROMISED ME! YOU PROMISED ME!"

He came straight up out of the water and stood rigid against the front of the tank, arms clenched across his huge chest, hands knotted into fists. His body shook with an anger born of a lifetime of doing all the things Abel Hitch thought he was supposed to do.

"YOU LYING-SON-OF-A- . . ."

And that's all I heard. The rush of the heavy tank cover covered the rest of his words as it thundered down onto the top of Abel Hitch's head, leveling his skull to the eyes. The cover slammed onto the top of the tank, the booming vibrating among the pews, shaking the windows. And then the sound was gone as quickly as it had come, the noise that had profaned the church soaked up by the darkness of the small auditorium. The old church seemed to welcome the silence and held it, close and warm, inside its walls. The golden floodlight shone warmly on the tank, the cover neatly in place. Water, tinted a bright red, dripped down the sides of the tank, instantly starting to dry.

And then, with a small crinkling sound, the golden floodlight burned out.

PART III

South Carolina

Bleeding on the Sand

⇜ Twenty-Two ⇝

The battered Triumph was jumping and making odd noises and each time I leaned it into a turn I wondered if the engine would still be there when I straightened up and tried to accelerate. It was difficult to tell when the Triumph was making odd noises. It made so many noises that a noise had to be particularly odd in order for me to notice. But I was noticing now.

I eased off on the throttle and let the old bike drift, down and off through the easy straight stretches and around gentle turns that seemed to have been built only to relieve the monotony of flat-road driving in South Carolina. The land had been ironed out, pressed down, the hills of Virginia and the western Carolinas pounded down to make the smaller hills that got even farther apart with each mile I rode toward the sea. Toward the sea, where I had never been. Then the hills broadened, shortened and became nothing more than rolling, hardened dunes supporting stands of tall, scraggly, long-needled pines that stood in the shadows, ranked and specter-like, their scent drifting, loaded on the warm air that flowed over my old Air Force goggles and pushed against my face.

It hadn't been hard to decide to leave Bean Camp. Like I said, I didn't have to decide at all.

When the cover of the baptismal tank slammed into Abel Hitch my first reaction was to run. Just run, anywhere. But I knew I couldn't do that. The heavy sound of the dropping cover kept thudding into the inside of my head and I knew I couldn't leave until I looked, until I saw for sure. I slid over the edge of the railing and dropped to the floor of the church.

The cover was as heavy as it looked. The water seeping down the front of the tank had a faint red tinge and when I gripped the dripping edge of the cover and lifted, my stomach knotted hard against my belt. The cover came up slightly and a pair of eyes picked up the loose light of the church and glittered back at me. Abel's eyes. I dropped the cover and vomited down the front of the tank. I believe that was the only time I ever made a donation in church.

But I didn't run. Not right then. I guess I just had to see. I got my stomach under control, closed my eyes and pushed the cover all the way back and it balanced there, just like before, just like Abel had done it. And I looked down into the half-face of Abel Hitch, floating in the water.

His chin was against his chest, his lips pulled back in some twisted snarl of an unformed curse. His eyes caught the light and stared into the ceiling, the faint glimmer of surprise still fading in the depths of them. There was nothing above his eyes. His head just stopped there, a sharp angle careening away above his eyebrows, leaving the face a mutilated work of a mad sculptor with nothing more to be seen in water turned red and cobbled from the blood and brains of Abel Hitch.

I lowered the cover, and I ran. There was no telling what they might do when they found Abel Hitch. No telling what Ruth Ella may have said after I ran from the church the night before. No telling what Luther might think, or what he might do.

I did the only thing I could think of. I sneaked back to Eli's barn, snaked in through a busted window at the end of the equipment shed, and waited.

There was no one there.

In less than fifteen minutes I was on the old Triumph.

Pine branches hung claw-like over the road and rained dead needles on the pavement where the wind would sweep them along, gathering them in shallow rows and patches, their dry color blending with the faded gray of road tar that baked in the Carolina sun. Several times, as I leaned into a turn, I felt the wheels of the motorcycle struggle to keep traction and once, in the late evening, when I was not paying attention, the front of the bike slid straight to the right, scooting off the road and into the sand and loam of the berm, digging a small trench and whipping the back of the bike off behind it. I gripped with my knees and fought to stay upright. The bike cut through and off the berm and down across a shallow ditch, finally stopping in some low pines, branches reaching for my face. The engine was still running. I got back on the blacktop and rode on, wide-awake now and adrenaline-pumped, for another hour.

I was free and I was heading south and if the bike held up I would see the ocean and I loved the whole thought of it. What more could I ask. Black Hawk Ridge and Crum and Bean Camp and Ruth Ella and the body of Abel Hitch and the religious fanatics were all behind me and I began to realize, sitting on the cracked and hardened seat of the Triumph, that all my life the most important thing was to have things behind me. And I wasn't even twenty-years-old.

When would that ever change?

Maybe I was changing. It was hard for me to even think about the things I had thought about in Crum.

Except for Yvonne.

The land, at least, had changed. It had changed color. I had never actually thought much about the color of land, of dirt. On Black Hawk Ridge when we turned the earth to grow the scraggly corn and the thin runner beans the dirt was gray, sometimes black, and always loaded with stones polished by the wearing down of mountains and the wearing down of men. At the edge of the small fields and into the woods there didn't seem to be any dirt, just layer upon layer of the stuff of which forest floors are made, the refuse of hundreds of years of the grinding turn of life in the near-darkness of dense stands of Appalachian hardwoods. The woods made their own floor, their own dirt.

The dirt of Black Hawk Ridge was sometimes downright personal. Like the dirt they took out of the grave when they buried old Cousin Elijah. Cousin Elijah had died with his face between the legs of one of the widow women from down on the lower end of Turkey Creek. His heart gave out at the very time the widow woman was giving out and Elijah began to thrash and twist, driving his face harder into the crotch of the widow woman, making sounds like the grunting of a pig, his head almost buried inside her, jerking. She had never known anything like what Elijah was doing and in her eagerness to help she raised her legs and wrapped them around Elijah's head. All summer long the widow woman had plowed her own ground and worked her own bottom land, walking the long furrows behind the mule, and her legs were like bands of iron around Cousin Elijah's head.

Elijah died just like he wanted to, and just where he wanted to. Some said it was his heart. Uncle Long Neck said he suffocated.

When they dug Elijah's grave the men swung their mattocks against the black earth in the hole, then shoveled it out into the pale light just beside the grave. In the hole the dirt had been alive, black with loam and time and all manner of living things. But as it dried in the sun it turned gray, the right color for being stuffed back into a grave.

The next day, when they buried Elijah, the rain misted through the trees and into the grave, turning the gray earth black again and then making it thin. A small rivulet of the runny dirt spilled down and spurted into the grave, splashing into the dark water already gathered there. And then more earth slid in and then more and the preacher was afraid the grave might cave in, so he cut the preaching short and the men just grabbed the long wooden box and tried to slide Cousin Elijah into the hole but the rain sluiced through their eyes and the black-slick mud climbed their legs and ran into their stiff Sunday-meetin' shoes and they stumbled against themselves like corn stalks twisting together in a high wind.

The soft edge of the hole gave way under Cousin Inis' feet and he went into the grave in front of the coffin. The other men, already sliding the thick pine box into the grave, dropped it in on top of him.

It took them a while to get Cousin Inis out and he nearly drowned in the liquid mud before they did. They had to put a rope around the box and raise one end of it, and one of the men stood on the coffin in the process, adding his weight to the coffin and dead Cousin Elijah, all pressing down on Cousin Inis, who was screaming from underneath the coffin that he could see the devil down there. His voice made bubbling, gargling sounds and we all thought maybe the devil had actually grabbed hold of him. Turned out to be the mud in his mouth.

They finally squeezed Cousin Inis around the side of the box and dragged him up out of the grave by his coat. One of the coat sleeves ripped off as he came sucking up out of the mud. Cousin Inis stood there in the rain by the side of the grave, blowing mud from his nose and digging chunks of black stuff out of his ears and eyes. He appeared to be angry.

The man who had been standing on the coffin took a shovel and levered the box flat again, then climbed out of the hole. By then, all the commotion had caused the mud to partially refill the grave, most of the mud under the coffin, and dead Cousin Elijah was in the hole only about half as deep as he was supposed to be.

And that's when they realized the coffin was lying flat, all right, but it was upside-down.

Cousin Inis, who didn't really like Cousin Elijah all that much anyway, ripped off his one-sleeved coat, threw it into the grave, grabbed a shovel and began to fling mud down on top of it. He had completely covered the coat and the box before the others joined in.

And so Cousin Elijah ended up in a shallow grave exactly as he had spent his last hour on earth. Face down.

≈ Twenty-Three ≈

The sun was running low behind me and evening light flowed through the pines, soft heavy bands of gold mixed with the black greens of the woods. It didn't seem to be a time to ride fast, so I slowed the old bike almost to a walk, cruising lazily through the easy turns and the thick air.

He was parked on the other side of the road, back under the trees, and I didn't see the car until I was sliding past it on the highway, the Triumph backing and barking a little. But I noticed the single red light centered on the top and the ornate lettering on the door that said "Sheriff."

There was nothing for me to fear. I wasn't speeding and I hadn't run over anybody. And then I remembered that I didn't have a driver's license, the bike didn't really belong to me, and the license plate was so old I could have sold it as an antique.

He looked at me as I went by, his face hidden behind the mirrored sunglasses cops always seemed to wear, but he didn't move and I didn't change the speed of the bike, just drifted on down the highway and around a flat curve and out of sight.

My breath came full and deep and I realized my shoulders were tight, bunched and pulling my neck down between them. Memories of Crum and Constable Clyde Prince and his pistol played across the front of my mind, so vivid, so alive they blocked out part of the road the Triumph was rolling on. Clyde was a man born with a pissed-off attitude and when he grew up someone gave him a gun and made him a lawman and said "Clyde, boy, don't you ever lose that attitude." And he never did.

And I had just passed another one in a car, sitting back there. Just like Clyde Prince. I didn't even have to ask. I just knew.

They sent me down to Benny's house to get a chicken for Sunday dinner. Benny lived on the high riverbank at the upriver end of Crum and his mother kept the largest chicken coop on the river. I didn't like to go down there and get chickens. I didn't like to get chickens anywhere, didn't like watching them hunt and peck their way across the bare dirt yards in front of the tiny houses, didn't like the chicken shit that ended up on my shoes, didn't like the sight and smell of them crammed together in a coop, rushing in a hysterical pack at some sick and fallen bug that pinged through the wire and plunked onto the hard-pack. The only way I liked chickens was dead, blood-squeezed, dipped, fried hard and dry and piled on a plate beside a football-sized glob of mashed potatoes.

But getting the chicken for Sunday dinner was my job and I went down early to get it over with.

Constable Clyde Prince came out on the porch and leaned against the railing, a cup and saucer in his hand, the coffee steaming above the rim. I had never seen him at Benny's house before. He wasn't Benny's father, and it was too early for him to go a-visitin' on Sunday morning. I wondered where Benny was, then remembered he usually slept in the barn out behind the house. Now I knew why.

Clyde stared silently. He raised the cup, tipped it, and let the searing black coffee run down the side and into the saucer. He blew gently across the saucer then sipped from its edge, slurping the coffee in shallow draughts. He never took his eyes from me, squinting in the early light.

The chickens moved warily as I eased inside the coop. I always wanted it to be easier, but it never was. Selecting the target, edging up cautiously, and then the final lunge, trying to trap the chicken between me and the fence. Always took two or three tries to make it work. Always got covered with chicken shit. Always felt like a goddamn fool. But, finally, I caught one.

I stood outside the coop, holding the chicken in both hands. Clyde was standing there when I turned around, right in front of me, no coffee cup, his arms hanging loosely, his face a flat mask of mean.

"Goin' to wring its neck, boy?"

"No, sir, constable. Guess I'll just take it back to Mattie and let her do with it. She likes to tend to all that stuff herself." I hated wringing the necks of chickens, even more than I hated chickens. And Clyde knew that.

"Well, boy, I think you ought to wring out that chicken. Mattie would probably 'preciate the help."

I eased to the side, still holding tightly to the chicken. There was no way I was going to wring that damned chicken's neck, not now, not ever. I was getting ready to run.

"Wait a minute there, boy." His voice dropped a notch, down to some level of evil I hadn't heard before. "How I know you ain't just stole that chicken?"

"Wha . . ."

"That's right. Stole. That chicken, there. I just come out on the porch to sip my coffee, and there's you, a-sneakin' into the chicken coop, right in broad daylight. How do I know that's what you was supposed to be a-doin'?"

"Listen here, c-c-constable," I stuttered. I had never stuttered before and it surprised me. "Mattie sent . . . I come down here ever Sunday . . . she always buys these Sunday dinner chickens . . ." The son-of-a-bitch. The-son-of-a-bitch. The-son-of-a-bitch.

"I just may have to arrest that chicken, boy," he said, a kind of low chuckle down underneath the words, his hand drifting behind him, "hold it for evi-dence." Almost lazily he pulled a huge pistol from his back pants pocket.

"Now, you just hold out the evi-dence and let's have a look at 'er." He flicked the barrel of the pistol at the chicken.

I jerked my head to the side, looking at the house, then back at the barn, at the chicken coop, anywhere, everywhere, looking for somebody, anybody. There was no one. Clyde was going to kill me.

"I said, boy, let's see her." He motioned at the chicken again, the barrel of the gun swinging slightly toward me.

The chicken was quiet, moving its head in little jerking motions, looking at Clyde in that sidelong stare that chickens have, the beady eye glaring out from the side of its head. My hands went forward slowly, shoving the chicken out toward Clyde.

"Shit, boy, I can tell this chicken's a out-law, just by the look of it's eye." He pulled the gun up higher.

And then he cocked the hammer. The cylinder turned easily, smoothly, and I could see the dull leaden noses of the bullets nestled in the little holes, waiting.

Click. The hammer locked back.

"Chicken, you under arrest now. Afraid I'll have to take you down to Wayne and put you in jail for a while, just to see if you can lay any evi-dence." He laughed aloud, a sound that must have sounded good to him but, to me, sounded like some-one gargling in the bowels of hell. The chicken suddenly pan-icked, one wing busting free from beneath my hands and flog-ging the air. I held on. The chicken quieted instantly.

"What's this? A-tryin' to e-scape, as sure as I live and breathe!" And Clyde put the pistol to the chicken's head and pulled the trigger.

The thunder of the pistol rolled across the river and bal-looned into the Kentucky ridges and then back across the flat river bottom and the tin roofs of the tiny houses of Crum, rush-ing away in a wave down the valley, rattling windows. The chicken's head exploded. I was holding the chicken out almost between Clyde and me and fragments of bone and beak and squirts of blood came back into my face, stinging. I closed my eyes, squinting against the gore that ran down my face and across my lips, ears ringing, stomach churning.

"Well, reckon that one won't get away, hey boy? Now, you just hold her upside down 'til you get back to Mattie's, and she'll be all drained out proper like. Just right for pluckin'." He was still laughing to himself and I could hear him walk away across the dirt and up the stairs to the porch. The screen door squealed lightly open and shut and he was gone, me still standing there in the Sunday new-born sunlight with my eyes closed against the gape and maw of the pistol and chicken blood painting tiny stripes down my chin and into the top of my only Sunday shirt.

A mile or so later I managed to get my shoulders un-bunched and things seemed okay, until I looked in the mirror vibrating on the handlebar. The car was back there. Gaining.

He didn't have his red light on but he slid in behind me, tight against the bike, his bumper only a few inches from my rear wheel. In my mirror all I could see was the mass of the car, dancing just behind my wheel, outlined from behind in the gold of the late sun. If he made one wrong move, if I made one wrong move, his bumper would touch my rear wheel and I knew the bike instantly would do strange and dangerous things that I wouldn't be able to control and several pounds of my ass probably would become a permanent and painful part of this shitty Carolina back road.

I cracked the throttle a little more and the bike opened up a small gap. He closed up immediately. If he was determined to stay that close, more speed was not the answer. Anyway, I was pretty sure the Triumph couldn't outrun the car on these flat, lazy roads. Up ahead I could see a wide space off to the right where cars had pulled off and then run for a while at the side, making a rough patch in the dirt. I eased the bike a little to the right and when we came to the wide place I darted off into it and got the bike out wide away from the patrol car, then hit the brakes hard, fighting with the Triumph on the rutted hard-pack. He wasn't expecting it, and he didn't seem to care. He went by without ever touching his brakes.

On down the highway, the patrol car rolled to an easy stop. It sat there, engine idling. The Triumph was back on the blacktop and I sat there, too, watching the car. I could see his outline clearly now. He sat straight in his seat, content with watching me in his mirror. Even at this distance I noticed the width of his shoulders and the height of his bulk; his hat must have been touching the ceiling inside the car. Big bastard.

I sat, engine idling. I had no place to go, nothing to do. I could wait.

The sun moved a few clicks farther down and it seemed to push the car, which started to roll slowly on down the road. I watched it go. And I would let it go. No reason for me to jump in behind it. It drove out of sight.

Every muscle I had was cramping. I rolled the Triumph off the side of the road, shut down the engine and got off, lifting my sweat-fogged goggles to my forehead and fumbling for my fly. I was ready to piss in my pants. But I held it in long enough to listen hard into the distance for any sound of the car. I could hear nothing. I pissed in the direction of the patrol car.

Probably, I had waited long enough. I had drained my bladder, walked around the road, stretched, done everything I could think of to take up a little time. I considered turning, riding back the other way, but I thought the deputy in the patrol car had just been trying to break the boredom of road patrol. Was probably halfway back to the office by now. Couldn't wait to tell the other boys about the hick on the motorcycle. I swung my leg over the seat and pulled down my goggles.

It was there, but I didn't want to hear it. The sound grew gently at first, then became harder, then a heavy, dull roaring that was the engine of a car in full tilt. For a few seconds I sat there, not wanting to believe. And then the patrol car came into view down the road, pointed in my direction, coming hard. He wasn't faking it. If he kept up that speed he wouldn't be able to stop when he got to me. Even if he wanted to. And I knew he didn't want to.

I began to pound the starter lever. In a panic I rose above the damned lever and slammed it toward the road. The bastard Triumph had always been hard to start but now it wouldn't even cough and each time I rose over the lever I knew the patrol car had covered another heartbeat of distance toward me. The bike and I were at the edge of the pavement and the car dived over in front of me, not slowing, coming hard down my throat. On the lever one more time and the engine turned and I dropped the gear shift into low and gunned the old bike hard into a digging right turn, off the road, the rear wheel spinning and slashing at the earth and I was into the trees and on a narrow dirt track that twisted down through the soft rolling land, the trail blackening in the fading light.

Tires screamed and screamed and I knew the big bastard with the sunglasses had thrown the car into a sliding turn and would be coming back. The noise of his engine rose and fell as he wrestled the car into the trees and onto the dirt, gunning the engine when he could and braking hard when he came to the tight little turns. The surface of the track was soft and covered with pine needles and twigs and some small fallen branches and the tires of the bike would bounce and then dig in, and then bounce again and in the space of a few seconds I thanked Eli a million times for those tires, those wonderful tires, the only things on the bike that were truly new. And in the middle of it all I remembered that I had never thanked him properly, not really, and wondered if I would ever see him again.

And then the car was just behind me, driving hard at my back wheel, the red light on and spinning.

The track made a sharp turn to the right and I didn't, plowing off into the brush and blasting through some thickets and heading for a pair of trees that stood just far enough apart for me to shoot through. I shot the gap and, just on the other side, hit a small deadfall. My front wheel bounded up into the air, a whirling, useless thing, and then the back wheel hit the log and I was down and over, still upright, fighting the bike across earth as soft and sticky as biscuit dough, gunning the engine and then backing off, low hanging branches slicing across my face.

The engine quit. I twisted the dead bike into some brush, turned off the key and laid it down. I lay down beside it. The black silence of the pine forest was thundering.

Off through the trees I could hear the soft rumbling of a big engine, idling, waiting. And then the rumbling slowly faded and was gone. I couldn't hear the patrol car but maybe he stopped somewhere back there, might be on foot, following me though woods he probably knew well, not hearing my engine, knowing I might be out of gas, and maybe . . . Christ! He really had me spooked.

There was no way I could stay there. I picked up the bike, hung my goggles on the handlebar, pushed on through the trees, found another path that led generally toward the east, and kept walking in the dark.

I thought I could smell the ocean. Only, I didn't know what the ocean was supposed to smell like.

≈ Twenty-Four ≈

The light of a fat moon drifted down through the pines and I was lost in the sweating effort of pushing the motorcycle along a road that seemed to become softer as I went, and I was at the edge of the pathetic collection of plank shacks and rough cabins before I knew they were there. It was some sort of tiny village, a shantytown, abandoned and rotting there in the damp lowlands. The cabins were scattered along both sides of a wide, flat lane, a sort of common front yard carpeted with pine needles and twigs. But even through the carpet I could see old tire tracks, the marks of wide, heavy cars that had pulled up between the houses. Off to one side at the edge of one of the buildings a round, metal table and some chairs, all rusted into a uniform stage of decay, leaned at odd angles and cast soft shadows in the warm light of the moon.

The shacks sat like fat sleeping storks, crazily balanced on pilings that kept their floors up off the damp earth. Some of the pilings were stone, some were heavy pieces of wood, and some were wired-together collections of things I didn't recognize, junk gathered together to support the small, leaning hovels with their sagging porches and gapped walls.

The dog came out of nowhere. Honest to God, I never saw him. He was suddenly there, on the other side of the Triumph, his angry barking splitting the night and the moonlight. I shoved the bike over toward him and he yelped, jumping backwards. I dived under the nearest shack.

The earth under the floor was soft and ran up toward the far corner of the shack. There were some old planks and pieces of wood under there and I grabbed one, dragging it with me as I crawled, finally squeezing myself into a back corner. I twisted around and held the plank in front of me. But the dog didn't follow me under the floor, at least not very far. He was growling now, his bulk in silhouette just under the edge of the shack. He had me trapped. He was in no hurry.

It didn't matter. If he could wait, I could wait. It was cool and quiet under there and, in spite of one rat that I saw clearly, I fell asleep.

The singing awakened me. I crawled from underneath the house and out into the dim light and the fog and looked for the dog, who apparently had gone on to other chases. The singing came from the house next door, a slightly larger building than the others squatting in the gray dawn. The building was a church, clapboard, unpainted, pale in the early light, with no panes in some of the windows. A rickety wooden cross was nailed and wired, leaning, at the front of the roof. Lord, a truly joyous building.

And the incredible singing — the rocking, ecstatic singing — seemed to raise the dust from the sagging front porch and its broken railing. I sneaked across the porch to get a look inside. I was hypnotized, my mind locked blindly to the sound of a hundred swaying black people singing praises to the Lord, dancing words of faith and happiness. The sound of that singing is still in my mind, and it may have been the most beautiful music I have ever heard. I was very quiet, careful not to make the boards creak.

"I think you be out of gas, boy."

I turned and leaped off the porch, but it was too late. The largest man I had ever seen, of any color, was holding up my bike. He held it out in front of him, straight out and off the ground, his thick arms not even quivering. He was wearing bib overalls and no shirt and his arms jutted out from under the suspenders like thick pipes, just came down and joined the backs of his hands in a knot of muscle that didn't seem capable of bending. His skin was the color of milk chocolate melted under the warm light of a southern sun in winter. He had a round face and a bald head and his jaw seemed to meld into his shoulders with no discernable thing that could be called a neck. His trunk from his shoulders ran straight down to his hips and then flowed down his legs to the very earth that supported him. A tree. A warm chocolate tree a full head taller than me that could talk and hold a motorcycle straight out in front of him. He shook it like a toy. "Nosir, ain't a sound of no gas nowhere in this machine."

"I'm just a-passin' through," I mumbled. "Didn't mean no harm."

"Boy, you ain't done no harm to nobody. I heered you come in last night. Knowed the dogs would either tree you or put you under the house. Either way, knowed you'd be here in the mornin'."

"I'm sorry, mister. I thought this place was deserted."

"Nope, not deserted. Just dark, sometimes. Like us." He grinned. "See, boy, sometimes it be best to have the home place dark, 'specially when they's cars . . . or something . . . around where maybe they don't have no bid-ness. You understand?"

He said "under" and "stand" as two separate words, with emphasis on the "under." I nodded, but I had no idea what he was talking about.

Behind me, the singing stopped. I could feel the presence of people over my shoulder and turned slowly to face them. The sagging front porch was full of silent black faces. The faces shifted back and forth, each face trying to see the white boy standing down there in the yard. I had never seen so many black people in one place. I wondered where they all came from.

A slender young man in a dark suit stepped forward. "And that," he said softly, "is one fine looking motorsickle."

"I think this boy be out of gas," the giant said, again shaking the bike. "And I think he be from off. And I think he be scared."

"I ain't from 'off'. I'm from West Virginia," I mumbled. "Come down through Kentucky."

"Wes' 'Ginia," the giant mused to himself. "That be pretty far north . . . "

"There be nothin' to be scared of, boy," the man on the porch said. "We know where you belong, and we know it ain't here." He ducked under the frail railing and stepped off the porch, lightly, like a dancer.

"And, truth to tell, probably know why you be hiding under our porch. We preachers, we know things like that." The fleeting cast of a grin slipped across his lips, then disappeared.

Jesus God. Another preacher. "I just want to go on," I said. "Don't want to bother nobody." I looked toward the giant.

He set the bike down, flicking it back and forth between his hands, as lightly as he would flick a broom.

The preacher took a couple of steps toward me, then dug his hand in his pocket. "Here, boy. Here's somethin' that was put in the collection plate this morning." And he handed me a dollar.

"I . . . I can't take your money. I don't know when. . . "

"This ain't no loan, son. This is a gift. From the church. You take it now and be on your way. Might not do, if you was to hang around here very long."

I looked at the people jammed on the porch. They stared at me. None of them said a word. Most of the men had on dark suits, but a couple had on something that shined in the weak light and I realized their suits were made of velvet, worn thin from use at weddings and funerals and from rubbing against their friends in the closeness of church pews. The women wore bright flowered dresses, splashes of color and happiness displayed before their God. I had never seen people in church wear such wonderful clothes. I wondered what the Reverend Abel Hitch would have said, but then remembered that the good Reverend was, himself, standing before his God. Naked.

A slender girl was partially hidden behind the preacher and she looked out past his arm. Her skin had the richness of strong coffee and her eyes, even in the early light, startled me. There was a depth to them I had never seen before, not in anybody. She caught me staring, and turned away. The preacher caught me, too, and again the grin quickly flickered in the morning light. I turned my eyes to the ground.

We stood in silence, the porch full of people, me, the giant and the preacher down there in the yard. About a year went by. Somewhere through the haze a dog barked. The giant turned his head slowly in the direction of the sound.

"Brother Jason," the preacher said softly, looking off in the same direction, "maybe it's best this boy be on his way."

The giant walked the bike over to me. "This be a fine machine, boy. A machine like this can make you free. You take the dollar, boy, and you buy yourself some gas, and you ride away, free."

He leaned the bike into me and I remembered how heavy the bike really was.

"And, boy," he said softly, "if I was you, I'd be taking me that path over yonder." He pointed away from the dim road, down between some houses and into a stand of trees. "It'll bring you out near town, some ways on. Don't have to cross no hard roads to get there, neither. See, they's a car parked on a knob over yon way . . . " He pointed in the other direction, up the road, out beyond the village and toward a small rise at the edge of the trees.

" . . . got one of them little bitty red lights on the top."

My stomach clinched and my throat tightened.

I straightened up the bike and rolled it slowly toward the path. The girl from the porch had moved out to the edge of the yard. She was tall and slender, built to bend in the wind and then straighten up again, stronger. As I passed her she kept her eyes locked to me and I could smell the faint scent of magnolias. I didn't know then that I was smelling magnolias, only that I was breathing in the most wonderful thing I had ever pulled down inside me.

At the edge of the yard I ran as hard as I could, shoving the bike beside me down the path. At the top of a low hill I stopped and looked back. The giant still stared after me, but all of the others were gone. Except one. It was the girl. She stood by the giant, motionless.

I lifted my hand in goodbye. The big man raised his arm straight over his head. The girl still did not move. I turned and pushed on and when I came to a downhill section I jumped on the bike and coasted. And then I was out of sight.

❧ Twenty-Five ❧

Just across the highway there was a tiny shack with grease and smoke smeared across the front and a faded Royal Crown Cola sign nailed crookedly across a gap in the boards over the door. Off to the side a mound of old tires leaned into the sun. A lone gas pump, the kind with the glass ball on the top, stood guard near the road. I pushed the Triumph up next to the pump and waited. It took him a long time but eventually a skinny black man wandered around the side of the building, not even looking surprised that I was there. He was wearing old cotton pants and a sleeveless undershirt, his bony arms dangling like broken parts. When he came up next to the bike I thought he was one of the men on the porch of the church back there in the village. But he couldn't be. How the hell could he have gotten here before me?

He just stood there and waited. He didn't say a word.

"Give me fifty cents worth," I said, trying to keep my voice low and down in my chest. He pumped the gas, still silent, not meeting my eyes.

"Thanks," I said, handing him the dollar. "Didn't think you'd be open on a Sunday."

"Wasn't." He didn't even look at the bill, just stuffed it into his pocket, then from the same pocket pulled out a fifty-cent piece. He dropped the coin into my hand, making sure, I thought, that his hand did not touch mine. I pocketed the coin and threw my leg across the bike.

"Boy," he said softly, "let me give you some benefit of my age. That fifty-cent piece you got there . . . you spend it in a white diner. Get yourself some food you like. Go on down to the middle of town. Lots of white diners down there."

"What's a White Diner? They got cheap food?"

I still didn't get it.

I didn't get the no-neck deputy parked by the side of the road looking for Northern license plates; I didn't get that anything north of the Carolinas was "north." I didn't get the back roads that led nowhere except maybe to some humped-up little black village on the edge of a swamp. I had never been to a black village before; there were no black people on Black Hawk Ridge, no black people in Crum, no black people in Wayne County, West Virginia. I didn't get the old man's single-pump gas station that was open only because he knew I was coming. I didn't get any of this. And I sure as hell didn't know what a "White Diner" was.

"I said, do they have . . . ." But he was gone.

I turned the bike out on the road, mist and dampness still clinging to the blacktop. The town couldn't be too far away.

I knew I must be near the beach, but I had never been near a beach and I didn't know exactly what to look for. I had never seen the ocean.

A series of small unpaved lanes drifted off to my left, lined with strange trees and small wooden houses that had screened porches and tiny patches of concrete outside at the edges of the porches, with hoses and pipes that led to shower heads. Showers. Right outside the house. This was strange country.

I was heading south in full darkness and I slowed the Triumph to a walk, trying to smell the air. The wind against my face was black and heavy with moisture, the whole thing tasting and smelling like the swamp back at the village. I knew the air was warm, but, still, I shivered. I started looking for a place to hole up for the night. Maybe an abandoned gas station.

I was on a low rise, a hump in the road that rolled up and then off down toward the distance, suddenly curving. I drifted lazily around the curve and was almost on top of the patrol car before I knew what the hell was happening. The car was parked on the side of the road, just behind another car, its red light on, turning, flashing. The deputy was standing beside the other car, leaning into its open window.

I decided to be cool, not slow down, not speed up. Just ride by.

It didn't work. As soon as he heard the sound of the engine he glanced up and then jerked upright.

My deputy. The guy who tried to kill me.

He knew it was me. He bolted for his car and I gunned the Triumph. The only thing I could think of was to put some distance between me and the patrol car before he got the big Ford in high gear.

There were some houses off to the left with narrow, sandy lanes that ran down between them. Heavy trees lined the lanes, their branches hanging over the small roads like the long wings of vultures, making the roads even blacker in the already black night. I flicked the bike's headlight off; no sense giving him a light to follow. I picked a lane that looked more narrow than the rest and slid through a sharp left turn and underneath the grasping branches. The lane was deep sand, a soft little side alley that sucked at the bike's wheels. I gunned the Triumph and pulled my weight back, trying to keep the front wheel from digging its own ditch in the sand, hoping to keep going, hoping to find enough room to ride but not enough room for the deputy to maneuver the big Ford.

Wrong again. He twisted the car into the same turn and jammed it through the limbs and brush. We were both going too fast in too small a space but I was desperate and he was crazy and the only way this could end would be for one of us to run out of gas, or room, or nerve.

The lane necked down to a tight fit. The sand seemed to get even softer and the bike labored through the drifts. The trunks of trees were lit with dancing light and I knew it was from the headlights of the patrol car, still behind me.

And then the road ended. It just disappeared into a low, long mound of sand and there was nothing I could do about it. The front wheel tried to auger in like a huge, twisting drill and I leaned back harder, pulling the bike out of the suck as hard as I could. I figured I could get over the mound and the Ford couldn't.

I was only half right. The bike made it over the ridge and labored down the other side, coughing and stalling. Then I heard a sound like a fist hitting a giant body bag, and the Ford blasted its way through the mound.

Its engine died.

I heard his starter grind. I kicked the bike's starter lever with a panic stroke and for once the Triumph knew I wasn't kidding. The bike came back to life and I took off down the hard packed sand that seemed damp to me, a strange sort of dampness that made the surface like a speedway. Lights swung behind me and I knew he was coming again, knew he could catch me on a fast, straight track, knew that the screaming of the engines would ring in my ears until I died.

I wasn't sure how to make a turn in this stuff, but the lights behind me grew closer and I didn't have a choice. I leaned into a diving left turn on the hard-pack. The bike twisted, the front wheel skittered out from under me and the old motorcycle just lay down and died, the foot-peg digging into the sand and stopping everything in its tracks. When the peg dug in I flew over the top of the bike and onto the sand, rolling and sliding, feeling the skin come off my arms and the side of my face.

The Ford shot past, inches from my leg.

I got the machine upright, kicked the starter and twisted the throttle as far as it would go, the rear wheel digging a rut in the wet sand as the bike shot straight into the darkness away from the Ford.

Before the I could get out of low gear, I hit the water.

Jesus H. Christ. Finally, I could see the ocean. It was all around me. It was black. I was in it up to my ass.

The bike had plowed into the gentle surf at full bore, splitting the water and then rapidly slowing as the bottom of the beach dropped away and the water rose onto the engine. I wasn't ready for the deceleration and I went over the handlebars in slow motion, flipping over the fender and landing on my back. Somewhere between the flip and the splash, the engine died.

When I stood up I was only waist deep, the gentle waves lapping at me. I stood motionless, feeling the Triumph against my leg, feeling the sting of the salt water against my bleeding face and arms, listening to the sound of the water, bracing myself as it gently pushed against me. Now and then a tiny wave would leap up, flicking drops of water into my face on my lips, stinging me again. For the first time in my life I tasted real salt water. I liked it.

The bike was under there somewhere. I could feel it. I groped for the handlebars and dragged the thing upright, then wrestled it around to face the beach. Walking the bike up on the beach was like wading in wet cement, but I damn well wasn't going to leave it in the ocean. It was my bike. I had built it. Out of the water, I eased the Triumph over on its side.

And then the lights came on. They lit up the beach in a long streak of golden yellow, showing up the bike in the perfect center of their glow. For a brief second I wondered where they came from, then watched them flicker gently as the engine caught and I heard the heavy horsepower of the Ford build into a roar. He was sitting not more than fifty yards down the beach. Waiting.

I grabbed for the handlebars but it was too late. The Ford shot forward and there was nothing I could do. He was coming straight and hard and fast. I let go of the handlebars, turned and crashed back into the water, hoping he wouldn't risk the Ford in the surf. A couple of steps and then I dived, trying to thrust my body through the water like a torpedo.

Before my head went under I heard the crunching of metal on metal, the bike under the wheels of the patrol car, the grinding death throes of an old bike that had sat in a barn in Kentucky for years, slowly rusting, waiting for me. I loved that old bike. And now, swimming and choking in the warm Atlantic, letting the tide carry me along the shore, on a night that should have become a painting on the back of my mind . . . I knew the old bike was trash.

It lay out there, waiting.

Not like the mountains. In the mountains everything changed from moment to moment, especially if I were on the ridges, watching the rise of the light against the west wall of darkness in the earliest of mornings. The mountains moved, heavy with the advancing light. As the light rose, the far ridges gave up their blackness and trees just an arrow-shot away lost the sinister fingers that had dripped from their limbs only minutes before. The light moved, turning the world to brightness long before the sun could climb from behind other mountains that I could not see, maybe would never see. As the sun climbed, the air turned warm and brushed a softness against my face unlike anything I could ever remember. In the mountains.

But not the ocean. It just lay out there, waiting. In the sunrise, it didn't grow brighter slowly, and with grace. It just burst into a full, flat reflection of the sky as the sun leaped up from beneath the horizon, a flaming ball slung loose from a cosmic trap. It had no subtlety. It excited the hell out of me.

I was sleeping behind a low dune, rolled up in a scrap of canvas I had found wind-wrapped around a tree. I sat up, crawled to the top of the dune and watched the sun lift boiling out of the ocean. There was nothing like this on Black Hawk Ridge.

Up the beach about a hundred yards I could see the pile of scrap that had been the Triumph being washed gently by the highest of the small, soft waves. The bike was bent into an L-shape, the rear wheel turned oddly up from the beach. I went down to the water and walked along the edge of the surf, thinking that I could always go back into the ocean if the deputy showed up. My face and arms were stiff from dried blood and I washed them gently in the salt water, loosening the wounds and making them bleed again.

I realized that looking at the bike was a waste of time, but there was something I thought I should do.

One of the rusted bolts that held the license plate had broken, but the other was still hanging on. I took off my shirt, wrapped it around the license plate and began twisting it back forth, feeling it get easier as the metal heated up. In a minute or two the plate came away in my hand. I sailed it as far out into the water as I could. Maybe he hadn't gotten the plate number — it wasn't even my plate. No matter, I didn't want to leave the plate. Maybe it was just symbolic, but I didn't care. Maybe he wouldn't come back, anyway. Maybe, after he trashed the bike, he just wanted to get away. Maybe he would go to hell. Maybe I would help him.

It should have been a sunrise that would last for the rest of my life, my first sunrise on a beach, shining brightly against the mirrors of my mind. I stood there, warming in the young sun, in a place I had never been, where I knew no one. I stood there, watching the waves creep higher and gradually cover the broken motorcycle. It finally disappeared, and so did my last thin connection with anything from before.

Black Hawk Ridge and Crum were gone.

Twenty-Six

It was wonderland.

Everything about it was new. Everything was something I had never seen before. The water, the sand, the huge trees with the thick, gnarled limbs that hung out over the narrow, sandy lanes that ran between the kind of houses I had never seen before, houses with screen all around the porches and shutters that actually covered the windows, that lifted up from the outside and hooked back against the walls, just hanging there through the heat of summer at the beach.

The light was new. Not like in Crum, where the light would creep across the far ridges and then seep down into the river valley, a syrupy silver color that lit up the tops of the corn stalks and then found the river hidden beneath the overhanging trees, brightening the water to a lighter shade of mud. The light was soft in Crum, apologetic, almost as though it didn't want to bring a glow to something that had never glowed in the first place.

But not at the beach. The light came hard and fast, a slap of brilliance across your face. It came up out of the ocean like a thunderclap. I thought I could hear sunrise.

The smell was new. I had never thought about how the ocean would smell, was supposed to smell. In the books I had read in the Crum High School library, there was no mention of the smell of wet, dead things, no mention of the stench sent up by the rotting of soaked, lifeless bits and pieces of strange things from the sea.

It was the worst thing I had ever smelled. I loved it.

The water was new. It didn't run anywhere, just came in and out and tasted like hell. It stretched away from me, and not too far out there the sky bent down and touched it. For the first time in my life I could see the horizon, the real one. At the horizon, the water just stopped.

On Black Hawk Ridge, when I stood on the high rock near Long Neck's whiskey still, I thought I could see forever. But all I really saw was more ridges, more rocks, more trees, green waves that fell off into the distance and all of them far away, very far away.

But it didn't matter, back there on Black Hawk Ridge, how far away things seemed when I stood on the rock and looked into the distance, because I knew where I was. On the Ridge, I knew what it felt like, what everything felt like. I knew the trees and rocks and what was in the trees and under the rocks. I knew the taste of the water in Turkey Creek and what the air smelled like on an autumn morning after a night full of rain. I knew that I would hear the creaking of the hinges on Long Neck's barn door not more than twenty minutes after first light. And how far away the hunter was, just from the sound of the gunshot that rushed through the woods, filtered and dampened by the trees. I was part of Black Hawk Ridge. I didn't belong, but I fit in.

But on the beach I was just a drifter, another piece of gnarled wood lying on the sand, on the surface of things. On the beach, I had no depth. I was not tied to anything. It was an odd feeling, not knowing anything about where I was, what I was doing there. In a way, I was free, floating. No one in the world who knew me, knew where I was.

I spent a few days just walking the beach, heading south, wondering what I would do and when I would do it. I was looking for a place. Not just a place for now. Not just any place. I was looking for a place for all time, a place to stop, a place to get used to, a place to be. And every so often I looked over my shoulder. I knew that big son-of-a-bitch was back there somewhere, or maybe up ahead of me, or out there in a boat, for all I knew. But he was there. I knew it. And I wondered if he had ever gotten a good look at my face, if he would recognize me.

I wandered down some of the sandy lanes. The lanes usually came from off toward the highway straight as a shotgun barrel down toward the beach. They were lined with small cottages, summer places, I guess, that weren't too close together. There seemed to be a lot of room to put houses and they were spread out all over the place. I knew that I was wandering from one little town to another, but sometimes I couldn't tell where one ended and another started. Just little cottages. And more lanes.

There were small stores scattered here and there. They sold beer and soda, ice, lunchmeat and bread and beach stuff like big towels and folding chairs. Some of the grocery stuff that got old they threw out back, stale bread and old lettuce, soft tomatoes. And that's where I ate, fishing through the stuff to find something that didn't look all that bad. After a while, I learned that it didn't matter what the stuff looked like, it was what it *smelled* like that counted.

Now and then I found a sun tan lotion bottle with a little goop left in it. I twisted off the bottle cap and walked along with the bottle turned upside down in my hand, the drops of goop trickling down into my palm. I took off my shirt and smeared the stuff on me, hoping I would tan, hoping I would look less like a mountain boy at the beach and more like the guys I saw walking and running on the sand, out there impressing the girls.

A couple of nights I slept in gas stations that were closed and boarded up, but they stank of oil and some other smells that I didn't recognize and I switched to sleeping on back porches of beach houses that nobody was staying in at the time. Once, dozing in the darkness on a back porch of a tiny shack near the end of a lane, I heard somebody coming around the side of the house. He was at the corner of the house before I got fully awake and there was no place for me to go. I got up and eased into a cane-bottom chair, leaned back and put my feet up on the railing. The beam of a flashlight stabbed here and there as the guy tip-toed to the corner of the porch.

"Hello," I said softly. "Might want to be careful with that light. Don't want to wake up the neighbors." I tried to sound older, and friendly. I didn't know how to do that, exactly, but I tried anyway.

He stepped back away from the porch and shot the light at me. I couldn't see him because of the light, but from way he held it he must have been a big bastard. *Another* big bastard. They sure feed these southern boys a lot.

"I *am* the neighbor," the guy said. He sounded sort of insulted.

"Well, howdy, neighbor. I just got in. Late last night. Couldn't get to sleep so I thought I'd just sit out here for a while." I wasn't sure he was buying it.

"You rent the place from Woody?"

Uh oh. I didn't know who the hell Woody was. But maybe I wasn't the only hillbilly from West Virginia who ended up down here. "Nope. My paw, he rented it from the man up there in . . . Huntington. Never got to meet Woody. Actual', paw didn't know who owned the place when he rented it."

"Well, Woody owns it, and I'm his neighbor. Sort of keep an eye on the place."

"Well, tell you what. In the morning you come over and paw and me'll make some coffee and we'll talk about it. You can tell us about Woody, and we'll tell you about the guy in Huntington."

He played the light around the porch. I got up from the chair and stretched, trying to act it all out but not really wanting to reach for the screen door. I didn't know if it was hooked from the inside, and if he waited there for me to pull the handle either the door would open or not. Either way, I didn't have a next move after that. Except to run.

"Well," he muttered, "sorry I bothered you."

Jesus, he bought it.

". . . and I guess I will drop by in the morning. Just to see there's anything you might need." The flashlight backed off across the sandy yard, weaving back and forth.

"Sounds fine," I called after him, not too loudly. "We'll probably be up by about nine, paw and me. Y'all come on over." I thought that last part sounded southern.

The light faded around the side of the house. I could see the faint reflection of it, playing around up near the front yard.

"Hey," he sort of half-shouted. I could barely hear him. Where's y'all's car, anyway?"

I heard that plain enough. I vaulted over the porch rail and hit the sand running.

And the girls were all new.

I took off my shirt and tied the sleeves around my waist, strolling along the beach trying to act like I belonged there. The girls came down to the beach wearing their one-piece bathing suits, the suits with the wire around the tops and they would keep adjusting the tops when the wire punched into their tits, hooking their thumbs under the wires and pulling them out from their bodies, then giving that little shake with their shoulders, jiggling their tits into the cups, just so. And letting you see them do it. Letting you know they had tits.

Before the beach, I had never seen a girl in a bathing suit. In Crum, there was no place to swim except the river, and most of the girls never went down there. If one did, and if she went into the water, she sure as hell wouldn't wear a bathing suit. She would go into the water in full battle gear — loose jeans, heavy shoes, a blouse buttoned all the way up to her neck. Only one time did I ever see a girl in the river in anything but jeans. And she was wearing a dress.

I was up to my ass in the thick, brown water of the Tug River, looking at Ruby standing on the bank. All I had on were my jeans and the hot August sun was baking my head and shoulders. I had been standing there for ten minutes.

She still wasn't moving, but I kept talking to her, trying to convince her, pleading, almost begging. Hell, I *was* begging, trying to get her to come into the river.

The river bottom was soft under my feet and I backed up a couple of steps, the water creeping up over the tops of my jeans. I looked down at the water, so loaded with silt that I couldn't see my belt. I don't know what made me think of it; it just seemed like something to do. I reached underwater, unfastened my jeans, and took them off. I pulled the dripping pants out of the water, rolled them into a ball and fired them at the bank.

She couldn't believe it, Ruby Harmon couldn't, standing there on the bank wearing her thin cotton dress, the sun behind her, lighting the cloth like silver and printing the outline of her legs solid and graceful. A dress that might as well not have been there, hiding nothing. She couldn't believe I had taken off my pants, that I was standing naked in the Tug River, the town of Crum just up and beyond the riverbank, people going about their business.

She couldn't believe it, and after I did it I knew it was the only thing that would get her attention, would trap her mind. It was different and she knew it so she waded into the sluggish river, slowly, not liking the water, not liking the smell and feel of it, but wanting to have her part in this, knowing it might never happen again.

As she came forward the water caught her dress and floated it up around her waist. She never touched the dress, never took her eyes from my face. I stood still, waiting, not really believing that I would finally have her, finally have Ruby Harmon. And I knew I *would* have her. That, and only that, was what this river business was all about.

She dipped her hands in the water, cupped them, filled them and brought them up to her breasts. She folded the hand-cups of water onto her chest, one hand neatly on each breast, and let the water soak in and down, let it dribble down across her belly. Her hands slid slowly away and her breasts were there, high and firm, her nipples hard against the vanishing cloth.

Christ. I thought I was going to faint.

Our eyes were locked and she took another step toward me and then they weren't locked anymore, Ruby snapping her head a little upstream, beyond me, her eyes widening. I didn't want to turn my head from her, didn't want anything to change what was happening here, but she clapped both hands across her mouth and staggered backward. I had to look.

A dead horse was floating by, a gray horse, a horse spinning gently from the soft pull of the current, a horse floating on its side, its stomach bloated and riding high above the water, pulling one front leg into the air, a horse with one dead eye staring sideways at the sky spinning above it.

I heard Ruby retching behind me, but I couldn't take my eyes from the horse. Only in the Tug River, I thought. Only in the Tug River.

And when I finally turned around, she was gone.

Sure, I had seen pictures in magazines of girls in bathing suits, but I hadn't seen one in the flesh, so to speak. I had seen naked girls in the flesh, but that's different. There was something different about a naked girl and the same girl wearing a bathing suit. It just wasn't the same. Not that one is better than the other. Just different.

I had seen Yvonne naked. Yvonne, the only truly beautiful girl in Crum, more beautiful than Ruby, more beautiful than anyone. Yvonne, with her black hair and brown eyes and legs that could move like silk; who had more brains than anyone I had ever known; who had wanted to get out of Crum worse than I had; who said she would do anything to make the money for a bus ticket to get the hell out of Crum. Anything.

She said she would fuck her way out of Crum, if anyone was interested. And had the money.

We made love in the gold light of a full moon patterned over thickly by clouds, leaning on the railing of her front porch on a hillside high above Crum, me a little crazy, wanting to let everyone know we had done it, wanting to scream out over Crum that I had made love to this woman, this beautiful woman.

Probably the most wonderful night of my life.

For part of the night, anyway.

I just didn't understand. I didn't understand about the fucking and the money and leaving Crum and who fit into that plan and who didn't, who should pay and who shouldn't. And I ruined it. I ruined the whole thing.

The last time I saw her, she was driving her brother's car out of Crum. And she tried to run over me.

I knew what to do with a naked girl, but not with girls who were only partly naked and who lived in cities and went to college and knew how to talk about things I had never even seen. I walked far out around them there on the beach, giving them plenty of room, never coming close to them stretched out on their beach towels. And then I realized I didn't have to do that. I could walk right past them, right up to them, almost right on them, and they didn't care. They were on the beach and I was on the beach and it was anybody's beach and no one gave a damn. I kept right on walking close to them, strolling by, breathing in the suntan-lotion-smell of them. But not really looking them right in the eye. I mean, if I did, and one of them said something to me, what the hell would I say back?

I wandered down through Cherry Hill Beach, and past some other beaches and on into Myrtle Beach.

The farther south I walked the thicker the houses got and then I started running into motels that sat back from the beach, one-story buildings with lots of screen doors and little porches and air conditioners sticking out of the windows. By the time I got to Myrtle Beach, the buildings stood shoulder-to-shoulder and you had to walk between them just to get away from the beach.

There were lifeguards scattered along the beach. I figured I could be a lifeguard if all you had to do was sit around with a whistle. I talked to some of them about how to get their kind of work. Most of them just laughed at me but some talked about tests and training and waiting lists and jobs going to in-staters and there were two or three guys already wanting every job there was and did I have a local address and the summer was already underway . . . and who the hell would hire a hill-billy, anyway. They were all tanned and slick and trim and they all said they went to college and the only reason they wasted their time on the beach was the girls.

One of them said to try back up at Cherry Hill. Banger would hire anybody. And I looked like anybody.

It took me two days to get back to Cherry Hill Beach.

I didn't know who Banger was or where to find him.

A pier jutted out into the ocean, a wooden centipede on stilts, tip-toeing across the low surf, a creaking, shit-stained landing site for seagulls. On the beach, just back from the end of the pier, was a building I would remember for the rest of my life. It was the pavilion.

It had a name, but all anyone ever called it was "the pavilion." It was famous along the beach. It was a place to be, the *only* place to be at Cherry Hill, except on the beach or the pier. It was the meeting place, the drinking place, the place where you went to cool off for a while, to meet women, to buy a hot dog, to hang out. It was a place to sit in the shade and sip a beer and stare out at the water and watch people stroll on the pier and along the beach.

The pavilion looked like a square barn with the sides missing. There weren't any windows; the sides were just missing, all the way around, even behind the bar. Each morning someone would come out and un-bolt the sides, the huge wooden shutters, and drag them behind the building, just pile them there until closing time. When the sides were gone, you could sit at a table and drink beer and hang your arm outside, flip cigarette butts onto the sand, watch gulls strafe the beach. The building was one huge room with a small storage room at the back, a plank floor, naked rafters running across below the ceiling, bare light bulbs hanging down from wires. A bar ran the full length of the beach side and tables and chairs were scattered all over the place. When the clean-up guy swept it out in the morning, he shoved the tables out of the way and kept on sweeping. The tables just stayed wherever they landed until someone else moved them. At the far end, away from the entry, a huge jukebox stood on a plywood platform. In front of the jukebox an open area served as a dance floor. When the place was full, you could get a couple of hundred people in there.

At night, it was the place where everybody gathered, the kids, their parents, the college types, everybody talking, dancing, drinking beer, making out in cars parked at the far edge of the sandy parking lot. The pavilion's lights spilled out onto the sand, throwing a glow all the way to the beach-end of the pier. Banger had even put a couple of lights on the roof and now and then you could see a couple out on the beach, dancing in the glow of the pavilion.

As the night wore on the parents left the pavilion, and then the "older" college types, bored with the music and the energy of the high-schoolers.

Eventually, the high-schoolers drifted off into the dark.

And then only the hard-core types would be left, the ones with absolutely no place to go, and endless days to go there.

Like me.

Tomorrow would be another day on the beach. Another day exactly the same.

I got to the pavilion in the early morning and the sides were already off and piled behind the building. A thin black man was sweeping out the place and he turned away from me when I came up the short flight of stairs to the deck. I started to speak to him but never got to it. A short, stubby guy with shoulders the width of a car came out of the storage room and walked in my general direction, down behind the bar. His hair was cropped down to his skull and his face looked puffy. He had on a t-shirt and jeans and the t-shirt was a size or so too small, gripping his chest and wrapping tightly around the little roll of fat that was beginning to show at the top of his belt. He had a pack of cigarettes turned up in the sleeve of his t-shirt, and the shirt was so tight it was bending the package.

"We ain't open yet," he growled, walking past and not even looking at me.

"That's okay. I'm just looking for Banger," I said, sliding onto a stool.

"He ain't open yet, neither." He kept walking. I noticed the black guy had stopped sweeping.

"Look, the lifeguards down at Myrtle said I should come up here and look for Banger. Said he might need another life-guard."

I had learned that the locals just used one name for the beaches. Myrtle Beach was just "Myrtle". Cherry Hill was "Cherry."

He turned toward the black man with the broom, who still had his back toward me. "What you think, John? We need another lifeguard?"

The black guy still did not turn. "Looks that way to me. You done run one off yesterday." He started sweeping again, working toward the back.

"Yeah. Sure did. Caught him with his finger in the till."

"No shit," I said, trying to sound interested. "You mean he was stealing your money?"

"Nah, dumbass. *Nobody* steals my money. He had his fin-ger in the till. Mary Jane Till. Her daddy owns the biggest house in Cherry and one of my very own lifeguards was sitting down there on the beach with his finger in Mary Jane Till all the way up to the last knuckle. Her daddy find out about that, I got a lotta trouble. Had to fire that boy's ass."

"Well, I'm ready to take his place. I do my fingerin' in private. And I don't know nobody named Till."

He shuffled along the bar until he was across from me, just standing there and looking. "What you think, John Three?"

he said sideways along his shoulder, not really looking at the black guy. John Three?

A car rolled up outside and I heard the engine die.

"Might as well," the black guy said. "He look strong enough to me. Keep the girls coming in."

"Yeah, well, he got to pass the test, first."

Shit. The test. I wondered if all the swimming I had done in the Tug River would be enough to get me through. I wondered if the ocean were different. I wondered if I would drown.

The guy reached under the bar and came up with a ball bat. In one smooth motion he swung the bat across the bar, straight at my head. I rolled backward off the stool, the bat whistling over me, and hit the floor on my back, my breath exploding out of me. I thought the fucking guy was crazy and that he probably would come across the bar so I rolled over and came up on my knees, gasping for breath, my arms covering my head, waiting to feel the bat.

The guy was leaning over the bar, laughing. He turned toward the black guy. "What you think now, John Three?" he said, dangling the bat over the bar in front of me.

Another guy had come up the steps and was standing there watching, leaning against the door frame. He was so big he almost blocked out the light. I only glanced in his direction. I really didn't pay any attention. I had a few problems of my own, kneeling there with my arms over my head.

"I think your swing is still good and level, Banger, but you got to move your hands up on the grip a little," John Three said. "Never could get you to choke up proper." John Three was almost at the corner of the dance floor. He turned and looked straight at me, grinning. It was the preacher, the guy who had given me the dollar.

"Okay, boy. You hired," Banger said. "What they call you?"

"Jesse. Jesse Stone," I said, almost whispering, still on my knees.

He stretched across the bar and touched me on the shoulder with the bat. "Well, get up Jesse Stone. And from now on, you a *lifeguard!*" And he touched me on the shoulder with the bat again, like he was knighting me. It was a plastic bat, the kind you buy for little kids to play with in the backyard.

The preacher was in front of me now, bending over a little, taking me by the arm. "Come on, Jesse. Looks like you done pass the test. Get you something to take down to the beach with you."

He pulled me up, a tight grin on his face, and led me toward the back of the pavilion. I started to turn and say thank-you to Banger but the preacher felt the motion and tightened down on my arm, keeping me going straight toward the back. When we got back there he stopped me at the door to the storage room.

"Take a look around in there. And take your time."

Somehow, when he spoke to me now, his voice was different. His eyes flicked toward the front of the building. I followed his eyes and saw the big man leaning on the bar, talking to Banger. He was bigger than Banger, heavier, with more weight in his chest and a trim waist. He had on a sport shirt and his slacks looked new, but there was a gun in a holster on his belt. Through the far door I could see the huge Ford with the red light on top. I slid into the storage room, leaped across to the other side, opened another door and jumped outside.

The deputy. That fucking deputy. And he had heard me tell Banger my name.

I pressed back against the wall of the pavilion, listening for sounds of someone coming into the storage room after me.

No one came. I stood there and shook for ten minutes.

I heard the Ford start up and drive away.

I was a lifeguard.

The deputy knew my name.

The preacher was nowhere to be seen.

Twenty-Seven

Banger had swung his magic baseball bat and decreed that I was a lifeguard. He said I could start any time I wanted. He didn't even take me down to the water to see if I could swim. He didn't even *ask* me if I could swim.

I spent the morning looking around the pavilion. Banger told me the pavilion was actually named the Sha-Boom, said he named it after the song by the Crew Cuts, but he told all the tourists that he named it after the sound the waves made when they piled up the beach and smashed into the side of his pavilion. Only the waves never did that. Not in anyone's memory, anyway. And I found out later that Banger re-named the pavilion almost every year. Didn't matter. No one ever called it anything but "the pavilion." Banger was full of shit.

The preacher had said there was some stuff in the back room I might be able to use, so I poked around in there for a while. I rummaged through some boxes of junk, old towels, mostly-empty bottles of suntan lotion, broken beach chairs, punctured inflatable floats and other beach stuff I had never seen before. On a nail by the door I found the whistle Banger said was there and I took it and slowly shuffled my way out onto the beach, not knowing exactly how to act, now that I was a lifeguard. At the moment, it didn't matter much how I acted. The only people on the beach seemed to be more interested in walking than in swimming or sitting in the sun and none of them paid any attention to me. It was still early but even in the weak light I could feel the heat of the sun beginning to focus on the beach, beginning to sear the color out of everything it touched.

Banger told me there was a white wooden chair down there, not too far from the restrooms, a chair not much higher than a baby's high chair. It was my chair, he said. The other guys had chairs up and down the beach, chairs they had staked out, chairs they had carved their names into. Most of them had their chairs on parts of the beach where their favorite girls stayed nearby in beach cottages, Banger said. One of the benefits of the job. But don't carve my name in a chair he said — I probably wouldn't last long enough to stake an actual claim to it.

He told me to check out the restrooms and the beach rental shack, a tiny plank structure that stored the umbrellas and floats that the lifeguards rented to the tourists.

I was halfway to the chair before I realized I didn't have any swimming trunks; I was still wearing my jeans.

Back at the storage room I found three pairs of men's swimming trunks I thought I could wear. One of them had the ass ripped out; another had some sort of stain down the front, right over the crotch. The third pair looked okay. It had a sort of jock strap sewn right inside the trunks, a net-like sling that kept your balls from falling down and out the leg. The trunks were a little large but I took them anyway and changed my clothes there in the storage room. There were no windows and the light switch didn't work, but if I opened the outside door I could see just fine. As it turned out, I would change my clothes in that storage room for as long as I worked for Banger.

I sat stiffly in the lifeguard's chair, staring at the water, the whistle lanyard around my neck, my hands gripping the chair arms, wondering what I would do if I saw something I was supposed to blow the whistle at. Or something I was supposed to rescue. In the middle of trying to figure that out, I dozed off.

I heard them giggling before I opened my eyes, the sun burning against my eyelids, my legs dangling over the front of the chair, my chin fallen down against my chest. I pretended to stay asleep, straining to hear more. Very slowly I eased up one eyelid, like you did when you were a kid, pretending to sleep, but really trying to see what your parents were doing. I could see legs strolling by, legs that were the legs of my dreams, legs that went all the way up to firm rounded asses and crotches covered with thin swimsuit material, crotches that rolled back and forth gently as the legs strolled by the chair.

They all giggled. Somewhere up above the legs, up where I couldn't see without giving myself away, there were tits and faces and mouths and giggles, little bubbling sounds that came up from slender necks and out between lips that I could only imagine. And they kept walking by, and they kept giggling. It was time for me to "wake up."

My head came up from my chest and I stretched my arms, casually, as though taking a nap in the lifeguard chair was something I did all the time. Several of the girls had stopped, just standing near the chair, all of them looking at me. Other girls came over. A small group had formed to inspect the new lifeguard. Damn, Banger was right. I'd have to fight 'em off with a stick. There really were some great benefits to being a lifeguard, benefits that were hard to measure. All I had to do was sit there and let 'em walk up. I began to pick out the ones I'd talk to first, if I could figure out what to say.

One of my legs was a little numb from hanging over the front of the chair, and when I eased forward to rub it some of the giggles got a little louder. And then I realized that my swim trunks were pulled up tight against my crotch, the jock had slipped, and one of my balls had squeezed out into the light, just hanging there against my leg, baking in the sun.

They giggled some more.

And so it began. Life on the beach.

There were four lifeguards who worked for Banger, including me. Two of them I never really got to know because I only saw them sometimes in the late evening, after they came back from their girls' cottages. Most of the time they didn't come back at all. But the fourth guy was Hugo, a dark-haired jock from Charlotte who came down to Cherry every summer to work as a lifeguard and hang out. His real name was Francis, but he thought that wasn't manly enough for a lifeguard, so he changed it every summer to Hugo. He was slender and fast and you could read the map to every muscle in his body. He had one of those skins that tanned deeply and quickly and before the summer was half gone Hugo was so dark he got odd looks from some of each week's new visitors to the beach.

Hugo's chair was the next one down the beach from mine and we could see each other, tell how the other was doing. We even arranged a bunch of hand signals for things like "I need help with these women," and the like. If I saw Hugo's "I need help" signal, I would wander over his way to see what was going on.

No one ever drowned while I was doing that. I'll never know why.

Every day on the beach was pretty much the same. We would get up, go to the pavilion and scrounge something to eat from Banger, then wander down to our chairs. We would open the rental shack and drag out some umbrellas, chairs and floats, pile them next to the shack and just let them lie there. Now and then someone would rent one. Banger wouldn't let us take the money; we had to send everyone to the pavilion to pay. In the evening we put everything away — and that was it. Another completion of our appointed rounds; another hard day at the office.

The lifeguard chairs were far enough apart that the lifeguards didn't get to talk much to each other during the day, but that didn't matter. There were dozens of girls to talk to. When we weren't trying to cadge food from them there in the beach, we were trying to talk them into taking us home with them, getting into their beds, getting into their pants, and, the best thing of all, getting into their refrigerators.

Getting the girls to feed us was important. Banger didn't pay us enough to live on, and by the time he deducted our tabs for beer and other junk at the pavilion, there was hardly anything left. We had to beg food, but the women had to think it was a game. We couldn't let them know we really *needed* the food.

Naturally, we didn't have enough money to rent a place to stay. The lifeguards, all four of us, or whichever of us didn't have some place else to sleep, slept in the men's restroom.

The restrooms sat back at the edge of the beach, a few yards from the pavilion, partially hidden by overhanging trees and some shrubs that the town planted there, a squat, cinder block building with a door and one small window on each end. Inside, a thin partition ran across the middle, men on one side, women on the other.

Banger didn't like the restrooms. Before the town built them the only structures on the beach beside Banger's pavilion had been the little rental shack for the umbrellas and floats.

The people on the beach had to come into the pavilion to take a leak. Banger liked that. He would say things to them that made them feel guilty if they pissed in his restroom but then didn't buy anything. He sold a lot of worthless crap like that.

I guess the restrooms belonged to the town but Banger considered the restrooms his, even though he hated them, and he gave us permission to sleep there. There were some cots on the wall that were suspended with hinges and chains, and folded down when we needed them. They were supposed to be used for sunstroke victims, only no one on the beach ever got sunstroke while I was there. It's a good thing. None of us knew what sunstroke looked like or what to do about it.

So we slept on the cots. There were some first aid blankets on each cot, but they were so thin we were always chilly, even in the middle of summer. The restrooms never got much sun and the dampness of the concrete building never went away. But what really kept the restrooms damp was us. Every night when we turned in, the place smelled like piss. So we took a two-inch fire hose and blasted the walls, the floor, everything. Except the cots. The place never quite dried out, but the dampness and the chill were better than the smell.

There was no place to put our clothes in the restrooms. I found an old canvas bag in the storeroom and I used it as a closet, cramming my stuff in there in a wad of confusion. I left the bag in the storeroom. If I wanted to change clothes, I had to get to the storeroom before Banger locked it for the night, or I had to wait until next morning. It wasn't much, but it worked.

The partition that separated the men's side of the restroom from the women's was made of some sort of concrete junk, and we spent the summer boring small holes in it using nails, bits of wire and even an honest-to-God drill that Hugo found in Banger's tool box at the pavilion. We worked at night, always careful of the noise. Every time we got a hole all the way through, Banger would catch us at it and knock us around a little. Strange. He never caught us *while* we were boring the hole, only after we had finished. And he never seemed to try to plug up what we had drilled. By the end of the summer there were so many holes you could feel the breeze blow through them.

I always felt a little odd, sneaking into the restrooms and peeking through those holes. The routine was simple — wait until some girl who was really a knockout went into the restroom, then saunter in there yourself — it didn't matter what was happening on the beach. If there was another guy in there, you couldn't peek through the holes. But if there wasn't . . .

I saw a lot of women with their bathing suits down around their ankles, wiping themselves. I saw them changing Kotex pads. I saw them put Kotex pads, Kleenex and other soft things I didn't recognize down under their breasts, shoving them up and out over the tops of their bathing suits. I saw them rub suntan lotion on their faces and their legs; and once I saw a woman rub lotion into her cunt, standing there in front of the mirror, rubbing and rubbing until she came.

I saw two women kissing and feeling each other up. I remember thinking at the time that they were really good looking women and I couldn't figure out why they were wasting time fooling with each other. If they would just spend some time with me, I was sure I could show them what real love was like. I was sure of that.

I didn't know much.

After a while the whole thing didn't do much for me and I quit going in there. There weren't any secrets in the restroom, nothing the women had to hide. Everything just hung out in the open with no drops of sweat and no grinding motion against your hips, no open mouths and heavy breathing, no fingernails digging into your cheeks. You could peek through the holes and see a lot of tits, but the fun part of it just wasn't there.

But Banger never quit. The funniest thing on the beach was to see a good looking woman go into the restroom, Banger noticing from the pavilion. Then see Banger sprint from the pavilion to the restrooms, trying to get to a peeping hole before the woman finished up and left. Some of the girls we knew saw Banger running back and forth, but they never caught on. They thought he had a permanent case of the shits.

We slept in the restrooms for almost two weeks before Banger began his sunrise raids.

The first time he sneaked in it wasn't full daylight and the restroom was gray-dark, stinking in the dampness. He tiptoed silently to the main water drain in the center of the floor. The drain had a heavy, perforated metal cover held in place by a single, large screw. The screw was always missing. Banger lifted the cover and carefully laid it aside. He didn't make a sound. The others were asleep, rolled and packed into the narrow cots, trying to fend off the dampness. I wasn't asleep, but I wasn't really awake, either. One part of me wanted to just lie there, letting my mind drift. The other part of me wondered just what the hell a grown man was doing in the darkness, sneaking silently across the floor of a public restroom.

There was a metallic click and then a tiny, bright flame, the unmistakable process of a Zippo being fired up. Another click and the flame went out. I heard the cover slide back on the drain. There was no longer any reason to sneak — Banger jumped up and ran for the door, disappearing into the early morning mist. I started to sit up, wondering what all the small noises were. I never got all the way up.

The explosion came.

Whatever the thing was, it went off in the drain, a monstrous, compressed cannon firing at point-blank range, pounding the sound into the walls and slamming back and forth across the commode stalls and down the row of urinals. The blast drove the iron cover into the air and dropped it back onto the concrete floor, clanging, spinning and ringing like a giant coin flipped up from hell. In the middle of it all I heard Hugo scream and one of the bunks slammed back against the wall. For long seconds after the blast, the cover bounced and rang on the concrete, underlining a pain in our heads strong enough to make our eyes bulge. Hugo moaned for a long minute after the blast, and then walked slowly out of the restroom.

Banger had used an M-80, a monster firecracker shaped like a short piece of pipe, the fuse sticking out of the side. The dammed thing could blow the bottom out of a five-gallon can. Banger would sneak in, drop it into the drain, then slide the cover back on. It was his preferred way of waking up his lifeguards.

I couldn't stand it.

Banger always tried to sneak into the restroom in the early morning, before the mist had rolled off the beach and the eastern light bounced its way around the concrete corners and doors and into the stalls along the walls opposite our cots. As time went on he would get more careless, sometimes just walking up to the door and flinging the M-80 inside, then leaning against the wall and waiting for the reaction.

The rules were simple: if you complained, you weren't a "sport," and your days as a lifeguard were numbered.

Knowing Banger would be there in the morning, we trained ourselves to be awake before he arrived. We would sit on the edge of the cots, listening for Banger. When we knew he was outside, we would pull the blankets over our heads and press our hands over our ears. Once the explosion was over we would stagger out of the restroom, pretending dizziness, giving Banger his laugh for the day. It was all pretty stupid, but, all in all, it was an easy way to get something *we* needed. We needed the jobs. We needed a place to sleep.

Still, I couldn't stand it. After a week or so I sneaked out of the restroom at night and began sleeping in the tiny rental shack. I rigged a lock on the inside to keep Banger out, but it wasn't necessary. He didn't give a damn whether I was there or not.

≈ Twenty-Eight ≈

Sitting beside the Tug River where it slid under the green, tangled overhangs with Crum just up and over the bank and waiting there for me, sitting there on that damp riverbank I would pretend that the Tug River was the ocean and I was sitting on a beach.

I had never seen a beach, never seen an ocean, had no idea what they really looked like. The books in the Crum High School library had a few pictures, but I knew that pictures of an ocean, like pictures of the Grand Canyon, couldn't really show me what it was all about.

And now I was a real lifeguard on a real beach with a real ocean just there, at my feet, where I could go down to it and roll in it, no willowy tree limbs in my way, no dead horses floating by, no pig fuckers over there in Kentucky waiting for me to swim across.

No cannibals.

Well, maybe I wasn't a *real* lifeguard. I didn't know much about what a lifeguard was supposed to do, or how to rescue people, or anything like that. I had the lifeguard chair and the whistle and white ring-float on a hook on the back of the chair and those goddamn people weren't supposed to go out there and get their asses in trouble in the first place, Banger said.

What little I did know I learned from watching the other lifeguards, especially Hugo. Hugo could swim better than anyone I had ever seen, better than any of the guys back in Crum who used to swim every day in the Tug River, better than anyone I ever saw at the beach. I could swim, but Hugo taught me how to really swim, what to do in the surf, how to protect myself, how to hold people and pull them toward the shore, hold them so they couldn't thrash around and get at my head and arms.

Gradually, as the days went by, Hugo and I began to feel that we really were lifeguards. Just maybe knew what we were doing.

Now and then I would wander down to Myrtle and hang around the lifeguards down there. I didn't let them know I was a lifeguard at Cherry, that I worked for Banger. They didn't like Banger much, thought he was an asshole, thought Cherry Hill Beach was so far out of the action at Myrtle it might as well have been in New Jersey. I stayed out of their way, but I hung around close enough to see what they did when someone had trouble in the water. What I found out was, hell, Hugo knew more than most of those guys.

It was Hugo who invented the Jellyfish Rodeo.

We were always looking for ways to impress the girls on the beach, make them think how manly we were, we lifeguards, we men who were ready to risk our lives to save those in danger.

We worked on our tans, ran up and down the beach, twirled our whistles, stood up on the chairs and stared at the water, apparently on the verge of initiating a risky rescue. And I guess we always tried to be 'cool' but we really had no idea what 'cool' was.

And then one day Hugo found the jellyfish. It was washed up on the beach, a gelatinous mass of some sickening thickness, a glob of sea snot on the sand. It was the ugliest thing I had ever seen.

Hugo had been dozing on his lifeguard chair when he heard a small squeal from down near the low surf. He jumped down off the chair and by the time he got to the squealer — a tiny girl with huge breasts, her legs clamped tightly together as she stared at the jellyfish — there were other girls there, all of them dancing from one foot to the other, like people do sometimes when they have to take a piss.

Hugo saw the jellyfish. He knew he would have to be cool, he told me, knew this was an opportunity, but didn't really know what to do about it. So he just let it play itself out. He looked up and saw me in my chair. He gave me the signal.

By the time I got down there, Hugo was explaining about the jellyfish, how dangerous they were, how, now and then, one of them washed up on the beach. And how the lifeguards had to risk their very lives getting rid of them.

I didn't know what the hell Hugo was talking about, but it didn't matter — Hugo didn't know, either. What we both knew, though, was that the girls were entranced, scared out of their wits, and were pressed up against Hugo and me for protection from the beast that lay, dead, shrinking and stinking, at their feet. All the girls wore similar bathing suits and I figured they were from some school, or camp, or something, maybe even a church. All there on the beach together. I hoped they were from a church. Hugo said church girls were the best and the horniest, not being able to do much of anything back home because they all had to hang out at the church. When they got down here to the beach, they went nuts. He said.

One of the girls wasn't a girl. She was a woman. She was taller than the others and more rounded, her shape pushing slightly against the straps of her bathing suit, dark brown hair glistening. She was good looking, but a little severe, restrained. Ah, I thought. The counselor. Or one of the mothers. Whatever . . . this one was no kid.

"Are they out there, in the water where we swim?" one of the girls wanted to know.

"Well," Hugo started, standing up straight and pasting a serious look on his face, "sometimes they are, sure enough. Not too bad when they *stay* out there. It's when they come into the beach they're a problem. Like to come into the beach, these things do. Like to hunt here."

The girls were hooked, not taking their eyes from Hugo. Except maybe for the counselor, who stood off to the side, her face totally blank.

"We can't let 'em do that," Hugo said seriously, "can't let 'em come in and mess with our beach, not *our* beach." Hugo sounded grim, a protector of women and other small life forms. I don't think he noticed the counselor.

And then the damned fool told them we, we lifeguards, had to go out and get them, swim out there and take in all the jellyfish we could, scare the rest of them off, make the beach safe for mankind. Womankind. Girlkind. Any kind that might feed us or fuck us. Hugo didn't say that last part, but I knew that was what he was thinking.

"When are you going to do that?" It was the counselor. I knew it would be.

"Well . . . have to wait for a school of them to come by, so we can get a lot . . ." Hugo noticed her for the first time. He got a little nervous.

"*When?*" She wasn't kidding around, her eyes boring into Hugo. The other girls were looking, first at her, then back to Hugo. "I find this very interesting, from a scientific standpoint, of course." She wasn't buying a damned word of it.

"Well," Hugo said, squeezing his lips together, "I guess maybe tomorrow. At least we'll go out and scout around. See what we can find."

The goddamn idiot. What the hell did we know about jellyfish?

"We'll be here," the counselor said. "Always interested to see demonstrations of . . . beach science. " And she walked away, taking the girls with her. I thought she had a tiny smile on her face, but I wasn't sure.

We didn't know what to do. All those girls were going to be down here on the beach, and if we didn't do *something*, and if the counselor really called our bluff, and if all those girls told all the other girls . . .

Hugo and I met at the rental shack to talk it over. In the end, it was simple. We would just take a couple of the inflatable beach floats and some fishermen's dip nets, borrow a couple of knives from Banger, paddle out beyond the surf a ways, pretend to look for the jellyfish, dip the nets around a little, and then come back in. We would simply declare that there weren't any jellyfish to be seen, probably because we had scared them all away. We had, at great risk, made the beach safe.

The girls came back to the beach. They sat in a clump on their blankets, down near the pier. The counselor kept looking at us, at Hugo, then at me, then back at Hugo. I began to get a little nervous. Once, she stood up, her arms folded across her breasts, looking directly at me. An unbeliever. We thought we would make her wait a while.

About mid-morning I saw Hugo's signal. We each picked up our floats and nets and walked stoically down to the surf, right in front of the girls. We did not look at them. Hugo and I adjusted the belts our knives hung from, took deep breaths, looked off into the surf, sadly. But heroically. We shook hands, long and solemnly, our grip lingering. And then we picked up the floats and nets and waded into the surf.

We were out beyond the tiny break of the surf, the tide low and changing, the water almost still. It was almost like a lake out there, the air quiet, the water moving only in gentle, low swells that rocked us easily on our floats. We paddled around a little, lying face-down on the floats, looking into the water, dipping our wooden-handled nets now and then, bringing them up and looking at them. The floats were short, mine only reaching from my neck to just below my hips. In the gentle water, it didn't matter.

Once, Hugo stuck his face right into the water, apparently looking for ravenous jellyfish. I thought that was almost too much — we didn't have diving masks. But it looked very heroic so I did it, too.

We were only a few feet from each other, shooting the bull about nothing in particular, wondering how long we would have to stay out there just to make our point. We were bored. We decided to start back to the beach, take our chances with the girls, try to fake out the counselor.

"What the hell," Hugo said, "let's just make it up as we go along . . ." And he stuck his head in the water again. One last look, for the benefit of the girls on the beach.

His head snapped instantly back into the air, as far back as he could stretch his neck. His mouth was open and he was screaming before his head cleared the water, the scream bursting out of the water in a mangled stream of bubbles. He was clawing at his face and he bent his legs at the knees and held his feet up above and behind him so that no part of him dangled in the water.

He choked off the scream. "Jesus Christ!" he gargled, "Jellyfish! Honest to God! Jellyfish! Hundreds of the fuckers!"

I paddled to him, thrashing my hands in the water, then realizing what he had said. I jerked my arms out of the water and held them down at my sides. By this time, both Hugo and I were trying to keep all parts of our bodies out of the water, balancing ourselves carefully on the tiny floats. Hugo was wiping something off his face, a thin strand of sticky ugliness that had strung across his cheek and now clung to his fingers. He looked into the water, made sure there were no jellyfish there, then splashed himself in the face a dozen times. Even before he was finished his cheek showed an ugly red stripe.

His eyes were wide. He pointed into the water between us. "Look at 'em! Look at the sons-a-bitches! Look!"

I looked. Just below the surface of the warm Atlantic the gray, rounded humps of jellyfish ghosted in the swells, inches from our faces, waiting. There really were hundreds of them.

"Goddamn! Let's get the hell out of here!" I whispered loudly to Hugo, afraid the girls had seen our panic, afraid they could hear our voices.

We carefully turned our floats toward the shore. "How fast do we paddle in?" I didn't want us to look like idiots, thrashing in the surf.

"As fast as we . . ." He stopped in mid-sentence. "Wait a minute. You know anything about jellyfish?"

"Me? Shit, Hugo, I know about deer and squirrels. Best I know, there ain't no jellyfish in the Tug River."

We hadn't started paddling yet. I was getting nervous.

"Look," he said, "these damned things can't even move, let alone bite anything."

"What about the stingers?" His face was swelling, but not very fast.

"Fuck the stingers," he muttered, rubbing his cheek. "I want to try something."

He pushed the dip net out in front of him, holding the short wooden pole that served as a handle across the surface of the water. He looked into the water. And waited.

In less than a minute he saw what he wanted. He slid the net gently under the surface, twisted it, lifted it. He had netted a jellyfish as big as a volleyball.

I towed Hugo back to the beach. I had taken off my belt, tucked the knife into my trunks, and used the belt as a towrope. I paddled hard, making it look difficult, Hugo riding along behind, the net held above his head.

When we got to where we could stand up, we strode solemnly — heroically, I thought — up on the warm beach. Hugo dumped the glob of jellyfish on the sand, heaving a sigh of relief, making sure the girls saw the red stripe on his face. I took the knife out of my trunks, slipped off the sheath, and sunk the blade into the jellyfish and down into the sand. I kept the hell away from the stingers.

Neither of us had looked at the girls.

Hugo and I shook hands. We turned to go back to our chairs, walking past the girls, sitting there, their mouths open, their eyes wide.

As we walked by I said, almost casually, "Probably should take you down to Myrtle, to the hospital. Have that sting looked at. Cut out the poison."

"Nah," Hugo breathed heavily, "don't worry about it. Been stung so many times it really don't matter no more.

"Oh," he said to the girls, over his shoulder, as though just remembering, "you can go in the water now. It's safe. Don't go out past the end of the pier, though. Never know . . . "

And we walked away.

The tall one, the counselor, came over to my chair the next day. She hadn't been in the water yet and her hair was still full and flowing, tiny sparks of red flickering in the deep brown in the late afternoon sun. She stood there, hands clasped behind her back making her breasts rise and spread under her swimsuit, letting me look down into them.

"I . . . didn't really know anything about jellyfish," she said, her voice softer than I remembered. "I just didn't want the girls to get into anything . . ." She took in a deep breath. Her breasts pushed out harder.

I jumped in. "Well, ma'am, it's our duty down here on the beach to protect the gir . . . the bathers. Just part of our job." I smiled down on her, trying to keep my eyes away from her breasts.

" . . . so I went down to the library this morning and looked it up, jellyfish I mean." The tiniest hint of a smile flickered across her face.

Caught. We were caught. This damned smartass woman had gone and done homework, for Christ's sake, *homework*, down here on the beach. I opened my mouth but nothing came out.

"I also talked to some of the commercial fishermen."

Fishermen? What fucking commercial fishermen? I hadn't seen a commercial fisherman . . .

"Seems that most of the jellyfish around here aren't dangerous at all. Can hardly move. Mostly float with the tide. Only cause trouble if you push yourself against their tentacles. Rarely get washed up on the beach. And if they're on the beach, they're already dead. Hardly need to stab them with a knife." She was enjoying the hell out of this, listing off the stuff about the jellyfish. She stopped and turned her head slightly, her chin lifted, still looking at me. Waiting.

"Shall I go on?"

"Well, uh . . ." I started out, "that doesn't mean that *every* jellyfish is, uh, is . . ."

Shit. I didn't know what the hell I was talking about. I climbed down from the chair and stood directly in front of her.

"Truth is, ma'am," I said softly, almost under my breath, "I don't know anything about jellyfish. Probably don't know much about anything else, either. Hugo . . . he just wanted to meet the girls. Me, I wanted to meet . . . you." I lied — that last part, anyway.

She stepped up, right in front of my face, almost right against me. She was close enough to kiss.

"Do you ever, in your whole life, tell the truth?" She was so close I could feel her warm breath on my face, taste the sweetness of it.

"Ma'am?"

"Do you ever tell the truth? You didn't want to meet me. You wanted to meet those girls. Those *little* girls. Those little girls with their tight asses and their hard little tits."

Jesus, I had heard a grown woman say things like that only once before, and it tore me up then, just like it was tearing me up now.

What the hell could I say now? There we were, standing in the sun, this woman so close to me. Any other time a woman had been that close to me she had probably been taking a swing at me, or maybe we had been kissing, were going to kiss, or something. I had never had a woman stand that close to me just to talk. I didn't know what to do, this woman just standing there, almost touching me. So I said something stupid. But honest.

"You bother me, ma'am. Standing this close. I don't know what I'm supposed to do."

Her face relaxed. "*That* is the first truthful thing you've said since I walked up here. Now . . . do you have a girlfriend?"

"Well, uh, I don't know." I thought of Yvonne, back there when we were in Crum, but she had tried to run over me with a car and she was long gone and I figured she didn't count as a girlfriend.

"You don't know? You don't know if you have a girlfriend? How the hell can that be?"

"You're right, ma'am. It can't be. I don't have no girl-friend."

"Any girlfriend."

"What . . . ?"

"*Any* girlfriend. You don't have *any* girlfriend."

I understood. "Yes, ma'am. My English ain't . . . isn't very good, sometimes."

"Probably because you don't want it to be."

"Yes, ma'am."

"Now, touch me," she said.

"What?"

"Touch me. Gently."

"Touch . . . " God, all of a sudden I wanted to touch her, wanted to do anything she asked. "Where . . . touch you?" I was almost mumbling now.

"Where do you want to touch me?"

"I want . . . everywhere." The last word came out in a whoosh of air.

"Maybe. Later. But you'll have to work up to that. For right now, just touch me on the arm, up here." She lifted her hand and touched my upper arm.

My hand seemed to come up all by itself. I touched her arm, running my fingers along silky skin, feeling, remember-ing. I had never felt warmer skin.

"I just wanted you to know what a woman feels like." She was smiling now.

"One more thing," she said, "and I want you to be sure you tell this to Hugo, too. Those girls that are with me are in a drama club, from a school in High Point. I bring the club down here every year and they stay with me at my cottage. And they're leaving in two days. I want you and Hugo to keep your dicks in your pants until they're gone."

I was totally caught by her. She knew that Hugo and I and the jellyfish were all full of shit and she didn't really care. She was playing the game better than we ever had. And she was in total control.

She turned slightly, as if to go, and my hand dropped from her arm.

"The girls are leaving, but I'm not. I'll stay for a few days, maybe a little longer."

I hadn't moved, frozen in place on a hot beach by a woman who probably could make me do anything.

She raised a finger to her mouth. The tip of her tongue peeked out from between her lips and touched the finger, circling the tip of it. She turned her hand and reached out toward my face, the finger glistening. She touched the wetness to my lips.

"My name is Rosalind," she said.

And then she walked away.

Anyway, that's how the Jellyfish Rodeos got started. Any time Hugo wanted to impress a girl we would get our floats, nets and knives and head out beyond the surf. We would thrash around out there for a while, then — if there were any jellyfish out there at all — one of us would net a big one, head back for the beach, and do our number in front of the girls.

Pretty soon the other lifeguards got in on it and competitions started, all of us out there netting jellyfish and no one watching the beach. We would stash a couple of cans of beer in our nets or trunks or wherever we could hide them and sip them as we floated around just out beyond the end of the pier, a flotilla of net-mad lifeguards. Jellyfish killers.

Since the jellyfish only grew so big, we gave up trying to find a really big one and started going for numbers — seeing who could bring the most jellyfish back in a single trip. Small, stinking mounds of putrefying jellyfish grew on the beach during the rodeos, but the mounds always disappeared, the jellyfish seeming to melt in the sun, oozing into the sand and disappearing.

When the girls stood around looking at the jellyfish we would talk about "jellyfish barbeques" and "jellyfish fries" and "jellyfish roasts" and "jellyfish fritters." We would explain to the girls the best ways to skin them, cut them up, soak them in oil overnight, cover them with corn meal before we deep-fried them. We talked about jellyfish salads and jellyfish sandwiches. Every now and then we would actually put a jellyfish in a bag and carry it away from the beach, on its way to some imaginary barbeque.

It worked. It worked all summer. The girls never got tired of looking at the jellyfish and the lifeguards never got tired of the rodeos. Some of the all-summer girls, girls who lived at the beach all the time, figured out what we were doing and why, but even then, knowing we were just fucking around to impress them, they didn't care. Hugo said he had one of them trained. Said all he had to do was say the word "jellyfish" and she would fall backward on her beach towel, her legs in the air, a damp spot showing through her bathing suit between her legs.

Banger caught on to the game and added a Jellyfish Burger to the list of stuff on the menu painted on the boards up behind the bar at the pavilion.

I never saw anybody order one.

❧ Twenty-Nine ❧

In my entire life I never expected to see her again.

Now and then Banger would give us a morning or an afternoon off — usually on a rainy day — and I would wander around the side roads, sometimes hitching down to Myrtle Beach and walking the streets like a real person, a man of means. I usually had maybe five dollars in my pocket, but that was more than I had on Black Hawk Ridge or in Crum. Especially Crum.

I would find a soda fountain, a bookstore, a guy on the beach selling hot dogs, or something — anything that I couldn't find back at Cherry Hill Beach — to spend my five dollars on.

The sign said "Wimpo's." It hung out over the sidewalk from one small chain and a piece of wire; the wire was longer and the sign hung at a crazy angle. The place was a beach-side bar and hamburger joint that I had often passed, but had never gone into. Wimpo was supposed to be fat, dumb and mean, maybe crazy. Probably related to that fucking deputy, I thought. Hugo said not to go in there, that Wimpo didn't like the guys from Cherry Hill coming down to Myrtle and messing around, thought guys from Cherry were just that — cherries.

So I stayed away from the place. Usually. But, what the hell, sometimes I was a slow learner.

I went in.

Wimpo's was big and airy, some ceiling fans turning, windows propped open to let the ocean breeze push the cigarette smoke and stink of stale beer out the other side. There were some booths along the street side, some tables in the middle. The bar was on the ocean side and when you sat on a bar stool you could look over the top of dirty whiskey bottles and get a clear view of the water.

I sat at the bar and had a beer, sipping at the cold bottle, wondering who Wimpo was and how he got here, and looking out through the windows at the beach and the gray water beyond. It felt odd to me, somehow, knowing that on the other side of that water there were people I had never seen, who spoke different languages, who thought different thoughts. People who would never, in their entire lives, lay eyes on me. But if we both, at the same time, went down to the beach and put our feet in the water . . . we were connected. Somehow.

I thought a lot of weird shit, there on the beach. I thought if it was weird, it was deep.

But thoughts like that made me feel good about being at the beach, about being able to look out on the water and know that others were out there, about having choices and directions to go if I didn't like where I was. On Black Hawk Ridge, I knew something else was out there. I just didn't know in what direction.

She hadn't been in the bar when I came in. She must have just come to work. And now she was there behind the bar, wiping at it lightly with a damp rag, her hips swaying slightly to the music from the juke box as she moved gently, slowly, in my direction. The light from the windows jumped into her shiny black hair and flicked at the edges of her face. She was calm and relaxed and I could tell she liked it here, liked what she was doing here at the beach, liked being on her own, liked knowing she would never see me again.

Her eyes snapped down the bar toward me. She wasn't close enough for me to see their color but I knew they were brown, the brightest brown I had ever seen. I had seen those eyes as closely as I had seen the eyes of any human being. I had been inside those eyes. They had been inside me.

Yvonne.

I wondered if she were still a whore.

We had been sitting on the porch of Luke's Restaurant in Crum, watching it get dark and hoping that the dark would cool the heat that smothered the valley. We were talking about getting money and leaving Crum and what we would do if we could do that, and I don't remember seeing Yvonne so interested in anything. I had never known that she wanted to leave until that day, and it sort of surprised me to hear her talk about it.

She kept talking about money, and how much bus tickets cost, and how far you could go if you had a hundred dollars. She was wearing a pair of her brother's jeans. They were too small for her, pulling up into her crotch. Mule was staring and Yvonne knew it, only for a change it didn't seem to bother her. For once, instead of crossing her legs like a lady, Yvonne would open her knees and let Mule take a good look at her crotch, at the part where the tight jeans pulled up into her, a tiny fold of the material disappearing right up inside her.

Mule was a born troublemaker and finally he just couldn't help himself. I guess the heat got to him. He sat up and looked straight at Yvonne.

"Can I feel your cunt?" He said it quietly, almost as though he were waiting for Yvonne to belt him, or something. I almost fell off the steps.

She knew it was me. I could tell the second that she knew, the second when those eyes went hard and her back went straight and her hand went towards her own throat. I could tell that I was her worst vision, a worthless slag heap piled somewhere in her future, with smoke rising somewhere out of her past. She thought she had lost me, and now I was here.

"How much do you want to feel of it?" She spoke quietly, with a halt in her voice.

Mule blinked. "I want to feel it a lot. I really want to feel it good."

Yvonne sat there, thinking about it. Finally, her words came very slowly and carefully. She said quietly, "How much would you pay to feel it?"

"I ain't got but thirty cents."

She looked at Mule, then at me. It was quiet again in front of the restaurant and the hushed tones of the questions and answers seemed to add to the stillness.

"Okay," she said, "you can feel it for thirty cents."

I was watching a whore in the making. She would let Mule feel her crotch for thirty cents. He might not get to fuck her — not for thirty cents — but he could feel her, and that might be the next best thing. In Crum, to get your hand in a girl's crotch, well, you could brag about that. It was like . . . if you held it in your hand, you owned it.

Mule stood up and dug out the thirty cents, held it out to Yvonne. She let the coins fall into her hand, then sat looking at them for a moment. Mule sat down beside her and reached for her crotch.

"Not here." She got up and walked quickly away, around behind the restaurant. Mule was right on her heels, and I got up to follow.

At the corner, Yvonne turned and looked at me. "Not unless you've got money," she said softly. I stopped dead in my tracks. I was broke, and Yvonne knew it. She looked at me for a second, then turned and went around the corner of the building, Mule close behind.

When all this had started, she wasn't my girlfriend. After she left Crum I used to remember her as my girlfriend, but she probably never was. She was no one's girlfriend. She was always above the rest of us, always reading books and laughing at the way we pronounced our words and not really caring what we did or didn't do. Maybe she was marking time. Seems now that she was. But Yvonne was maybe the most beautiful girl I had ever seen. And I guess it made me feel good, or big, to think of her as mine. Maybe it made me feel worthwhile.

There I was, standing in the darkness at the side of a run-down restaurant, knowing Yvonne was back there in the darkness with Mule, and he was feeling her cunt.

I didn't have thirty cents. I didn't have anything. All I had was the burn behind my forehead to get out of Crum, by doing whatever it took. I never knew that someone else could want out of there as badly as I did, but there she was, back there in the heat of an Appalachian night, getting her cunt rubbed for thirty cents. There she was, back there, a girl who would do whatever it took.

Here she was, with a dirty towel dangling from her hand, behind a warped and dented bar in Myrtle Beach, South Carolina.

Her hand dropped back to her side and her face went pale and calm. She stood still for a long minute, not really knowing what to do. So help me, I thought I could see the pulse beating in her long, slender neck.

She started up the bar toward me, haltingly, hating every step she took.

A couple of minutes later Yvonne came out from behind the restaurant. She went past me, glanced unsmiling in my direction and walked away down the dirt lane in front of the restaurant. Mule came out of the darkness.

"It's hard as a rock! It's hard as a fuckin' hot rock! She's got the hardest pussy I ever had my hand on!" Mule said.

I grabbed him and pulled him down to the steps. "Did she say anything about fuckin'? Did she? What did she say? Can you buy it?" I kept shaking Mule by the arm.

Mule just looked at me. "Five dollars," he said. "She said five dollars."

I looked away and after Yvonne as she grew smaller in the distance down the dirt lane, passing into the full darkness beyond the glow of the porch light on the restaurant.

She really was good looking. And it was hard as a rock.

Five dollars.

Five dollars.

Yvonne had found her ticket out of Crum.

She stopped directly in front of me. She wasn't pale anymore. The blood was rising in her face and she struggled to stay calm. She reached for my empty beer bottle, absently wiping the bar with the damp rag.

My mouth wouldn't work right. "Uh . . . howdy . . . Vonny."

She pulled her arm back and swung the beer bottle. I saw it coming in a brownish blur that cut an arc across the bright light coming in from the windows. I saw it coming in the light from her eyes and the heat of her body. I saw it coming in what she owed me, in the great justice of my being there on that bar stool within reach of her. I saw it coming, but I couldn't move. The bottle caught me cleanly on the temple and I crumpled off the bar stool, tumbling downward. My mind clicked to another time, some place far removed and safe, a place where there were tall hardwood trees with vines in them and I was swinging on one of the vines, clinging to the end of it, my body cutting great, sweeping arcs out and through the sunshine and far over and above the forest floor. And then the vine broke.

I fell into a pool of left-over mop water still standing in a depression in the wooden floor of the bar. I hit the mop water face first.

For days on end the sun would not shine, unable to cut through the layer of insulation that hung above the valley and prevented spring from moving through the hills. The browns stayed brown and the mud stayed mud, except when it was ice, and the cold never let you forget that you were only minutes from the edge of wilderness.

I stood on the railroad tracks, a cold winter rain blowing against my face. There was nothing for me anywhere. I had gotten out of Black Hawk Ridge but I would never get out of Crum. I think I knew that for the first time, there in the rain. I was there for life. Either there, or back on the Ridge.

I had nowhere to go except back to the shed on the back of my cousin's house, a shed I slept in.

I sensed her before I actually saw her. When I looked up, Yvonne was standing there by the railroad tracks. She was coming back from the general store trying to keep a big brown paper sack dry between her arms. The rain had blown in under her hat and the drops clung to her face and made it glisten in the cold light. She stood there, the water running down her legs and into her shoes and she was beautiful. More important than that, she wasn't saying a word, not a word. Maybe she didn't think I was just a hillbilly. Maybe she didn't think I was stupid.

"Your house. Can I come up to your house?"

She just stared at me.

Sounds crept into me. I could hear some guy yelling, distantly, that someone should get a towel, that my head was bleeding. There were some scraping noises and some sounds I couldn't identify. I tried to tell them I was there, inside my body, that I really wasn't all the way knocked out, that I could tell them what hurt and where it hurt. I tried to tell them all that, but it only happened in my mind. I could hear them, but I was a prisoner inside my head. I never uttered a sound.

Yvonne's house was built along the side of a hill, with a porch that ran all across the front. On nice days you could sit on the porch and put your feet up on the wide, low railing and look out over most of the town.

She was wearing a white blouse and a full, blue skirt, but she didn't have any shoes on. Somehow, her bare feet made her look like she really belonged there, like she had been waiting all day for me to come home. It was one wonderful feeling.

We had the house to ourselves.

The living room was heated with a small, open gas stove that sat in a fake fireplace in the corner. She had the heater turned up high, the flames making the ceramic grate glow. We turned off the lights and sat in the glow of the heater . . .

Later Yvonne went into the kitchen and got a bottle of beer and a couple of glasses. We split the beer and sat on the sofa, sipping at the glasses and leaning toward each other until suddenly the glasses were on the floor and Yvonne and I were wrapped around each other, crushing each other back against the sofa, working mouth against mouth. Our mouths stayed together through the droning of the winter rain, through the tangle of arms and legs, through the rolling and turning. We were deep within the pillows of the sofa, twisting and reaching, groping, making low sounds.

They were moving me. Hands pushed under my chest and lifted and my head flopped down against the floor, back into the slimy mop water. The hands got me up again and I was dragged along the floor to a cot. I could feel a blanket being pulled over me and I tried to tell them that my head was broken, that somewhere inside there was a piece knocked loose that I couldn't quite get hold of. I tried to tell them.

Sweat poured from my forehead and her face glistened as we pressed together. She forced her hands between us and unbuttoned my shirt, peeling it from me. I felt her warm breasts against my chest and I realized they were bare, too. And in another instant she was naked. I couldn't help myself. I pulled back and sat up on the edge of the sofa and explored with my eyes. I pulled off the rest of my clothes and lay beside her, running my hands over her, wanting to know her in the smallest detail. She moved under my hands, only slightly, helping the hands along, helping them explore. She looked steadily into my eyes, with nothing to hide, and then she rolled me on top of her.

When it was finished we lay pressed together for a few minutes, neither of us wanting to make the first move to get up. Then she sat up and so did I, the two of us sitting on the sofa, naked, as though we had done this many times and it was the most natural thing in the world for us to be sitting there like that.

I couldn't make them hear me, so I quit trying. I lay there on the rickety cot with a damp blanket over me. Now and then a sound came through to me but my eyes wouldn't work and the darkness was like a shield that kept them from me. There was something warm on the side of my head and I knew I was bleeding. I wondered if anyone else knew that.

I lay there thinking. And then I remembered why she hit me.

She really wasn't a whore. Nobody ever fucked her. Nobody. Not for a while, anyway. Sure, she took Mule's thirty cents, but that isn't fucking and none of us in Crum ever had five dollars for the real thing and I think she knew that. She just used the five dollars to establish one very clear thing — that she wanted out of Crum as badly as anyone.

For the rest of the summer and through the bad parts of the winter Yvonne kept her distance from the rest of us. She was a soft, curvy, olive-skinned girl drifting through the fog of Crum High School, waiting. I would sit with her, now and then, when she would let me, and tell her about Black Hawk Ridge and she wouldn't believe me. Nothing, she said, could be as bad as Crum. It was times like that when I thought she was my girl.

I picked up my pants, but she put her hand on my arm and held it there until I put the pants down again. The small room was warm from our bodies and from the gas heater and our sweat stayed on our skins and glistened in the dim reflection of the flames. The rain had stopped and the silence that comes after a rain was on the house and the dark town. Through the window I could see that heavy clouds were moving down the valley and that, somewhere up there, a bright moon was struggling its way through.

She kissed me, then got up and walked toward the kitchen, her step like a dancer's, holding her sweat-shining body perfectly erect. I followed her into the kitchen. She went to a shelf and got a couple of glasses and then opened the back door and took a large pitcher from the cupboard that stood outside on the back porch. The pitcher was full of buttermilk and she poured it into the glasses. We sipped the buttermilk and walked back into the living room, then across the room to a window that looked out on the front porch. Down the distance we could see the tiny town lying there in darkness, with only a kerosene lamp or two flickering, or a bare electric bulb hiding behind a drawn window shade. A shaft of moonlight broke through the clouds now and then, dropping directly onto the valley floor.

I stood beside her, holding her hand. She stepped in front of me and pressed herself backward, firmly. Her hips rubbed against me and then she stepped away and disappeared down a short hallway. In a moment she was back, wearing a bathrobe that was so big it trailed the floor behind her. It was one of those bathrobes made out of terry cloth like a big soft towel. She took my hand and led me to the front door. We stepped out on the cold porch and she pulled me to her, wrapping me inside the bathrobe. We stood there, swaying slightly, tiny cold drops of rain brushing us, and I could feel myself hard against her stomach. We shuffled over to the railing. We shivered slightly from the cold, but it wasn't nearly as bad as I thought it would be. I was almost too warm.

No, she wasn't a whore. But I made a goddamn awful stupid fucking hillbilly mistake and I wanted to die for it but when I got the chance I jumped out of the way.

I think maybe on the night we made love that I was as close to her as I had ever been to any other human. I was with her, beside her, inside her. And she was inside me, as surely as if she had drifted on naked wings in through my eyes and floated across my mind, down, then rode the currents of my breathing to land softly in some warm and silent place that I hadn't known existed. She was inside me, and I didn't know where.

I think I loved her then. Maybe I loved her now.

She scooted herself up on the flat board that ran the length of the railing, opening her legs as I moved forward and then wrapping the bathrobe tighter around both of us. And then she pulled me inside her.

I still had a glass of buttermilk in my hand. I fumbled around, trying to put it down, but she took it from me. She held it under her left breast, leaned forward, and tilted the glass onto her, coating her breast with buttermilk. She locked her legs around me and leaned backward, her head and shoulders suspended above Crum, above the valley, her white, dripping breast pointed straight at the dark sky. She held the glass over her and gently tilted it, dripping buttermilk on the other breast and onto her stomach. As she raised herself the buttermilk ran down her stomach, down between her legs and onto me.

Jesus, where did she learn stuff like that? There sure wasn't anything like that described in any book I'd ever read. Yvonne sat up and pressed herself against me. The buttermilk made us slide across each other and we had to hold tight to stay locked together. And in the middle of all the sliding and holding, of all the moving from side to side and up and down, in the middle of kissing her breasts and finding myself with buttermilk all over my face . . . in the middle of all that, she came, her head back and her neck arched out over the dark distance below. And in the middle of coming, she screamed. It wasn't a true scream, just a sound of some sort of deep pleasure rolling up from inside her and out into the night.

I knew Crum. I knew someone down there was out on the porch, watching the clouds drift across the moon. And I knew they had heard Yvonne. I hoped it worried the hell out of them.

Light was coming in. I could feel my eyes work in their sockets, the lids fluttering. There was the soft feel of moving air against my face, air that smelled like beer. It wouldn't be long now.

When my eyes finally opened she wasn't there. Some big guy with a beer belly was bending over me, waving a bar towel in my face. He was a fat man, but one of those fat guys who had all the fat on the outside. You could tell, underneath, that there was some hardness in there. Muscle.

"You alive, boy?"

It must be Wimpo, I thought. No one else could be that fucking stupid.

" . . . " I opened my mouth but nothing came out. At least my jaw worked.

"Yah, looks like he's alive, awright. One you boys fetch me a glass of beer. Let's see if that lubricates him a little bit."

I heard feet scurry away.

"Now, boy," Wimpo said, grabbing my shirt and lifting me up in front of his face, "just what did . . . GOD DAMMIT, this here shithead's a-bleedin' all over my floor!" His voice had taken on a high whine and he dropped me back on the bunk. The guy with the beer showed up.

"Throw it on the floor! Get it down there 'fore that damn blood stains everthing!" The beer hit the floor.

Wimpo leaned over me and started to reach for my shirt again, thought better of it, and placed one big hand on each side of the bunk.

"Now, boy, let's you and me try this again. Just what the hell did you say to Yuh-vonne that got her so goddammed upset?"

We were indoors again. She sat on the edge of the sofa and leaned against me and I wished that I lived inside her. The air in the small room seemed close and heavy from our bodies and I wondered if her mother would notice. I looked hard at the room, trying to soak up the details, wanting to remember it years from now. I savored the stillness and the dark, I savored the warmth of the heater and the glow of the grate. I savored the buttermilk. I savored Yvonne. She drifted out of the room. I didn't want to, but finally I pulled on my clothes.

I was standing there with a five-dollar bill in my hand when Yvonne came back into the room.

She was dressed, fresh and soft. For a moment she didn't see the money. I hadn't meant for her to see it, honest to God I hadn't. I had remembered that it was in my watch pocket and I had pulled it out to look at it, wondering why I had ever put it there in the first place. Don't ask me why I did it, I just did. So I stood there, a simple fool, feeling the blood in my face and watching Yvonne turn to stone.

I think she saw the money from across the room but it didn't really hit her, didn't really register, until she was standing in front of me. But she saw it then, for certain.

"Oh, God," she said, "oh, God, you've ruined it. You've ruined it. Oh, God . . . "

Her voice trailed away and the tears came, pushed down her face by deep, throbbing sobs. I reached out to her. She stepped backward, quickly, sharply, not wanting me to touch her, not wanting my hand to contaminate her, not wanting to admit that I was alive. And I probably wasn't. She was trying hard to choke off the sobs, to stop the tears. She wasn't going to cry for me.

There was nothing else I could do. I *was* a fool. I had ruined it. I opened the door, the awful dampness and cold cutting through me instantly. I knew I had to leave but I didn't want to and I kept trying to think of something to say, something that would explain the five-dollar bill. But the miracle didn't happen. I was speechless again.

"I said 'Howdy', was all I said."

"Oh, sure as shit, that's all you said, boy. I just know a good girl like Yuh-vonne would drop your sad ass with a beer bottle just because you said 'Hi'. Now why don't you tell me the truth."

"Ask her. Ask Yvonne."

"I'll do just that," Wimpo growled, and he left the room, flapping the bar towel against his leg.

I was alone. The others, whoever they were, had left before Wimpo. I guess there was nothing too interesting about just another beach kid lying on a creaking cot with his head open and dripping. Happened all the time.

She stood in the door. I don't know how long she had been standing there. The light came in from behind her, drawing her curves within the straight frame of the door. She was there, just across the room. She lived here, in Myrtle Beach, somewhere in a small room that I could find and fit into. She lived here.

Maybe I had found the place I wanted to be.

"Wait."

It was not a request, it was a command and I turned in the doorway, half gladly, half warily, the tone of her voice shaking me. She walked to the door and stood in front of me, her face flat and unfeeling, her eyes dark solid points of pure hardness. She held out her palm.

"Give it to me. Give it to me. It's mine. I earned it. I can do whatever I want with it."

She was standing there, demanding her rightful pay, a price negotiated in advance and brought with me in the watch pocket of my jeans. I pushed the five-dollar bill toward her. Very slowly she reached for it, gently curled her fingers around the bill, increasing the pressure until she was squeezing the paper with white knuckles. Then in a smooth, furious motion she jerked her arm backward, ripping the bill from my hand.

"From now on," she hissed, "you don't have the price. You'll *never* have the price again!"

I didn't go to school for two days, and when I did Yvonne wasn't there. After school I walked in the cold and dim light down past Yvonne's house. I could look up the hill and see the railing where we sat and I wondered if there were buttermilk stains on the boards. There were no lights on in the house.

The narrow highway was empty and I shuffled on the pavement past the tiny rough-plank garage where Yvonne's brother parked his old Chevrolet. The doors were open and I could see the grill of the car grinning out at me. The rest of the car was hidden in darkness. I felt uneasy, walking past Yvonne's house like that. I didn't belong there; she had made that clear. I stopped in the middle of the highway, intending to go back.

But before I could move I heard the engine of the Chevrolet grind into life. The car rolled forward and turned in my direction on the road. It stopped, the engine idling. I wondered if Yvonne's brother was going somewhere, anywhere, out of Crum. I wondered if he would mind giving me a lift. But I didn't wonder long. The car's gears pounded and it lurched forward, the engine racing. Straight at me.

The whole thing didn't register. I didn't realize that the car was coming for me. I was standing there minding my own business. Hell, it *couldn't* be coming for me. But it was.

The car didn't have the lights on and the distance fooled me. I almost stood there too long before I moved, and then I leaped sideways, slamming into the side of the road and bouncing onto the gravel. As I rolled over I heard the car slide to a stop; I heard the door open. I stood up and looked at the driver. It was Yvonne.

All the way back to my shed I thought about Yvonne closing the car door and driving away. I had stood by the side of the highway until I couldn't see the car anymore. And I knew that Yvonne was gone.

Gravel fell out of my shirt and blood oozed from some odd places as I shuffled back to my sleeping shed on the back of my cousin's house. I fumbled in the darkness trying to open the door. As the door swung inward something caught my eye and I lit a kerosene lamp. A five-dollar bill was nailed in the center of the door. The nail was a railroad spike, driven straight through the face on the bill and through the door, two inches of the rusty iron sticking out into my room.

For a long time her glowing silhouette hung in the doorframe. She seemed to be staring at me, but with the light behind her I couldn't be sure. One thing I was sure of — she was slowly and gently rubbing her crotch.

I could see her hand down there, massaging, pushing the soft material in between her legs. Her shoulder came away from the doorframe and there was light on all sides of her, soft rays of it flowing past her into the room and painting muted golds on the dirty walls. She stepped into the room, being pushed by the light, and moved slowly toward my cot. I had never seen anyone move like that, one leg coming around the other, each foot placed on the floor as though she were walking on frozen crystals of memory, easing across the creaking wood of the floor, in perfect grace. And her hand never left her crotch.

She was beside me, in front of me, standing over me as I turned my head and looked up at her delicate hand still massaging her crotch. I couldn't believe it. My head still rang and my eyes watered but I could see what I could see and it was Yvonne standing there, making a damp spot on the front of her dress as she rubbed her hand into her cunt.

The cut on my head had stopped bleeding and I lifted my hand away from the stinking towel across my head and reached slowly for her hand. She waited. When I touched her she lifted her hand from her crotch and took mine, holding it gently, moving it away from her.

And then she slapped me across the head, full across the cut, a slap of blinding speed and blinding anger, a slap that almost made me pass out again.

My eyes clamped shut against the dizziness and I waited for more slaps but they never came. I lay there for long minutes, feeling the blood ooze across my face again, trying to get oriented, trying to remember where the hell I was and why my head hurt so much. When I figured it all out I forced my eyes open again. She was gone. I never heard her leave the room.

I waited a while longer, thinking Wimpo would come back and help me patch up my head. But he never did. Finally, I tore a piece off my shirt, wrapped it around my skull, and pulled the knot tight. I eased myself up from the bunk, held on to the wall for a couple of minutes until I could get my stomach under control, then went out a side door.

With any luck, I could catch a ride back up to Cherry Hill before it got too dark.

❦ Thirty ❧

Rosalind took my mind off things for a while.

If there ever was a woman who could take your mind off something, anything, anything at all, it was Rosalind. Sometimes, when I looked at her, my mind started to see Yvonne's face where Rosalind's was supposed to be, but it never stayed that way long. Rosalind just wouldn't let it.

She was some older than me. I don't know how much older, but when she invited me to her cottage she talked sometimes about when she had been in college and about when she worked in New York and Florida. I wanted to know more, I wanted to know everything, but I never got the chance.

It's strange, thinking back on it. She was like a friend, not like a girlfriend. We would talk about a lot of things, but never in such a way that meant we would be doing something together down the line; not as though we were making plans together. We had a few days of summer, that's all, Rosalind was going to go away, and both of us knew it. And it was okay.

Fact is, Rosalind just liked to fuck.

A friend, not a girlfriend . . . and yet we would end up fucking, always, every time I was there. Sometimes slow and quiet, easing into it, she walking around the house naked to the waist, making me want it, making me wait for it; sometimes locked together before the front door got all the way closed, on the floor, rolling across the rug and once knocking over a lamp.

"You really are a hillbilly, aren't you. You really don't know much. You've been spending too much time with little girls."

As so she taught me and taught me and taught me.

We kept at it until I got it right.

Her house was one of the larger ones in Cherry, on a big patch of grass with those trees that hung out and over everything. The house had a lot of rooms, some of them little guest rooms where company could sleep, some rooms bigger, some of them with kinds of furniture in them that I had never seen before. Sometimes I would come to the house for supper and she wouldn't answer the door. And I would go on in, locking the door behind me, knowing she was in there, somewhere. I would have to search the house, leaving my clothes strung out behind me in the various rooms, until I found her. I found her in closets, under beds, in a bathtub.

And, once, I eased into a kitchen lit only by a single candle and I found her naked, sitting at the kitchen table, eating chocolate ice cream directly from the carton. The stuff was melting and there was chocolate ice cream all over her face and on her breasts, chocolate ice cream running down her stomach, soft, sweet swirls of brown patterned across her white skin. Her legs were clamped together and there was chocolate ice cream pooled in her crotch, seeping down into her pubic hair.

Jesus Christ. I wasn't sure I could move. I had never come across anything like this. Even Slick Jesse would have been impressed.

She slowly parted her legs, letting the glob of ice cream slip down between them, running through her cracks, pooling in the chair she was sitting on.

I moved.

It took us all night to clean up the kitchen.

But one thing was clear from the very beginning: she was in control. Whatever we did, wherever we did it, however we did it, what we did after it . . . it was her decision, her timing, her choice. I never knew anything like that could happen, never knew anyone like her could exist. I loved it.

And then one morning she was gone. Just gone. I got up and pulled on my jeans and shirt and walked barefoot into the kitchen, then the living room, then through the other rooms, knowing it wasn't a game this time. Knowing she was gone.

I set the latch and pulled the door closed behind me, hearing it lock, knowing I would never be back in that house again.

The sun was above the trees now, getting hotter, and I wondered what the temperature was in High Point, North Carolina. And knowing I probably would never go there.

It was okay.

It was well into the summer before I noticed there were no black people on the beach. *Really* noticed it, I mean.

Before, I had noticed that there were no black people, but I didn't really check it out, just thought they were there, but were somewhere else, down the beach a ways, by some other lifeguard station, not liking it here near the pavilion where all the traffic was, where all the tourists came and went. They liked to be alone; several of the other lifeguards had told me that. I kept meaning to ask Hugo about it, but every time we got together Hugo had some story about some girl who was hanging around and I never got to it.

One day John Three came down to the beach for the first time since I had been there. He was carrying a rake, but he wasn't doing any raking.

"Hey, Reverend. This your day to rake the sand?" I got up and stood beside him.

"No. Just carry the rake as a prop. Don't want these fine folks to think I'm on their beach with no good reason." He said it quietly, his voice a smooth rich flow, smiling sideways at me while he kept an eye on the beach. Sometimes, when he talked, he used different words, different sounds. I had heard the other guys around the pavilion imitating black talk, and sometimes John Three sounded just like that. But sometimes not. And not when he talked to me.

"Reason? Why do you need a reason?"

"Because this isn't my beach. I have never been swimming on this beach . . . you really are new to this place, aren't you," he said gently. It wasn't a question.

"Yeah, well, I guess I don't understand much about it, Reverend, about how I'm supposed to act around here."

"Well, these local folks, they will educate you soon enough. And, incidentally, I'm only a reverend out in the Homeplace. These white folks don't recognize my rev-er-end-ship." He strung the word out, being careful with each piece of it.

"Homeplace? They call that place Homeplace?"

"No. *We* call it Homeplace. *They* call it Niggertown."

I didn't know what to say. I had never heard a black man use the word "nigger" before. I had never heard a black man say much of anything. Long minutes went by, the two of us standing in the sun. People walked by and looked at us, at John Three. Some of them seemed to know him, nodded their heads, said howdy.

His full name was John Three Sixteen Hutchison. His mama surely did like the Book of John, he said, and named all the kids, all seven of them, after some verse of that Book. And everybody had to memorize his verse, John said, and repeat it whenever his mama wanted.

She was a good woman, his mama, John said.

"Does she live at Homeplace?"

"She used to. But people get born and people die and the only thing we got that we know will live for a long time is the Homeplace." He paused, breathing deeply. "Mama, she died."

I didn't know what to say. I didn't know if I was supposed to say how sorry I was . . . what to say to a black man. So I didn't say anything.

For the first time I looked at the beach, looked for black people. The white beach glistened in the sun, stretching smoothly north and south, gentle, inviting, undisturbed. The surf was hardly big enough to be called surf, lapping at the legs of people wading in the warm water. It was a calm scene, pure. And nowhere in that scene was there a black vision, not a single body, none.

"Do you . . . your . . . people, do they have a beach? I mean, how do people decide what beach is theirs?"

"We don't decide. You decide. And then we go where you tell us, and that's our beach."

"I guess . . . I . . ."

"Look, Jesse," he said, his voice showing some tension, "you can't be completely ignorant . . ." He looked at me closely. "Where did you say you were from?"

"West Virginia."

He got a look on his face that said, well, maybe I could be that ignorant, after all.

"Jesse boy, why don't you take a look for yourself. You know Murphy Beach?"

"Uh . . . somewhere north on the strand . . ."

"Right, just up the coast, not too far. Feel like it, come on up sometime."

He picked up the rake and slung it over his shoulder.

"Listen, John . . . Reverend. That day when I got hired as a lifeguard, and we were in the pavilion . . ."

He grinned. "Almost walked straight into the deputy, didn't you. You got to be careful of that boy, Jesse. He got no sense of humor, none at all. And him and Banger, they been friends since Banger starting coming here summers, some years ago. See, Banger picks up a lot of gossip at the pavilion and . . . " He let it trail off. "You think he knew you the boy on the motorsickle?"

"No. Don't think so," I said, but not really too sure. "Only times he really ever saw me, the first time I was wearing goggles and the second time it was dark." My voice didn't sound too sure about the whole thing.

"You know," I mumbled, "I never thought about somebody trying to kill me, somebody don't even know me. At least back home we get to know people, get to really hate 'em, before we try to kill 'em. Hell, we even call 'em by their first names. I mean, you hate a man so much you try to kill him, that's right personal. Need to call a man by his first name, you hate him like that. Make sure he knows you know, knows you got a killin' goin' just fer him."

"Different down here, Jesse. Down here, some people, they born with hate, get it pumped into them from the very first. Got a hate in them when they don't know your first name, or your last. Don't matter. Like the deputy there? Well, there's two things he really hates, hates worse'n anything. One of them is northern license plates." He started to walk away, tall and straight.

"Hey, Reverend," I called after him, "just so's I'll know. What's the other thing, the other thing he hates?"

He went on a few steps, then turned slowly and said, almost under his breath, almost so I couldn't hear.

"Niggers," he said.

I watched him until he disappeared, walking slowly, dignified, around the side of the pavilion.

≈ Thirty-One ≈

Sometimes, I thought the rainy days were the best. It didn't rain often down there on the beach, but when it did it settled in gray-dark and flat, everything blended into itself. The thick sky fused with the horizon, curving back into the ocean and pushing toward the shore until tiny streaks of surf foam provided the only definition, the only break in the gray.

I wondered where the gulls went on rainy days.

Banger didn't pay lifeguards for rainy days. No one in his right mind would be on the beach in this shitting rain, he would say, and if they are they can damn well look out for their ownselfs. I ain't paying lifeguards to watch out after crazy people.

So I would prop open the door of the rental shack and lie back inside against the beach floats and watch the rain on the water and the beach. Now and then someone would walk by down near the surf, or maybe a couple would go by, hand in hand, not looking at each other. Not needing to. If someone did walk by, they always walked slowly. I guess if you're on the beach in the rain there is no reason to hurry.

Once, in Myrtle, I found a bookstore on a side street. Used books were piled on the floor and ran out over the tops of cardboard boxes. You could buy any book in the place for fifty cents. I would buy a book each time I went into Myrtle and on rainy days in the rental shack I would read until I fell asleep, the rain sometimes shifting direction and blowing through the door, soaking me awake.

When I finished a book I would lend it to Hugo. He never gave them back to me. He would keep a couple of them by his chair, usually one lying open to some part he had picked out that he thought would impress the girls. Now and then he would trade a book to a girl for food and when he did he always shared the food with me. I'd rather have had the book.

Banger kept the pavilion open on rainy days. Actually, he liked rainy days better than any other. There was nothing to do in Cherry, and if the rain kept people off the beach the only thing they could do was hang around the pavilion, drink, eat, play the jukebox, and dance. There was a song on the jukebox called "Mexico," sung by a bunch of guys whose name I could never remember. It was one of Banger's favorite songs and he would reach behind the jukebox, hit the free-play button and play "Mexico" over and over. It got on my nerves, everybody's nerves. It got so bad I saw people pay Banger not to play the song.

Like I said, on rainy days I would wander around a lot.

The rain had stopped and I was standing inside the used bookstore in Myrtle. I had two books under my arm and was wondering what to spend my last dollar on. People were back out on the streets now, wandering through the shops, some of them even heading back toward the beach.

I went down the street and past the front door of Wimpo's, slowing down enough to get a good look inside. Yvonne wasn't behind the bar. Neither was Wimpo. There was some tall guy with a bald head shoving beer across the wood, not really paying any attention to anyone. I had never seen him before.

I wanted to go in and ask about Yvonne, about where she lived, about . . . anything they would tell me. I wanted to see her again, wanted it so much that I could feel the want of it pounding through my stomach. But I didn't go in. I didn't think my head could take it.

A small hotdog stand sat at the edge of the sidewalk, a shack about the size of a good two-holer outhouse, one of those shacks they haul away in a truck come winter, put it back in the spring. The hotdogs cost a quarter. I always bought one, or two, or whatever, when I went into Myrtle. They were bigger than normal hotdogs, piled high with hotdog sauce or kraut or cole slaw or whatever else you might want, the stuff running out the ends of the bun and dripping over your hand. When they handed one out to you through the little window on the front of the shack, they always gave you a spoon, just in case. Before Myrtle Beach, I had never had a hotdog big enough to need a spoon to eat it.

Each wave of tourists that came into Myrtle would find out about the hotdogs and a line would form before noon and not run out until after two o'clock. There was a line there now but it wasn't too long. The rain had kept most people away.

I stood in line, the books under my arm. I would buy a couple of hotdogs, eat on a bench near the beach, and then get back to Cherry. Take a nap in the rental shack.

The lady in front of me was maybe the oldest person I had ever seen. She was older than any old I knew how to measure. I knew, if she had a son, he would be old, and even her grandson would be old, and maybe her great-grandson, he'd be old, too. I thought you would have to go through a lot of generations of her family to find someone related to her who was still young.

She stood a head shorter than me, probably more, and I could look directly down on the top of her head. Her face was a convoluted map of wrinkles that ran up and disappeared beneath the whitest hair I had ever seen. She was carrying a shopping bag, but I could tell she hadn't been shopping. The bag was full of stuff that looked like she had brought it from home, or maybe found somewhere. The rain had left the air thick and sticky, a heavy heat that made sweat form on my forehead, me just standing there; even so, she was wearing a thin shawl around her shoulders. I could tell she had placed the shawl carefully to try to hide the holes that I could see in it, just below her neck. Her dress came down almost to her shoe tops. It was missing a button at the top and she held her hand there, pulling the dress together, fidgeting with it, her hand a butterfly.

I wanted to talk with her, but I didn't know how. Back home, it would have been easy. I'd just say something like, Good afternoon, ma'am. You got any kin up on Black Hawk? But I wasn't on Black Hawk, and I knew this woman and I had no common kin. Not likely. So I said nothing, looking off to the side, checking out the three or four people in line behind us.

We waited our turns, inching forward toward the hotdog window, me, and this small, old woman. This tiny woman. This miniature black woman.

The guy in front of her was about the size of a pickup truck and he blocked our view of the window. When he got his hot dogs and left, the old woman stepped to the window, her head barely coming up to the counter.

She never got a chance to order.

"Sorry. Closed." The guy inside muttered just those two words, then slid the window shut.

Damn. I wouldn't get any hotdogs. I didn't have a watch, but I didn't think it was late enough to close. But, what the hell, it was his hotdog stand.

The old woman stood looking at the window for a moment, then turned and stepped aside, her movements graceful, gentle.

I started to turn away from the window, wondering where to go to spend my dollar. The window slid open.

"Hep you?" the guy inside asked, looking at me, his face blank.

I was a little confused. "Thought you was closed."

"Was. Just for a minute, there. But open now, open for business. Best hotdogs on the beach."

"Yeah, I bought hotdogs here before, but I thought. . ."

"Look, friend, they some people there behind you want to buy some hotdogs. You want to buy some?"

The old woman hadn't gone away. She had only gone back to the end of the line.

"Nah. Guess not." I stepped away and let the next guy belly up the window. I noticed that none of the other people had stepped out of the line. No one looked at the old woman.

The line moved forward one step, and so did the old woman. I went to the back of the line and stood behind her again. One step at a time, we moved toward the window. And then she was there.

"Sorry. Closed." The window slid shut again. The old woman stepped away and moved to the rear of the line again.

The window opened. "You back again? Change your mind about them hotdogs?"

"Don't know. This a White Diner?"

"White diner? This ain't no diner, but it sure as hell is a white hotdog stand, boy. Don't you see the paint?"

He reached out through the window and patted the side of the shack, patted the white paint, a smirk across his face.

"Now, you want them hotdogs, or what?"

"Nah. Guess not. Just wanted to go around again with the line." I stepped away from the window and went back to the end of the line, behind the old woman.

We did it two more times. Each time she got to the window the hotdog stand would be closed. And each time she would go back to the end of the line. The last time when I got to the window it stayed closed. He didn't even open it to ask me if I wanted any hotdogs. The window stayed closed until I left, went back to the end of the line. I thought about just standing there, waiting in front of the window, just to see what he would do. But I didn't really know what I was doing, or why, and I didn't know what I would say if he asked me, if I didn't want any hotdogs, then what the hell did I want?

It was one of those times in my life when I knew there was something I was supposed to do, but didn't know what. I was out of my element, out of my place, out of all knowing, probably out of my fucking mind. I was involved in something that was wrong, and I didn't know how to make it right. We were at the back of the line again, inching forward, and I guess I would have just kept that up, going around and around in the line because that was what she was doing, not knowing what I was doing or why I was doing it, only that it was a thing happening and I was in it.

Just kept it up because there didn't seem to be any way to end it that made any sense.

Somebody else ended it.

A hand gripped my arm, pulling me, squeezing hard, making sure I knew the pull and the squeeze were not suggestions that I step out of the line. They were commands.

I looked at the hand, the size of it, the arm that came down into it like a tree limb, with no wrist that I could see. I looked into the face of the deputy. My deputy.

He pulled me two or three steps to the side. I glanced back over my shoulder at the line. The old woman was still there, but no one had moved. And no one was looking at us. What I hadn't noticed before, a small crowd had gathered, not too close, but close enough to see everything, hear everything.

"What's your name, boy?" He still held my arm.

I knew enough not to try to pull away. I didn't even resist his grip. His fingers were crunching into my arm and I could feel the muscle tissue in there begin to separate, but I kept myself from flinching. "Jesse," I said, trying to keep my voice even.

"Don't I know you, boy? You work up at Cherry?"

"Yeah. Work for Banger. On the beach."

His grip loosened slightly. "What are you doing down here, stirring up trouble?"

Shit. I was beginning to get the drift.

"Didn't mean to get any trouble going. Just wanted to get a hotdog. Best damn hotdogs on the beach." I pasted on a stupid grin.

"Where you from, boy?"

"You know — up at Cherry. Work for Banger."

"Don't get smart with me, boy. I mean *where* are you from?" His grip got tight again.

"West Virginia."

"Shit. That explains most of it. You hillbillies come down here, clutter up our beaches . . . Well, at least you got a job.

"Tell you what, boy. I'm going turn you loose, send you back up to Banger. You do that, you hear? You go back up to Banger, tell him I turned you loose."

"Turned me loose for what. What was I being held for?" I couldn't help it, should have kept my mouth shut, should have just walked away. His face went a deep red and his flat piggy nose seemed to turn up even more.

"We don't have to explain things to outlanders down here, especially *hillbilly* outlanders." He began to twist my arm a little, leading me further away from the line.

I looked back at them, all the people back there, all of them looking forward, toward the hotdog stand. As far as they were concerned, the deputy and I were not even there.

He kept pulling me. We stopped near a trash can sitting at the edge of the sidewalk. I saw the big Ford parked just down the street.

"Tell you what, boy. I'm going to give you the benefit of the doubt this time, seeing you work for Banger." We stopped on the sidewalk and he twisted me around to face him. "But I think from now on, you want a hotdog, you buy it from Banger. You hear?"

He took the books from under my arm and looked at their covers, sneered, and threw them in the trash can. "What are you reading that trash for, anyway? Should be looking out for people on the beach, people maybe having trouble in the water."

I opened my mouth, but nothing came out. I was trying to figure out what to say . . . something that wouldn't get me pulled into the Ford, but something that would let him know he wasn't scaring me. Even though I was scared shitless.

I never figured it out. His hand came up out of nowhere, a hand the size of a side of bacon, slapping me across the side of the face, a slap that rattled my brain — I could feel it shake inside my head. My vision went out of control for a few seconds, my eyes refusing to focus on what was standing in front of me.

He raised his hand again, but this time patted my cheek where he had hit me, patted it several times, patted it like an uncle trying to teach an unruly kid.

"I didn't quite catch your comment there, boy. Now *where* did you say you going to buy hotdogs?"

"Banger's. Gonna buy them hotdogs at Banger's. Best goddamn hotdogs on the beach, them Banger dogs. Love 'em. Hell, I could eat them hotdogs . . . "

He shook my arm and patted my cheek again. "Yep. That'll do it, boy. All I wanted to know." And he turned me loose.

I walked backward away from him a few steps, then turned and tried to amble down the sidewalk. But my knees shook and I knew he had seen them shake and there was nothing I could do about it. Maybe it didn't matter.

There was still a line in front of the hotdog stand.

The old woman was gone.

"Boy!" I heard him call sharply behind me. "Just been wondering. You ever been to New York?"

I pretended not to hear.

≈ Thirty-Two ≈

Hugo and I didn't have the money to buy suntan lotion, so when we couldn't beg lotion from the girls we slicked ourselves up with motor oil. For a while, we worried what the girls would say if they found out we were using motor oil, but then one day a girl saw Hugo slathering the stuff all over him and she made gagging sounds and wouldn't touch him when he held out his arm for her to feel. But she didn't leave. Hugo told her it was a lifeguard secret — using the motor oil — and that she shouldn't tell the other lifeguards that she knew about it. That they would get mad at him for letting her in on it. Within a week, half the regulars on the beach were using motor oil. It got to be a thing. Got so you could smell some of those girls coming.

I never told Banger about the hotdog stand and the deputy. I knew the deputy would tell him, and I didn't want Banger to think it was anything that I was worried about. For a couple of days I would catch him looking at me, wrinkling up his face and squinting, but he got tired of that and after a while he quit.

The fact is, Banger just didn't care, didn't give a shit, about me, about hotdog stands, about anything.

I've often wondered if Banger loved anything, even *liked* anything.

He was from an island near Ft. Myers, down in Florida, and he went back down there every autumn after the beaches closed in South Carolina. That's where he got the big seashell that hung over the bar, said he found it right on the beach, said the beach was the only place on the whole island where you could see more then fifty feet. Trees and vines and even the damned weeds grew higher than your head, way higher, he said, and so thick you need a big knife just to hack your way through. The only way on the island you could see anything, *really* see, was to get in a boat and go out on the water. Then you could look back and really see the island, the low line of dark green that hung just in back of the line of delicate lacy surf that pushed the shells up on the beach.

In other words, Banger said, you couldn't see a goddamn thing and no one could see you. He loved it.

I thought I might want to go down there someday, but only if I was sure Banger wasn't there.

For the whole summer, Banger never said anything about kin or friends or anybody else down there on that island. It was as though he went down there every winter, and hid.

Well, there was one thing I knew for sure he liked, even loved, but it didn't really count.

Banger loved firecrackers, all kinds, but his two favorites were the M-80s and cherry bombs. He seemed to have them around all the time, in his pockets, in his car, dumped into boxes in the storage room. Once I even saw him put some into the cash register. For just in case, he said.

And he liked those little ones, too, the ones he called ladyfingers. He kept a supply of them in a large seashell that sat on the shelf behind the bar, next to a neon Budweiser Beer sign. He would reach into the shell, grab a ladyfinger and play with it at the bar, toss it into the air, wave the fuse around next to his cigarette. Now and then he would take the cigarette out of his mouth, put the firecracker between his lips, light the fuse with the cigarette, then roll the whole thing into his mouth. The women would scream and the guys would try to act casual, like they saw guys swallow miniature bombs every day. He would turn and spit the firecracker, fuse still burning, over the shelf and out into the junk piled behind bar where it would explode, an empty popping sound all but muffled by the noise from the bar.

People would edge away from the him, trying to be casual, trying not to show Banger that they wanted the hell out of there before he accidentally swallowed the dammed thing and blew his stomach up through his mouth.

Once, there was a drunk sleeping out there in the junk, curled up inside some cardboard. Banger spit the firecracker through the window and it dropped inside the cardboard and went off against the drunk's chest. Drunks didn't sleep out there much after that.

Banger made me uncomfortable. Yeah, you might say that.

Banger would take a life preserver ring off the back of one of the lifeguard chairs, prop it up on the beach, and practice throwing cherry bombs through the hole in the center, fuses lit and sputtering. He made a big deal out of it, wrapping two fingers around the bomb like a miniature baseball, lighting the fuse, taking a quick wind-up, and then flinging the thing straight through the preserver, laughing all the time. He seldom missed, but when he did the cherry bomb would hit the ring and carom off in wild directions, scattering everybody who was watching the action. I didn't mind the cherry bomb throwing. It was his goddamn crazy laughing I couldn't stand.

And he was the sand-crab-launching champion of Cherry Hill Beach.

All it took was a cherry bomb, a cigarette, and a little patience. Banger would lie belly-down on the beach, not too far from a good-size sand crab hole. He would light the cigarette, and he would wait.

The crab was always cautious. It would poke itself out of its hole, scuttle sideways a foot or so away, then make a dash back to the hole, all the time watching Banger, who would not make the slightest move. He would just lie there, the cigarette burning, not even smoking it.

And the crab would get cocky. He would dart out of the hole and run farther away, watching Banger all the way, then back to the hole. Banger knew it was only a matter of time.

Always, sooner or later, the crab went too far away from the hole.

Slowly, Banger touched the cigarette to the cherry bomb fuse. When the fuse burst into sparks, Banger leaped to his feet and made a mad dash for the crab's hole in the sand. The split second that Banger moved, the crab, too, dashed for the hole. The race was on. But it only lasted for a second or two.

Usually, Banger beat the crab to the hole, his arm raised all the time he was running. At the last second, he flung the cherry bomb into the hole and dived off to the side. The crab, not knowing what that meant to his life cycle, dived into the hole on top of it.

The explosion was muted, but effective. The hole in the sand tripled in size as the crab was blasted into the air, bits and pieces of crab legs, shell and sand flying in all directions. The people on the beach would turn to see what the noise was all about, just in time to see Banger pull a scrap of paper and a stub of pencil out of his pants pocket, to chalk up another kill.

I went up to Murphy Beach.

Some weeks had gone by since John Three had invited me to do that. I saw him almost every day at the pavilion but he never said anything else about the black beach. I finally figured out that, once John Three had invited you to do something, he didn't feel he had to keep pushing it.

So I went. Besides, I was curious. A whole beach with no one on it but black people. I thought John Three was kidding.

I hung around the pavilion until Banger got the grill fired up, ate a hotdog for breakfast, and then walked out to the highway and stuck out my thumb. I was tanned, trim, wearing cut-offs, t-shirt and sunglasses, all of which I had found on the beach. I thought I looked like a bitchin' beach guy. The first car that came along stopped and picked me up.

The driver was a woman in her thirties, good looking, tired eyes set deep under a head of blond, faded hair that had been out in the sun too long. When I slid into the car she looked me full in the face, then let her eyes drift down over my legs. Measuring. I thanked her for stopping and then we didn't say anything for a mile or two, until she asked me where I was headed. I told her Murphy Beach. She stopped the car and put me out.

I was only about a mile from Murphy, so I didn't bother thumbing. I cut through between some houses and out into a deserted area, rough, high dunes with clumps of some sort of hard grass, the dunes twisted, eaten by the wind. I slogged around them and popped out on a sand flat, more tough grass growing, higher this time, ragged edges filing at my arms, and nothing else in particular to look at. I thought if you had to run through this stuff you would lose a few pounds of skin in the process. A little further on the grass stopped instantly and I stepped out onto a narrow, ugly stretch of hard sand.

Murphy Beach.

The breeze seemed to be stronger here, pushing against me. The people lying on the beach had coolers and legs of beach chairs holding down their beach towels, not really paying any attention to the wind. There was no pier, no pavilion, nothing but the hard beach and the people scattered along the strand, talking, playing their battery radios, laughing. A few of them were in the surf, a short vicious chop that lapped angrily at the sand. And every one of the people was black.

I edged out onto the sand, away from the dammed grass, and strolled along, acting cool behind my sunglasses.

Nobody said anything to me. They saw me, they watched me, they stopped talking when I went by, but nobody said anything to me.

I kept walking up the beach, my hands stuffed into my pockets, trying to be casual. I looked at the black faces as I went by, thinking maybe I would see John Three, but I saw no one I knew.

Until . . . there he was again. Brother Jason.

He was lying up high on the beach, away from the water, his bulk not really any smaller because he was lying down. He was wearing sunglasses, his face turned full up into the sun. His chest rose and fell with his breathing; a chest so large that I couldn't tell where it ended and his stomach began. He was wearing a sweatshirt with the arms cut off and some sort of pants that came down to his knees, no shoes. His legs seemed like ebony logs joined at the top, lying v-shaped, too thick to meet anywhere except at his hips. He was a great black whale, stranded, and not caring about it at all.

I was glad to see a face I had seen before, even if it was the giant. I walked over.

She was lying behind him. I hadn't even seen her at first, Jason's bulk shielding her. But as I walked over I could see the tips of her breasts rising on the other side of him, and then one perfect, slender leg, and then all of her lying there, the girl from the village, at the church, her eyes closed, the rise and fall of her breasts pushing gently against her bathing suit, a suit so thin, so light, so sky blue, so perfect . . . Her blue sunglasses matched the color of her suit. Her nipples showed against the silky material and down at the top of her legs the suit pulled up into her crotch so tightly that the hair under there made a soft mound in the material, the material dipping into a gentle slot in the center of the mound.

The white girls at the pavilion wore suits that had wires in the top, the cups for their breasts lined with padding so thick it would drip for ten minutes after they got out of the water. Their suits sometimes had little skirts around the hips, like you weren't supposed to know there was flesh under there. At their crotch a thick roll of material curved around the top of each leg, so tight that, when the girls weren't pulling the wire away from their tits, they were pulling those thick rolls away from their mounds, sometimes, when they thought no one was looking, sticking a finger up in there and wiggling it back and forth, trying to get some circulation going.

There was not an extra square inch of material on the black girl's bathing suit, no wires, no rolls. Everything I saw was her, just her.

They seemed to be asleep, both of them breathing regularly, gently. I stepped closer.

"White boy like you get close like that, I begin to think he up to some thing." He said some-thing, two words. He hit the last word harder. Other than his jaw, he didn't move, didn't turn his head. "Why don't you close you mouth. Sand fly get in there, we never get him out." His voice came from the bottom of some heavy, wooden barrel, the words deepened and colored up out of the dark places.

"No . . . no . . . I just . . . "Damn. I was tongue tied, trying not to look like a fool, trying to pull my eyes away from the girl. She hadn't moved.

"What you doing up here this beach anyway, boy? You lost? You need some hep finding you way out . . . again?"

"No, not lost." My mouth was working better. "Just looking around. Rever-end John Three said I should come up here sometime, just look around." He still hadn't moved. Neither had she.

"Oh, I can see you looking. You looking at all the right things. You like that color blue? That be Evangeline's blue."

He must have meant the bathing suit. Evangeline's. Of course he meant the bathing suit. Here I was a white boy, on a black beach, looking down on the most beautiful woman on the beach, maybe on any beach, and she belonged to the black Moby Dick. Who would probably get up and kill me any second now.

"Sure, you like that color blue. 'Specially on Evangeline. She make that suit herself."

He rolled his head to the side and looked at Evangeline. "She don't move 'til I tell her it okay, see? She trained to do that, not move, not change her face, not adjust anything. When a white boy around."

What the hell was he talking about?

"See, white boys, they think when a black girl shift her legs, she got juice running down inside her thighs. Think she sayin', 'Come get it.' Think they got the right to think that, to do that, to go get it."

Jesus H. Christ. "Look, Brother Jason, I didn't mean nothing. I just wanted to see what John Three was talking about. I'll leave you alone. Don't want no trouble."

He rose from the ground and was standing beside me. That's just it — he *rose*, he didn't get up, he didn't stand up, he rose. His bulk came up off the sand in one fluid motion, no pushing with his arms, no thrashing around with his legs. One second he was lying there, the next second he was standing beside me. I glanced around, trying to pick an escape route. Other people were looking at us, some of them moving quietly in our direction.

"Don't fret, boy. You ain't going to get any trouble. See, you practical a friend already, you being chase by Deputy Pork and all. Anybody chase by Deputy Pork, well, he practical a friend from the very first."

"Deputy Pork? You call him Deputy Pork? That really his name?" I heard Evangeline giggle, softly, deep in her throat. The sound of water bubbling through silk.

Jason draped an arm over my shoulders, a log pressing me down into the sand. He lifted his other hand and flicked his fingers and the other people turned back to whatever they were doing before.

"Well, no, name ain't really Pork. It *P-O-L-K*," he said, drawing the word out slowly, making sure he got the L in there. "But we have some trouble with that word, so we just make it easier. Call him Pork. Kinda fit, you think? Flat stubby nose, little nostrils facing straight out, red face, thick neck, bristly hair with no curl to it." He was laughing now, really into it.

The girl — Evangeline — limbered up from the sand, stretched, stretched, took off her sunglasses, looked at me. Those eyes again. My God. She dropped the sunglasses, balled up her fist and punched Jason in the center of his chest. Her fist bounced off. Jason grinned at her and she strolled off toward the water. I tried not to look at her, feeling the huge arm tighten slightly on my shoulders, but I couldn't help it. Her hips worked gently back and forth, more than they needed to, and the material of her bathing suit pulled up between them. Everything about her was hidden under the suit. Nothing about her was hidden under the suit.

I dropped my eyes. "Sorry," I mumbled.

"Boy, you don't have to be sorry. She the best looking woman here, maybe anywhere. You can look all you want. Right proud to have her for my sister."

"Sister . . . "

"Sure, boy, what you think? You think she my woman? Sure wish I had a woman, look like her. See, we got different daddies, but she my sister, sure enough."

His sister. Evangeline was his *sister*.

We sat on the sand and Brother Jason explained the facts of life. This was a black beach. White people had their own beach — their own beaches. White people had more than one beach, black people had only one, Murphy Beach. White people didn't come to this beach. Deputies, like Deputy Pork, would drive up and down the beach roads now and then, just to make sure, just like they drove up and down the roads at the white beaches, just to make sure no black people were going to those beaches, or even thinking about going to those beaches. Any black man going down to one of those beaches better have a rake in his hand, Jason said.

He usually grinned when he talked, but I thought behind his sunglasses his eyes weren't grinning.

I decided I could say anything to Jason, anything at all. I don't know why I decided that. Maybe it was because the man was sitting on the sand beside me, telling me things I never knew existed, things he wished didn't exist. Maybe it was because I felt comfortable there with Brother Jason, two guys who had absolutely nothing in common, just sitting on a beach. But maybe we did. Maybe we were two guys who never had anything, maybe never would have anything, maybe didn't know where we belonged, maybe didn't give a shit about all the things that everybody else gave a shit about. Maybe there wasn't any place for us.

There was something wrong here, down here, on these beaches and in these towns. And I knew what it was. I just didn't know what to call it, what to say about it, what to do about it, how to act about it. So I didn't say anything. I just sat there on the sand and listened to Jason talk, watching Evangeline play in the surf, wishing I could go down there and be with her and knowing I couldn't.

Brother Jason rolled back on the sand, turned over and started digging with his hands. He uncovered two cans, buried in the damp, cool sand. He handed one to me. Well, at least we can have a beer, I thought.

"Tomato juice," he said, grinning. "Cold can of tomato juice. Ain't nothing like it in the world."

They were going to send me to Crum to stay with people named Oscar and Mattie and I didn't want to go. I wanted to go farther than Crum, farther than the Tug River, maybe farther than any of us had ever been. But they wouldn't let me and I knew it.

Uncle Long Neck took me to the general store in Dunlow for the last time. We went in his old truck and he let me drive, me sitting on an old blanket so I could see over the steering wheel, fighting the odd-sized tires and the ruts, wrestling the grunting machine around the tight turns that followed Turkey Creek.

When we got to the store Long Neck talked with the men on the porch for a while, then went inside. He was out quickly and went to the little stream that flowed past the store and drained into Twelve Pole Creek. The stream was spring-fed, cold, rising less than a mile up the hollow behind the store, running through the moss-covered rocks, dripping from leaves. Long Neck put something into the water.

An hour later, after we had eaten a sandwich on the front porch, and Long Neck had talked all he was going to, and we got ready to leave. He put a couple of gunny-sacks of groceries in the back of the truck, then went to the stream and pulled something out, two tin cans. We walked slowly down to the creek bank and watched the dark green water of Twelve Pole creep by. We both knew it was maybe the last time we would ever go to the general store together. Maybe anywhere together.

Long Neck pulled out his pocketknife and punched holes in the tops of the cans, handed one to me. Tomato juice. A cold can of tomato juice. It was, he said, one of the great secrets of life, a cold can of tomato juice. Tasted better than real tomatoes, all that red, smashed, delicious life filled up in that tin can, sweat on the outside from cooling in the water. Nothing like it. Nothing better in the world. Not even 'shine, he said, and that surprised me.

We drank the juice in silence. We had said all we ever needed to say to each other, Long Neck and me.

And he was right. About the juice. And about everything else.

"Nothing better in de whole damn world. Best liquid thing de good Lord ever made. Not even beer be better," Jason grunted, sucking the last of the juice from the can. "Well, maybe one thing be better. Maybe licking the sweat off Sweet Julie Johnson's belly, maybe that be better." He was laughing now, still sucking on the can. I didn't know who Sweet Julie Johnson was, but she must be something, to be better than cold tomato juice on the beach.

The sweat on Slick Jesse popped into my mind. I had licked the sweat off just about every part of her. Yeah, it was about the only thing better than cold tomato juice.

He sucked on the can again, a wet, rattling sound. "Listen to that, boy. Sound like a pig farting in a rain barrel!" He fell over backward, laughing harder, pleased with himself.

His sister. Evangeline was his *sister*.

He walked me back through the rough grass toward the road, sometimes clapping his arm on my shoulder, making my lungs jump.

"One more thing," he said, stopping and turning me to face him. "Deputy Pork, you get cross-ways of him and you think you fix him, go over his head, report him to some higher a-thor-i-ty. You forget that, boy. See, he be the sheriff's brother, his real brother. And he do whatever he want and get away with it. Pork, he just do what he want. And the sheriff, he don't ask."

"And another thing, boy . . . he look like a redneck, and he *be* a redneck, but he be a redneck that gone to college. He smart. And he gonna use that smart to make sure the South stay just like it is."

He shook my hand, holding onto it. Then he let it go and we stood there for a while, neither of us knowing what to do or say.

He put his hand on my shoulder.

"My friend, it truly has been a pleasure to have you here on our very own private beach," he said, his voice as smooth as hot chocolate over marble, all the southern inflection gone. "A beach for the personal use of us folks with the darker coloration. And I shall be sure to pass the good word around to the brethren, be sure that you are always welcome here, that proper hospitality is always ex-tended."

It was as formal a speech as I had ever heard.

"And you come join us at the Homeplace some Sunday afternoon, for our weekly picnic and cool libations."

He let go of may hand and walked away.

"A pig farting in a rain barrel," I heard him say to himself, " . . . have to remember that."

❧ Thirty-Three ❧

The beach is a naked dun stripe along the edge of the earth that forces you out into the sunlight or the night and keeps you there.

There is no place to hide on a beach, not even in the dark.

I was always good at hiding. Ten feet inside the edge of the woods that surrounded the farms on Black Hawk Ridge and I was gone, flowing down into the floor of the forest as I was born to do. I could stay there for days, living quietly, meeting no one, but hearing and seeing everything. When I was younger they came looking for me, up there on the Ridge, wondering where the hell I was, and why wasn't I home for supper. When I got bigger, they gave it up. I would come out of the woods, come home, when I was ready.

It was different in Crum. I hid out because I had to and I had my places all picked out and ready. Sometimes I hid in the small old barns scattered around the town, boards hanging from their sides by a single nail, holes in their tin roofs. Or in the little tool sheds that leaned against the houses. But the best places were down on the riverbank and in the woods above the town. Once I got into the brush, into the woods, no one could ever find me.

When I first saw the beach in daylight I wondered where I could hide, if it ever came to that. I wanted to have my place all picked out, be ready. But there was no place. Not even in the dark. In the dark there was nothing on the beach, no bodies, no dogs, no umbrellas, nothing to melt down through. In the dark you stand on the sand and nothing moves except a line of black surf at the edge of a black ocean and you are out there to be seen, a dark beacon in the blackness that can be found by anyone, for any reason.

At first, that's what I thought she was doing, trying to hide in the dark on the beach. I lay back in the rental shack waiting for the rain, my feet propped up on a stack of beach floats, my trunks still damp from my last swim of the day. It wasn't full dark, just a hard gray that made everything blend together, and I should have been able to see her clearly but she moved so slowly that I had to look hard to see her legs push through the edge of the surf as she drifted down the beach, her lithe form seeming to glide above the water. And then I realized she was wearing a dress. She was wading, about up to her knees, and the small waves would come up and lap at her legs and soak her skirt and she didn't seem to care.

Clouds had settled in over the beach about mid-afternoon and most of the people had drifted away, back to the beach cottages and motels, back to the latest copies of *Life and Saturday Evening Post*. Later, some of them had come out again, wandering into the pavilion, dropping coins into the jukebox, waiting for the darkness. I could hear the music and now and then the slick rolling of the swells beyond the low line of surf would catch the pavilion lights and send quick reflections shooting down the shoreline.

I had curled up in the rental shack and propped the door open, waiting for the rain to come, waiting for the gray to go black.

She was almost directly below me in the edge of the surf before I really noticed her, quick bursts of light from the pavilion finding her, outlining her, then losing her in the darkness between waves.

And then she was gone.

I lay there and listened to the low rush of the surf and the thin sounds of the pavilion jukebox. She was gone and I hadn't seen her go. She was a woman in the near-dark and I didn't know her name or why she was wading in the surf in a dress and I wished I had gone down to the water and talked to her, all the time knowing that if I went down there she would hurry on or turn and go back. Knowing I would break the mood. Knowing she didn't need me down there, with her, in the water.

I had never seen a woman wearing a dress wade in the surf. I would have liked to have known her.

A soft wind was building into something stronger and the rental shack shivered a little. I sat up and put my legs through the open door and stared down at the water where she had been, some vague feeling of loneliness washing over me, the female presence of her gone, the beach empty.

The beach empty.

I got up from the doorway and looked up and down the strand. The lights from the pavilion helped and I could see some distance in each direction, the gray light dropping quickly until the beach fell away under darkness. But I could see far enough, and she wasn't there, wasn't anywhere. She had been walking down the beach, away from the pier, just moping along. I couldn't figure it out; even if she had taken off running, she still didn't have time to get out of range. No matter which way she would have gone, I would have seen her.

And then I knew where she was and I didn't want to know and all summer long I had been playing lifeguard and drinking beer and chasing girls with plump little asses and now there was a woman in the water and I was going to have to be real and find her out there and I didn't know how to do that, didn't know how to find a woman in the dark water, a woman wearing a dress, a woman who didn't want to be found.

I lurched away from the rental shack and ran about halfway to the water, then slid to a stop. Maybe I should get somebody from the pavilion to help. Maybe I shouldn't. Jesus Christ, I was there on the sand and it was darker and there was a woman out there and the only thing she had going for her was a dumb hillbilly who pretended to be a lifeguard.

I stood there, my body locked and rigid, the water flicking shots of light from the pavilion.

I was looking too close to the shore. Farther out, just out beyond the end of the pier, I saw, caught in the middle of a reflected patch of light, a single arm, lifted, falling back into the water, not even flailing, just moving. And then the other arm. Then the light was gone and the arms were gone and all the lifeguard bullshit was gone and there was just me and the water and the woman and the blackness and I ran, panicked, toward the surf, screaming, screaming.

"Heeeaay! *Heeeeaaaaayy!*"

I split the surf as hard as I could, knowing that somewhere a very short distance from me something was happening that I didn't want to happen, that I couldn't live with.

I could see nothing. I could find nothing. I kept screaming, knowing she could not hear, would not hear me, but not
knowing what else to do. I screamed down and back through
the pathways of all my life and I knew that all I was doing was
making noise.

I had never been this far out beyond the end of the pier.
I didn't know how deep the water was and when I felt something brush my leg I had one of those moments when everything in your body shuts down, waiting. All the lifeguards had
told me shark stories, but I had never actually seen a shark.
And now I knew, I was positive, there was one brushing against
my leg in the blackness of water at night on the edge of rain.

But whatever brushed my leg stayed there and when I
shoved against it, it moved, and I reached down and grabbed her.

I pulled her up, rolled her over on her back, put my arm
around her and started swimming to shore, like Hugo had
shown me, like we had practiced together. But it was a lot
harder than when Hugo and I had been playing at it, and it
took me a long time to get to where my feet could touch the
bottom and by the time I got there I could hardly breathe.

I tried to pick her up and carry her but she was loose and
limp. She wasn't large, but her arms and legs hung and slid
everywhere, dangling, her head lolling backwards, her body
folding in the middle and hanging down between my arms,
her dress dragging the water. I gathered myself and tried to
heave her up higher, carry her higher, but one of her elbows
clubbed me in the mouth and I couldn't really get a grip on
her. I knew if I didn't try something else I would never get her
up on the beach. I put her back in the water and slid underneath her, rising quickly and draping her over my shoulder,
face down, hanging over my back. I crashed toward the shore
as fast as I could, jogging her up and down, and I felt her twitch
and she puked down my back and down the back of my legs. I
could feel it, warm and running, and I hoped she was only
puking water but I didn't really care. I thought probably she
had to be alive to puke and I wanted her to keep right on doing it. But she didn't.

When I got to the sand there was a crowd of people there,
come down from the pavilion, some of them carrying cans of

beer, and they all stood silently along the beach, the line of them outlined in the lights from the pavilion. No one came into the water to help.

I put her down like Hugo had shown me, face-down on the sand, her head turned to the side, her arm underneath her head. I straddled her back and pushed hard against her rib cage and a glob of water came out of her mouth and nose and I pushed some more times and some more water came and I gagged and tried to breathe at the same time and I kept telling her she shouldn't be wearing a dress in the water and I pushed some more waiting for her eyes to open, but they didn't.

Someone grabbed me by the arm and hauled me off the woman. Some guys were there in white coats. They carried flashlights and ran around a lot and messed with her, pushing against her, feeling in her mouth, talking tensely to each other, me just there on my knees in the sand, covered with vomit. Someone shined a light on her back and there was blood there, patches of it smeared across the thin material of her dress. They shined a light on me and there was blood painted in streaks down my chest. My lip was split and it was still pumping blood.

And then she puked some more water and then some other stuff and her eyes opened.

They had her on a stretcher, covered with a blanket. She was breathing.

By the time they started carrying her off to the ambulance the first drops of rain were blowing in off the ocean. She was looking at the faces in the crowd, ignoring the rain running into her eyes, her expression blank, recognizing no one, and I realized she did not know who had pulled her from the water.

The crowd split and moved around me, not wanting to be close to anything that smelled like I did, moved away with the stretcher toward the ambulance, some of them sipping beer as they went, hurrying now, pushed by the rain. When they got to the edge of the beach near the pavilion I heard some laughter drifting back from them and then they were all inside the pavilion and the ambulance was gone. None of them looked back.

I sat there on the beach where the woman had been lying, still feeling the presence of her, rocking back and forth on my knees, my arms wrapped around my stomach, shivering, tears forming in my eyes, wanting to hide and knowing there was no place to hide on the beach in the dark, not even in the rain, and telling her she shouldn't have been wearing a dress in the water, *goddammit*, that was no way to behave on a beach, squeezing the words out into the blackness through clenched teeth, head spinning. And then someone touched me on the shoulder.

"What do I have to do to get rid of you?"

I tried to stop my whimpering and look at her, her loose slacks and blouse beginning to stick to her, her hair down and falling around her shoulders in wet strands. That black hair.

Yvonne.

"Don't have to worry about that. Won't ever bother you again," I mumbled.

Her hand was still on my shoulder. She pulled it away and looked at it, her face screwed into disgust.

"You're covered with . . . stuff."

I stayed there on my knees, my arms still wrapped around my stomach. Maybe she would just go away.

"Where do you stay? Where's your room?"

I nodded toward the rental shack. For a moment, she didn't understand. Then she did.

"The rental shack? You sleep in the *rental shack*?"

All I could do was nod.

"My God," she whispered.

She took me by the arm and pulled me to my feet. I started toward the rental shack but she held me, pulled me back toward the surf, wading in up to our knees. She didn't even take off her shoes. She dipped water in her hands and poured it on my back and chest, splashing it down my legs. She did it carefully, not wanting to touch the stuff that was clinging to me.

The stuff wasn't coming off, not even with the rain and her splashing me. She took off her blouse and dipped it in the ocean, rubbing me gently with the silky material, cleansing me. She washed my back and my chest, then down my legs, dipping the blouse and then rubbing me with it, gently, all over, rubbing the stuff off me, rubbing me on the parts that were already clean.

She kept doing that, again and again, over my body.

She stood in front of me, standing close, like Rosalind had stood, her head tilted up, breathing into my face.

"I'm . . . sorry. Sorry about Crum . . . " I mumbled.

"Shut up," she said.

She was wearing nothing underneath the blouse.

❧ Thirty-Four ❧

There are times when you get a second chance. I had one now. Maybe I would get it right this time.

Yvonne still had her brother's old Chevy. She loaded me in the thing and drove to Myrtle, to her house, off on the edge of town where the houses were tiny and pushed together, where a waitress or a lifeguard could rent a place for a few bucks a week. She had been living there ever since she had come to Myrtle Beach, and she had come straight from Crum, almost two years ago.

She drove all the way over there, naked to the waist.

It was still raining when we got there. She pulled up into a small parking space beside her tiny cottage and hauled me out. When we got inside she didn't turn on any lights, just stood there with me in the dim glow of some faded light that filtered in from the street, just stood there touching me, water running from both of us, mingling at our feet; just stood there, me in my wet swimming trunks, Yvonne's breasts glistening in the silvery light, her sodden slacks slipping down on her hips.

I don't know how long we stood there. I could have stood there forever.

I ran my hand up her side and cupped her breast. With an unhurried motion she raised her hand and covered mine, pressing it into her breast, kneading the breast slightly.

Her hips were firm against mine and I ran my other hand down her side, feeling the top of her slacks. They were wet and sagging and it was easy to slide them from her hips. They fell around her ankles.

She stepped out of the slacks and led me to the couch, worked at my wet trunks, finally getting them to slide down and off my feet. She stood, wearing nothing but her panties, then carried my wet trunks and her slacks out of the room.

I lay back and waited.

When she came back into the room she was wearing pajamas, the tops and the bottoms, and was carrying a blanket.

She dropped the blanket on me, spread it out a little, covering me, tucking me in. I thought maybe I was supposed to be disappointed. But I wasn't. I was warm and dry and clean and, sure as hell, I was once again on the couch in Yvonne's living room.

My eyes started to close before she left the room.

She came in early, almost at daybreak, already dressed like she was going out somewhere. She had on a pleated skirt and a short-sleeved blouse and I thought if I ever saw a woman more beautiful than this I probably wouldn't be able to stand it. I'd just pass out from overload.

She sat on the edge of the couch and we talked and right in the middle of the talking my eyes closed again and when I woke up she was gone.

When she had driven the old Chevy into Myrtle Beach it had been late summer and she knew she had to get a job some place that didn't close down when the tourists left. Wimpo's stayed open all year, one of the few saloons that did. She said for the first time in her life she used her looks to get what she wanted. She tucked her blouse down tight into her skirt and pushed her breasts out. Wimpo took one look at her and she went to work behind the bar that same afternoon. Wimpo had tried to grab her a few times, but she kept pushing him off, pushing hard enough to get rid of him, but not so hard that he didn't think he could try again later. She kept her job that way. It wasn't hard.

She went to school in the mornings, she said. College courses. Tended bar at Wimpo's in the afternoons and evenings, all the time planning on something better. Something better than Crum. Something better than Wimpo's. Something better than me.

She didn't really say that last part, but I could tell she was thinking about it.

A few days after I pulled the woman from the water I was sitting at a table on the far side of the pavilion, sipping a beer and watching the moon slide around the water out beyond the pier. The crowd was smaller than usual, the music lower, the whole place sort of relaxed, even tired.

It was Yvonne's night off at Wimpo's and she had promised to come to Cherry Hill. I had seen her only a couple of times since the night of the rescue and we had only talked, nothing else. I hadn't touched her since then, not even held her hand. She wasn't my girlfriend, not yet, and I wasn't going to screw it up this time.

When she came into the pavilion she picked up a beer at the bar and walked toward me, her hips and legs moving in those dancer steps, those steps that fix themselves in your mind, a stopped movement in there, waiting, like a picture, anytime you want to look. Banger watched her walk, his eyes riveted to her ass. Across the room a bunch of college guys at a big table fell silent, just watching her move. One of them started to get up and follow her, then changed his mind.

The only person who had asked me about the rescue was Yvonne. I had told her the whole story, from front to back, and she had listened. No one else seemed to care. Banger never mentioned it. I don't think the other lifeguards even knew about it. I told Hugo, of course, but I'm not sure he believed me. Funny, I always meant to ask him that, if he believed me, but I never got around to it.

So I was surprised when Deputy Polk walked in. He looked at Banger, Banger nodded in my direction, and Polk came straight to our table and asked about it, asked about the rescue, straight out.

"You pull that woman from out the water?" He was looking at me, ignoring Yvonne. My hand was gripping my beer can so hard I could feel the tin start to give.

"Yeah, I got her out. Some other guys took her off, though." I was trying stay calm, wondering what he really wanted. Yvonne hadn't moved.

"Heard she puked her guts out. On you. She puke on you?"

"Don't remember. It was dark, raining, lots of stuff goin' on. Don't remember any puking."

"Heard she wasn't wearing any panties under her dress. You get a feel of that? Feel she wasn't wearing panties?"

His eyes flicked toward Yvonne. He wanted a reaction. He wasn't getting one.

"Don't know anything about . . ."

"Yeah, yeah," he muttered, "it was dark and all that shit. Never knew a lifeguard to rescue any woman without grabbing a feel.

"Anyway, got a guard on her at the hospital. Kept her there after she come around. Going to arrest her tight little ass soon as I get enough statements. Need yours."

"What kind'a statement?"

"Statement about her trying to commit su-i-cide and all," he growled.

There he went again, dividing up his words like he didn't want to miss anything in them.

Suicide. He was going to arrest the woman for trying to kill herself. How did that work, I wondered? How did it work when your life is so messed up you try to kill yourself, and somebody fixes it so you can't do that, and you live over the whole thing, and then they *arrest* you?

"Don't know about any suicide," I mumbled, paying close attention to my beer.

"Don't know? Hell, boy, you were the one pulled her out, weren't you?"

"Yeah, I pulled her out. My job. I'm a lifeguard, you know."

He didn't like it. He was used to getting exactly the answer he wanted. He leaned forward, his arms stiff, his hands knotted into fists, his knuckles planted on the table.

"What was she doing down there? Trying to find her panties? Washing her dress? She was wearing a *dress, goddammit*! Now, unless the two of you was doing something else," he growled, flicking another glance at Yvonne, "that's all I need you to say, that she was wearing a dress and she was trying to swim to Eng-land . . . "

"Didn't know her. Never saw her before. Don't remember a dress," I muttered. "If she was wearing a dress, must have been lots of other people saw it. Why do you need me to say it?"

"Because you the . . . *life-guard*." I could tell it pained him to have to call me that. "And I'm not worried too much about the dress . . . need you to say about the Eng-land part, that she was trying to swim to Eng-land, place she never make it to. She drown. She drown, on purpose."

"Don't know about Eng-land, either." I wondered if he knew I was mocking him. "Went out to get her, found her in the water out by the pier. Lots of people swim out that far. Can't say where she was trying to swim to. Seems like she just got too tired . . . "

"And what about this one," he interrupted, flicking his head toward Yvonne, but not looking at her. "Heard she was down there. She see her trying to swim to Eng-land?"

"She wasn't there," I said, a little stronger, my chin coming up.

"Well, now, why don't we just let Yuh-vonne talk for her-self," he muttered, looking directly at Yvonne again.

I glanced at Yvonne. Their eyes were locked on each other. It wasn't friendly.

"I can talk for myself," she said, her voice firm. "You should know that by now. And I didn't see anybody trying to swim anyplace, and certainly not to Eng-land." She mimicked his word.

Polk stood up, his face even redder than before. "Well, *ma'am*, would you excuse this gentle-man and me for just a minute or two?" He stepped back, expecting her to get up. "I'd like to talk to him privately."

She didn't move. "I don't think I can do that," she said.

Polk's hands clenched and relaxed, clenched and relaxed. A vein in the side of his thick neck pounded in and out from the force of his pulse.

"I could *order* you to do it, to move away from this table."

"Yes." But she still didn't move.

Polk stared at her for a long minute, then at me. He slowly straightened himself up, away from the table.

"Well, I'll see you back at Wimpo's, sometime, *ma'am*. Come and sit a spell. Have me a beer. Maybe two. Talk to Wimpo some. About life, and swimming, and Eng-land, and *employ-ees*, and all that."

He turned to me. "And when I find that motorsickle, I'll just run me a check on that engine number. Do some tracing back. See if I can't come up with a name." He paused. "And then we'll see, boy. We'll see."

He spun on his heel and walked away, not really in a hurry, but bumping some people on the dance floor anyway.

The motorcycle. He knew it was my motorcycle. Or did he? And how the hell would he know it was mine, if he didn't know where it was? The son-of-a-bitch was bluffing.

On the far side of the pavilion, over near the front door, a table full of college guys suddenly erupted, two of the biggest guys leaping up and grabbing each other. By the time Polk got there the college boys were clenched, wrestling, staggering, each trying to get an arm free to throw a punch. Polk stepped behind one of them and ran his arm around the front of the guy's throat, pulling back hard. As he pulled, he put his leg up into the other guy's stomach and pushed, sharp and vicious, popping the fighters apart easily. He held one guy up but the other one hit the floor. Polk hit the one he was holding, a short, hard, lancing shot to the kidney. The kid dropped like a rock. The other one bounced up, still trying to catch his breath, and Polk stepped into him, grabbing his arm and driving an open hand into the kid's chest. The kid spun. Polk was still holding the arm and as the kid spun he kicked the kid's feet, crashing him to the floor on his back, Polk still hanging onto the arm, the arm tucked into Polk's armpit now. Polk twisted. The guy screamed and his shoulder popped, looking deformed and enlarged.

It was over. It had taken about ten seconds.

The place was silent. Banger was behind the bar, not moving. The only sound was from the jukebox, winding down to the end of a song. I think it was "Mexico."

Polk said something to the rest of the guys standing there, then turned and looked at me. Then he just walked out.

"Jesus," I breathed.

"Fuck him." She said it quietly, letting her breath follow the words. "What was that about a 'motorsickle,' anyway?" she said, again mimicking Polk.

I leaned back in my chair, no longer interested in my beer. "Nothing. Guy just likes to give me a hard time. Never really figured out why." It was a lie. "He come into Wimpo's a lot?"

"He's a regular. Always hanging around, especially when he's off duty. Wanted to go out with me."

"Wanted?"

"Wanted. But I wouldn't. Didn't like him then, don't like him now.

"He and Wimpo, they do . . . things . . . together, get together in the corner and talk, like they're planning things." Her voice dropped off. "I'd worry, except I think they're both too dumb to do anything that requires too much thinking." She was silent for a moment. "But they're mean," she said quietly, "both of them."

Thirty-Five

The road led from the highway, wandered off through the trees, crossed one small, shallow creek and ended at the Homeplace, less than a mile from the blacktop.

It was a one-lane dirt road. At least, I thought it was dirt; the layer of pine needles on the road was so thick I could never really see the surface. There was a hole in one of my sneakers and as I shuffled along the narrow lane the needles would work in through there, sticking into my toes.

When I walked out into the tiny village flashes of West Virginia bounced off my mind, clattering around until I saw something that held the memory in place; fixed it. Like the houses. Most of them sat squat and gray, unpainted, the square little boxes I remembered from Crum and Black Hawk, the same houses I saw in Doane and out on the edge of Williamson. Two rows of them here, facing each other, as though someone had thought to place them so one could always watch the other, each house with a guardian neighbor across the flat, wide yard, almost like a park, that separated the rows, brooding pine trees hanging tall above everything. You could drive a car right up between the two rows of houses, but nobody did. They pulled their cars off under the trees and left them there, mostly out of the way, the cars that would run parked next to cars that wouldn't, cars that hadn't run in years, cars with chicken nests in the back seats.

It was just like it had been the first time, when Jason handed me my motorcycle, and John Three had handed me a dollar.

I had tried to get Yvonne to come with me, but she wouldn't. Said if Wimpo found out about it, she'd lose her job. Said I shouldn't go, either, not if I wanted to fit in.

They seemed to know I was coming. There were people on the front porches and in between the houses, sitting, swinging on porch swings that looked to have been hand-built. They were there, in their places, and they seemed relaxed, comfortable. But they didn't take their eyes from me.

A tall, slender man in a sleeveless undershirt was stirring a fire in a metal barrel that had been cut in half. He put a wire refrigerator shelf over the top of the barrel and started taking pieces of chicken from a bucket, dropping them on the shelf. Almost immediately you could smell them cooking. A woman in a bright flowered dress pushed a small child in a swing hanging from a pine tree. The swing was an automobile tire, hung flat, level with the ground, the center covered with a burlap bag tied loosely there, hanging down through the center of the tire, the child nestled down in the bag, laughing, watching the woman intently. From somewhere down the row of houses I heard a screen door slam and a child yell and a dog bark, both of them chasing someone, something.

I just kept walking, slowly, hoping I could find Brother Jason or John Three or somebody who maybe had seen me at Murphy Beach, somebody who would know I wasn't there to cause any trouble. Hoping I would see Evangeline.

At the first house on my right an old woman was sweeping her bare dirt yard, the broom moving in slow, short arcs in the sun, pushing the pine needles and the chicken droppings without raising dust, the heat of the dirt rising up around her long skirt. As I walked past her she stopped sweeping, holding the broom in front of her with both hands and turning as I went past, her face flat and open, unafraid. It was her. The old woman from the hotdog stand.

I thought I should talk to her, say something, anything, but before I could get any words in my brain and in my mouth I heard Brother Jason's deep voice from somewhere up the line of houses.

"Lookie here, y'all, we got ourselves our very own white boy come to Sunday dinner."

Brother Jason and John Three and Evangeline and a bunch of people I didn't know and me . . . we sat at a huge plank table in Jason's back yard, drinking iced tea from Mason jars. The ice came from a single block that must have weighed thirty or forty pounds to start with, but now was whittled down considerably as people took the ice pick and knicked off pieces to drop into their jars of iced tea, Royal Crown, and Dr. Pepper.

We had chicken off the refrigerator grill and a pot of greens that Evangeline cooked in her kitchen, brought to the table in the pot she cooked them in. There were fried potatoes served on a wooden plank and a bowl of light brown gravy made from the leavings of somebody's fried pork chops. Loaves of white bread lay opened around the table, most of the men using slices of bread as plates and napkins, picking up a piece of chicken and carrying it around in a slice of bread, and then eating the bread when the chicken was gone.

One of the women had made red Jell-O in a bucket and it sat on the end of the table, a ladle sticking out of it. Kids would walk by, drop a ladle of Jell-O on a plate, and disappear around the side of the house.

The afternoon was spent eating, visiting, and story-telling. The dinner went on and on, some of the people eating, waiting, and then starting over again after they had a walk around the houses or off through the woods.

I ate and talked and walked and generally felt better than I had in a long time, looking up now and then expecting to see Long Neck or Slick Jesse or maybe even Lard come walking by, just to say howdy. It was all just like home. Just a different color.

I was hungry — I was always hungry — but I tried not to eat too much. I was a guest and I didn't want to wear out my welcome, particularly since they didn't seem to mind that I was there, Jason and John Three getting a kick out of the way the other folks would walk by and check me out.

But Jason ate. Goddamn, Jason ate.

All the plates were in use but that didn't bother Jason. He took a serving bowl from a cupboard and ladled some fried potatoes in it, then poured some gravy on top. He ate with a serving spoon and it seemed about right for him. The men grinned and the women laughed outright, but that didn't seem to bother Jason. He just kept eating.

As he ate pieces of chicken he dropped the bones down beside him and I thought he was dropping them on the ground. Instead, he was dropping them in a bucket and as the day went on the bucket got full, actually full, of chicken bones. When he finished a piece he never even reached for another one. Evangeline or one of the other women would just put some chicken in front of him, and it would go the way of the other pieces, the naked, sucked-slick bones ending up in the bucket.

And he drank his iced tea from a two-quart jar . . .

Cyrus ate out of a serving bowl.

I loved to go to Cyrus and Lydia's house to eat. It wasn't the eating, exactly, that I went there for, it was the watching.

Cyrus was some sort of relation, like most everyone else up there on Black Hawk Ridge, but no one could ever explain it to me so that I could understand. A distant cousin. Maybe some sort of uncle. It didn't matter. All that mattered was that he was a relative, Long Neck liked him, I liked him, and he was no crazier than most of the other people on the Ridge.

What Cyrus could do better than anyone I ever knew, was eat.

On hot summer Sundays, they would set the table up on the front porch of the house, four or five long, stiff planks from the pile out by the barn laid across some saw-horses. You had to be careful sliding your hands along the planks because of the splinters in the rough-cut wood. Cyrus sat at the end, near the kitchen door, his huge hips spread down into the cane bottom of a rocking chair big enough to hold two men, a chair Cyrus had built himself. The table would be set up for breakfast, and it would stay there the whole day.

For breakfast, Cyrus liked store-bought cereal. He ate it out of a serving bowl, the bowl that Lydia used at dinner to put the mashed potatoes in. Lydia would buy the boxes of cereal a dozen at a time from the general store down at Dunlow. I don't remember what kind of cereal it was, maybe Cheerios, maybe Wheaties. I just don't remember. Whatever it was, Cyrus would eat half a box at a time, covered with sugar and fresh milk from his own cows, ladling it up with a serving spoon. In the fall, Lydia would slice up fresh apples, fry them a little with some butter and sugar in a cast-iron pan, and spread them on the cereal. When she did that, Cyrus would have a second helping, sometimes finishing a whole box of cereal.

I would sit at the table, eating a slice of warm bread covered with the fried apples, and watch Cyrus eat. It was a sight to be remembered.

At dinner, with people from the church dropping by, the table would be so loaded with food that the planks would sag. Cyrus would sit in the same place — sometimes I don't think he moved at all, not all day Sunday — talking and eating at the same time. At dinner, he ate from a huge platter, a thing about twice the size of a plate, and Lydia kept it loaded for him. Lydia kept everybody's plate loaded. In all the times I ate there, I never saw Lydia sit at the table. She was always in motion, drifting from the stove to the table, ghosting along behind the chairs, a bowl of something in her hand, looking for a blank space on your plate. When I started getting full and thought I couldn't eat any more, I would watch for Lydia and her bowl and then lean forward over my plate when she came by, so she couldn't ladle any more food onto it.

Supper, Lydia gathered all the things that hadn't been eaten during the day, and they ended up on the table. Cyrus and Lydia were usually alone at supper, unless I was there, but I didn't count as company. I was just there. If Cyrus wanted one of the leftovers, he picked up the bowl and ate from it, whatever it was, Lydia quietly shoving another bowl within reach.

When Lydia baked pies she cut them in half. She would take one half of each pie and cut it in smaller pieces, normal size, for serving to normal people. The other half, she left in the pie plate. For his desert, Cyrus would eat half a pie, right out of the pie plate.

In a way, Cyrus was something special. No one ever knew how much he weighed. Cyrus said he weighed more than the average man, but less than the average horse. But not by much.

Jason was different. There was something about him I couldn't figure out, something that didn't fit. He talked like black men talk in the movies, sing-song words that bubbled out mainly for sound effect. Except Jason's voice was deeper. Much deeper. And then, when things were quiet and calm, when there was just Jason and me or maybe Evangeline or John Three, there would be a different voice, words that were clear and correct with no rounded edges, smooth and crisp words, deep thick sounds, words that slipped off his tongue like dark rose petals falling.

And, once or twice, I heard something in his voice that had an edge to it, like maybe he was holding some feeling down deep in there where it was hot, simmering a little, hurting him.

"Heard you like hotdogs," he said. The movie-Negro voice was gone. "Heard you have trouble buying them, though. Something about supply and demand."

I wasn't exactly sure what he was talking about, but I got the general idea.

"I wasn't trying to start nothing. Guess maybe I didn't know exactly what I was doing, or why I was doing it."

"Heard you pulled a white girl out of the water the other night, down by the pier." He took a bite of chicken.

"Yeah. Did. Wasn't nothing. Just lucky to find her. Truth be told, didn't know what I was doing then, neither."

"Didn't have to pull her out at all. Wasn't really your problem."

I thought about that. "Couldn't just let it go, couldn't let her go. Long Neck wouldn't like it."

He stopped chewing. "Who?"

"Nothing. Never mind."

"Would you have pulled her out if she had been a black girl?"

"I never thought about her color. Just thought she was out there and I was supposed to bring her in." I thought I'd take a small risk ". . . and, besides, it was really dark. Ain't we all the same in the dark?"

He grinned at me across another piece of chicken. "Jesse, my man, I think you've got it figured out, only you just don't know it, yet. You see, the important thing is to do what's right. It might not even be important to know why you've done it. Strange how that works, isn't it?"

Evangeline sat by me at the big table, now and then reaching across me to get something, brushing her arm against mine, not looking at me a lot, enjoying the hell out of making me uncomfortable. I was trying not to stare at her, trying not to feel her presence, trying not to smell the nearness of her, the soft scent of something deep and southern curving down on me when she moved. I remembered her on the beach and the way her hips moved under the thin blue bathing suit when she walked away from me. She was so close I could hardly talk.

I tried not to stare at her but it was no use and I knew she was doing everything, making every move, on purpose. She was cooking me.

John Three sat under a tree and watched the whole thing, enjoying it. Brother Jason just kept eating.

The back seat had been pulled out of one of the old cars and tied against a tree with a piece of clothesline. John Three and I sat there, our legs stretched out into the sun.

"Uh, John Three, I don't mean to get personal and all, but how come you work at Banger's? I mean, knowing how he feels about . . . uh . . ."

He grinned. "How he feels about us gentle folk of color, you mean?" He was using his preacher voice. "See, Jesse, down here, most of us has got to work for the white man. Not many jobs down here the white man don't control."

I had never thought of anyone controlling jobs. I hadn't really thought about jobs in any other sense except just working them.

"What'll you do when the summer's over? Banger closes after Labor Day. Already told me I won't have no job after that."

"Some of us fish a little. Got a boat down on one of the sloughs.

"You know, you want to hang around, you might could get a job fishing. They's other boats down there . . ."

We sat silently, like two friends who don't have to talk. The sun slid down through the trees, warming our bellies and then our chests. We were both getting sleepy.

Somewhere up the line of houses I could see smoke rising gently from a front porch. A woman had built a small fire in a coal bucket and then dumped dampened wood chips in on top of it to make smoke, the smoke rising and spreading against the porch roof, drifting out into the yard, chasing away mosquitoes and other bugs that had begun to move through the woods.

It was Sunday.

It was Sunday back there in Kentucky, too, and Eli and those church folks would be eating out in Eli's yard, passing the huge bowls . . . And maybe Lard, too. Eli and Lard. To save my own ass, I had run away from them without a word, without a second thought, without . . . anything. I had just run. And now, they were back there in the shade of Eli's huge elm tree, eating, maybe now and then looking up at the tiny widow off there in the barn.

I never ate at Eli's house on Sunday.

But I ate at the Homeplace on Sunday.

"That Jason, he surely can eat," John mumbled, his voice drowsy.

"Reminds me of my cousin, Cyrus. At least, I think he's my cousin."

"You hillbillies have trouble keeping up with who's a relative and who isn't? I heard that about you folks." He wasn't using his preacher voice and he was enjoying himself.

"He sure does like chicken."

"Yes," John Three laughed, "and he sure does like hotdogs, too." He let his laugh trail off. "And so does his grandmother."

I didn't answer, and we trailed off into silence for a while.

"I think Evangeline likes you," he mumbled, his voice drowsy. He wasn't using his preacher voice.

"Well . . . uh . . ."

"Maybe you could take her down to the pavilion some night. Take her dancing. Buy her a beer." His face was turned to the sun, his eyes half closed.

"You really think I could do that?" I could see the pavilion, see the college boys, see Banger, see Deputy Pork.

"Only if you have a sincere desire to see your Maker, Jesse boy."

I waited. He said nothing else, and I realized he was asleep.

We were walking back toward the way I had come in, Jason and me. I always thought of myself as a big guy, big chest, big shoulders . . . big mouth. As far as size was concerned, walking beside Jason was one of the most humbling experiences of my life. He threw enough shade, your whole family could have a picnic and not get sunburned.

We got to his grandmother's house.

"This is as far as I go, white boy. Got to fix the railing on grandmama's back porch." Still in that voice that didn't have any black in it.

He stuck out his hand and I took it, held it.

"Thanks for the dinner, Brother Jason," I said seriously. "And for the . . . learning."

He gripped my hand — a little. I realized if he wanted to, he could squeeze my hand into pulp.

"Always glad to be of service," he said.

He turned and looked at his grandmother's little house.

"Don't it beat all," he chuckled, "how some women just have a way with flowers? I mean, they can just grow flowers *anywhere*." He let go of my hand and walked away, around the side of the house.

I looked at the flowers again, the colors spilling over everything, wondering how long it had taken her to get it all just right, just where she wanted. At the side of the steps leading up to the porch a large patch of flowers grew from some tangled mass of metal that she was using as a flower box, the whole thing sitting on top of a stack of broken cinder blocks. The flowers and small vines grew on it, in it, around it, up through it, dripping down off the sides, pushing and twining and reaching for the light. At first, I thought the metal was a bunch of old car parts.

Until I saw the handlebar sticking up through a batch of little yellow blossoms.

It was one of the best Sundays I ever had in my life.

≈ Thirty-Six ≈

The summer was coming to an end and if Hugo and I had let it alone it would have just run out on the sand, quietly, without any sort of notice, without even one of Banger's firecrackers. The days would have grown cooler, the people mostly gone, Hugo back home, in college. All of it gone without a whimper. If we had just let it alone.

But, no, we couldn't do that. We had to organize the Great Shark Hunt.

It was one of those days so hot, so still, that nothing on the beach seemed to have the energy to move. Sweat ran down my body, pushing out in little bubbles through my coating of motor oil; my brain groggy. Hugo was in his chair, struggling to stay awake. Even from where I was I could see his head nodding.

He must have heard the yelling before I did because I saw him leap out of his chair and run wildly toward the water, not even stopping to grab the float ring. A split second later I heard it — someone, a woman, I thought; a piercing scream that rode into the beach over the tops of some other yelling; deeper sounds, closer in.

I stood on my chair, trying to see what was happening. Hugo was in the water now, legs pumping high, trying to run as far out into the surf as he could before he dove into a swimming stroke. Out beyond him, almost to the end of the pier, I could see someone swimming for shore. I had never seen arms and legs flail like that before, a thrashing, churning motion that beat the water into foam as the swimmer drove for the beach. It was a woman, and each time her head came up for air she screamed something.

Several other people were in the water, but only about up to their knees, watching her, yelling, waving their arms. Some of them were men, their deeper voices underlining the shrieking of the woman. No one went into the water after her except Hugo.

The float ring was in my hand and I was running down the beach before I knew I was going. But by the time I got there the woman and Hugo had met in the water. Hugo said later that when he got to her, she didn't even slow down, just stiff-armed him out of the way and kept going. As she went by, one of her feet kicked up and hit him full on the nose. He felt the warm drip start to come. He said he rolled backward, out of her way, treading water, knowing that he was bleeding. He watched her go, hearing her screaming. And then he realized what she was yelling.

Shark! She was yelling *shark*! And he was bleeding in the water.

Hugo beat her to the beach.

C'mon, Jesse!" Hugo was whispering, leaning against my chair but not looking at me, trying to pretend he was concentrating on the water. He didn't have to concentrate very hard; there was no one swimming.

"Man, if you think the women went ape shit over that jellyfish crap, wait 'till we give 'em a shark hunt!"

He would talk me into it. Again. I knew he would. He had talked me into the first jellyfish rodeo, and now he would talk me into a shark hunt. In a way, I owed him. After all, the jellyfish rodeo did hook me up with Rosalind.

"How do we do it? I mean, *if* we do it — and I ain't saying I will, you know what I mean?"

He grinned. He knew he had me. "Easy. No sweat. We do it just like we do the jellyfish rodeo, 'cept we don't use any nets." He waited, for effect, I thought. "We use spears."

"Spears!? I ain't hunting no fuckin' shark with a spear! Nor with anything else, neither! You're out'a your fuckin' mind, boy!"

He looked at me like I didn't have a brain in my head. As far as sharks were concerned, I probably didn't. During the whole summer on the beach I had never seen a shark, had never had anyone report a shark — not until this woman the other day — didn't really know what a real live shark looked like. I had seen pictures, but, *hell*, these were sharks we were talking about, not pictures.

"Look, hillbilly, that woman the other day said she saw a shark, said she saw its fin, said the thing swam right between her legs. You wonder why people haven't been in the water much lately? Sharks, man. Sharks!

"Hell, Jesse, there probably weren't no shark out there in the first place. That's the whole point! We ain't got nothing to worry about. We can go out there, mess around a little bit with some old fishing spears, then come back in and be heroes again."

He would talk me into it again.

We were out beyond the end of the pier, balanced on our little inflatable beach floats, trying to keep our body parts out of the water. Each of us had an old fishing spear, the kind that the divers sometimes used. Neither of us knew what the hell to do with them.

Back on the beach a gaggle of girls stood at the edge of the water, motionless, some of them with their hands to their mouths. You would think, by now, they would know the game. They didn't.

Hugo and I paddled around in a circle, our spears raised, our faces tense, hunting sharks. Sunlight sprinkled the tops of the gentle swells, glinting, sparkling. Now and then one of us would viciously ram his spear in the water, and then jerk it out again, trying to look disappointed; another shark got away. Actually, we had agreed that if one of us saw a shark, or anything else he couldn't identify, he would tell the other and we would get the hell out of there, trying not to look panicked.

We had drifted in a little, almost to the end of the pier. Hugo paddled over to me, nodded his head toward the beach. "I want the tall one, the redhead. Which one you want?"

"Well . . . " I mumbled, not knowing where to go with it, thinking about Yvonne and Evangeline.

The sound of the gunshot cut me off, the thunder of it somehow flattened by the open surface of the ocean, but still loud enough to stop our breathing.

Both of us rolled into the water. I dropped my spear, clinging with both hands to the float. High above us on the end of the pier Deputy Pork leaned over the railing, a heavy rifle in his hands. He raised the gun slowly, pointed it down between us, and pulled the trigger.

In the woods, when Long Neck would fire his shotgun, the blast would be trapped among the trees, slamming back and forth past my skull until I thought I would fall down just from the pain of it. But out here on the water it was different; the sound cracked down against our brains and then was gone before the spray raised by the bullet fell back to the surface. He had fired the bullet exactly between Hugo and me.

"Almost got that 'en, boys! You got to get out of there. They's *sharks* all over!"

The lying son-of-a-bitch. There weren't any sharks, and we all knew it.

"Don't shoot!" Hugo screamed. "Goddammit, don't shoot!"

"Hell, boys, got to pro-tect you! That's my job!"

He was grinning, a gash of teeth across the front of his red face. And he was raising the rifle again.

About halfway back down the pier another deputy was blocking the way, keeping people from seeing what was going on. I knew they all thought Pork really was protecting us from sharks.

"You, black-haired boy!" Pork yelled down, his voice dropping a little.

"Yeah! What you want?" Hugo yelled up.

"I want you to paddle away, in toward the shore, away from those sharks there! You be safer!"

Hugo peeked at me from behind his float, then yelled up at Pork. "Okay! We can get going right now . . . "

"I didn't say *we*!" Pork shouted, "I said *you*! Now git!"

The rifle was pointed directly at us. "It's okay," I whispered over to Hugo. "He won't do nothing to me out here, not in front of all them people. Go on. Get moving."

Hugo hesitated, but he really had no choice. He began to swim for shore, pulling the float.

"Now, boy, I want you to hear me real good."

I looked up at Pork. He was leaning over the railing, the rifle dangling in his hand, not really shouting, but making sure I could hear every word.

"One thing we don't like around here is Northern white boys mixing in with folks they don't supposed to be mixing with. You know what I mean, boy? Mixing in. Visiting. Talking about stuff . . . ideas and things. Causing trouble. You under-stand, boy?"

Jesus Christ, he was talking about the Homeplace. How the hell did he know I'd been to the Homeplace? And what difference did it make, anyway?

I don't think I'm stupid. Really, I'm not. But there have been times in my life when things just went right by me, mostly because I had never seen them before, or maybe because I thought I would never see them again, or because what was going on was so strange to me that it just didn't register, didn't work its way through my skull and into that part of my brain where danger is supposed to register, where survival is supposed to live. I just missed it, somehow, whatever it was, and it always caught me napping, always caused me trouble.

Eventually, I learned. And I learned now, out here in the water trying to hide behind a piece of rubberized canvas directly beneath a man with a rifle who didn't know anything about me and who didn't care; a man who had a first name but I didn't know it but he hated me anyway; a man who could hate me for being born north of South Carolina and for having one of the best Sunday dinners I had ever had in my whole fucking life and having it with black people who took pity on me because they were all smarter than I was and probably figured I would never live to be twenty.

Unless I got out of South Carolina.

Well, fuck him. I wasn't going. I liked it here, liked this place with its funny kinds of trees and hard sand and salt water and thick sunshine. I liked knowing there was a bookstore down in Myrtle and places where I could buy a beer and not having to worry about re-chinking the cabin because winter might be hard this year, the squirrel tails being extra bushy, and all.

"Wasn't causing no trouble!" I was getting angry now. "Was just visiting with some folks . . ."

He wasn't listening, didn't really give a damn. He leaned farther out over the railing. "You trying to mess with my place down here, boy, mess with how we live. So, you know what I'm going do in return? Huh, boy? Well. . . I'm going to fuck with your des-tin-y."

And the son-of-a-bitch shot a hole through my beach float.

❧ Thirty-Seven ❧

Tuesday, the day after Labor Day.

We had closed the rental shack the evening before, carrying all the stuff up to the pavilion and stacking it in the storage room. When the rental shack was empty, all the beach floats deflated and gone, it was a bad place to sleep. Even for me. And besides, Banger always hauled the shack to some storage yard for the winter. So, last night, I had slept in the rest rooms. It had been quiet in there, deserted, no one down there at first light to get an early start on the beach.

The day before, while we had been were working in the storage room, I noticed a key hanging on a nail behind the door. It was a key to the back door and I doubted if Banger even knew it was there. I dropped it in my pocket. We were coming down hard on the end of summer and I wanted all the help I could get, even if it meant stealing a key to the storage room. Because Banger had made it clear: the day after Labor Day, nobody had a job. The season was over.

The sun was hardly up when I walked out of the rest rooms, carrying my old canvas bag.

Hugo was gone. We had shared a last beer at the pavilion — Hugo swiped the beer from the old cooler behind the bar when Banger went to take a piss — and then we just sat there for a while, staring out at the ocean. Finally, Hugo put his hand on my shoulder. I turned toward him, sticking out my hand, but he was already walking across the dance floor, then out the other side of the pavilion. In a few seconds he was gone into the darkness. Somehow, Hugo knew he would never see me again.

I was on the outside again, about to be locked out, standing there alone, with everything I owned in the world stuffed inside a bag that was stained, worn, and smelled like sun tan lotion and motor oil.

But something felt different. Usually, I like the idea of being outside, not belonging, wanting to be gone. And if I didn't really like it, I was at least familiar with it, used to it. Back at

Black Hawk Ridge, back at Crum, I would have been glad to be standing on a road with my bag packed, ready to leave. And here I was again, doing just that. But somehow it wasn't the same, this time. It just wasn't the same.

I hung the bag from my shoulder and started up toward the pavilion, shuffling along in the weak silvered light that separated the night from the booming sunrise of the beach. Banger owed me for my last week's work and I thought I would collect my money, wander down to the pier, take one last look, poke around a little. And then I would just walk the hell away from Cherry Hill, just walk away from whatever this feeling was that kept running down my back. Walk away. Doing what I did best. Leaving.

Maybe walk all the way to Myrtle Beach.

Maybe hitchhike farther down the coast, to one of those towns Hugo used to talk about.

Maybe get a job down there.

Maybe not.

When I got to the pavilion it was closed tighter than Banger's heart, all the shutters hung and locked from the inside. Without even thinking about it I knew Banger would be halfway to Ft. Myers, driving his convertible hard, the top down, the wind driving around the windshield and blowing out his mind. My last week's pay in his wallet. The son-of-a-bitch.

I fingered the key in my pocket but decided not to mess with the storage room door, not just yet. Maybe something else would turn up. Anyway, I didn't feel too guilty about having the key, now. I was broke because of Banger; the bastard owed me.

I turned down toward the beach and took a few steps out onto the sand.

And then I stopped. The sight sort of stunned me and all I could think to do was . . . sit down. I dropped the bag and melted down on top of it, my knees weak. What got to me was not something I saw, it was something I *didn't* see: for the first time in my life I was looking at an absolutely deserted beach. I was looking at nothing, absolutely nothing. There was the beach, of course, and the water, and the pier . . . but there were no people, not anyone, not anywhere. As far as I could see up and down the beach there were no walkers, no swimmers, no girls spreading out their towels in their favorite places, getting an early start on the sunrise; no one on the pier. The lifeguard chairs were gone, the rental shack hauled away. No umbrellas on the sand. Not a bottle. Not a forgotten towel.

No one.

Nothing.

It was the most beautiful sight I had ever seen in my life.

The tide was out and the water lapped weakly against the pilings of the pier. An offshore breeze pushed gently against my back. Far out on the water a fishing boat moved silently across the horizon, too far away for me to hear it, a ghost boat, a silhouette skimming the water at sunrise.

And right there, with nothing in the world that belonged to me but the junk in my canvas bag; right there, with the sun coming up and pouring light onto the best sight I had ever seen; right there, breathing air scented with some sweetness carried from the pine forests back of town; right there, knowing Yvonne was so close; right there . . .

Right there, I decided to stay.

All those years growing up on the Black Hawk, those years going to school in Crum . . . all that time I knew I didn't belong, that it was all a mistake; I shouldn't be there. In my mind I lived somewhere else, I just hadn't found it yet, hadn't had time to look, was too young to go looking, was not smart enough or tough enough to just get out.

I wasn't too young any more. And I was smarter. I had left Black Hawk, busted out of Crum, escaped Kentucky, and now here I was, in a place I had never really counted on, didn't know existed, a place where beautiful girls came every summer and where no one seemed to work, a place where the breeze smelled like something ancient and fulfilling, where the same ocean that washed the sand here was washing sand on a hundred other distant shores, places I could find out about and maybe go to one day. They were all there, just on the other side of the water, this water, this same water.

This water. During the summer I had learned that I could sit and just stare at it, sometimes for hours. There was something about it that was never the same, not any two times in a row, not ever. Each time, each look, it was a different ocean, always pulling me, always settling me.

I belonged here with this ocean.

Deciding to stay was the easy part.

After Labor Day, there was absolutely nothing to do at Cherry Hill Beach. No jobs, I mean. The day after Labor Day, the people didn't come to the beach anymore. They locked up their beach cottages, took the furniture off the porches, had the water turned off, shuttered the windows, went home, went back to school, went back to their businesses . . . whatever. I would learn later that a few of them did stay, did hang around to watch the winter creep up on the beach, but they were the hard-liners, like I wanted to be, people who liked the deserted beach and came down there only to walk on deserted sand, to watch the pier gather light in the morning. You didn't see much of them, and they liked it that way.

The pavilion was the only business in the area and when it closed Cherry Hill stopped functioning.

I went back up to the pavilion, made sure no one saw me, and opened the door to the storage room. I left the bag in there, walked out to the highway and hitchhiked down to Myrtle. I figured, if there were any jobs to be had, they would be down there. And, besides, Yvonne was there.

I didn't stay at Yvonne's house. I didn't even ask her. It just wasn't the time to do that. When the time came, I wanted it to be the right time.

For three days I went back and forth, hitching down to Myrtle in the mornings, back to Cherry at night, slipping into the storage room after it got dark and slipping out again before it got light. Banger had never fixed the lights but I wouldn't have turned them on anyway, afraid that someone would notice, and I crashed around a lot until I got the hang of the place. There was some stuff to eat in there, mostly stale buns and some cans of hotdog sauce. I helped myself. Thought Banger would never know. I checked the place out pretty well, looking for something I could use, but there wasn't much. I found a stash of Banger's firecrackers and some matches hidden on top of a stack of soap cartons, big boxes of commercial detergent Banger used behind the bar. They weighed maybe twenty pounds each and were stacked higher than my head. I was tired of Banger's goddamn firecrackers and I thought about throwing them out, letting them get wet. But I didn't. But I did stick the matches in my pocket.

The door from the storage room into the pavilion was locked and I didn't have a key, so I couldn't get in there to heat up anything. It didn't really matter. At least I had food, a place to sleep, and no one knew I was there. And I thought that, sooner or later, I would get a job in Myrtle and be able to work things out. Be closer to Yvonne.

Someone knew I was there.

On the fourth morning I awoke in the usual blackness, knowing that I had to get up and out of the room before full light. The air in the storage room was heavy with the smell of coming rain and I didn't even have to look outside to know that a thick layer of clouds was covering the area like a shroud. I pulled on my shirt and jeans and an old pair of tennis shoes, the same sort of clothing I had been wearing all summer. Everything else I owned — and it wasn't much — I kept stuffed in the bag, ready to go.

I stepped toward the door. A small sound from outside stopped me, the muffled closing of a car door, the sound it makes when you try to close the door without making any noise. But there is always noise. And then I heard the faint rattle of the lock being checked. Only, I knew, there was no lock there to check. That was the one problem of sleeping in the storage room. The hasp and lock were on the *outside*, which was okay for getting in, but, once inside, there was no way to lock the door. To make sure I didn't get locked inside, I brought the lock inside with me each night.

If you wanted to know whether anyone was inside the storage room, all you had to do was look at the lock. It wouldn't be there.

And now someone was checking the hasp, moving it back against the door.

I crawled behind the stack of soap boxes, moving a couple of them to hide me better, but they didn't really do the job. There was no time to do anything else.

I peeked through a crack between the boxes. With any luck, it was just some beach guy out there, noticing that the door lock was gone, some guy like me, some poor jerk looking for a place to sleep.

The door opened slowly. A shape filled the gap, a shape outlined against the gray and clouded background of pre-dawn, a shape I didn't even have to see all of to know what it was, who it was. All I needed to see was the hat.

No, it wasn't a guy like me, a beach guy looking for some place to hide out. It was Deputy Pork.

He eased through and moved quickly to the side of the door, his back pressed against the wall. He stood there in the dark, silent, motionless, waiting. I couldn't even hear him breathing. Whatever he thinks is in here, I thought, *whoever* he thinks is in here, he isn't afraid.

I heard the click of the broken light switch, and then another click as he tried it again. Then a brilliant beam of light bored through the gloom and hit a dead refrigerator on the far side of the room, then moved in little jerks back and forth across the walls, the piles of junk, the cardboard cartons, everything. He didn't sweep the light, he moved it quickly, a step at a time, stopping it, examining what it lit up, then moving it again. I could tell by the angle that he was holding the light as far away from himself and as far up as he could reach. And I wondered if he had his gun in his other hand.

The light hit the soap cartons and stopped and my breath caught in my stomach. Not in my throat, but in my stomach. How my lungs got down there, I'll never know.

The light moved on. I breathed again. And then . . .

"All right. You just keep hiding. I have plenty of time. I'll be right here when you decide to come on out."

He paused. I froze, hearing the voice, knowing I would never forget the sound of it, the way he said the words so perfectly, the smooth, low resonance of it . . . the anger that hid behind it.

"Be better on you," he said, still in that low cobra sound, "if you just come on out here. You haven't done anything yet that's all that terrible bad. But if I ask you to come on out here, and you don't come, well, now, that'd be resisting arrest. You know about that? Resisting arrest?"

He knew my name. I was sure of that, sure that he had known my name from the first time he ever saw me in the pavilion, knew that he would know all the names of people he thought he might come to hate. And, now, he didn't call me by name — so he didn't know who was here, in the room with him, waiting. If he had known it was me, he probably would have put down the gun, turned out the flashlight and just crashed around in the room until he found me.

And then what? He had tried to run me off the road once, me, a total stranger. He had fired a rifle at me, made me piss in the water out of fear. What would he do now, here, especially if he found out it was me?

And if he found out it was me, there would be no way I could stay on the beach, no way to stay in this county.

No way I could stay.

Dawn was coming, the heavy light growing in the door.

"Tell you what," the low voice said. And my hair stood up. He had moved right next to me, right beside the stack of soap cartons. I had not heard him move. "Tell you what. You don't want to come out, that's all right. Just makes things a little bit more interesting. But I haven't got all night, so I have to move things on a little bit. So what I'm goin' to do is, I'm goin' to let my friend here help me poke into all the dark corners."

His friend? Jesus, there was someone else with him, someone else in the room, and I hadn't even heard them come in.

He fired his pistol into the detergent boxes.

I fell, smashing back against the wall, just from the sound of it.

I don't think he meant to do that, hit a bunch of detergent boxes. He probably didn't know what the hell he was going to hit, but I'll bet he didn't mean to hit soap boxes. The damned things exploded, flakes of soap filling the air instantly, a white, choking cloud that seemed to be everywhere at once. I heard him thrash around, curse and cough and choke, all at the same time. I was hoping, over the sound of his coughing, that he couldn't hear the sounds of my gagging.

But, whether he knew it or not, he had found me. I had to get out of there.

I lit the box of firecrackers, the whole damn box.

When the first of the firecrackers went off he screamed and threw himself on the floor, another huge cloud of white rising from the falling of his body.

I leaped over him. "DIE! DIE, you son-of-a-bitch! Take that!"

The firecrackers were machine-gunning in the room, Polk squirming into a corner, his arms clamped over his head.

I pulled another box of soap over onto the floor and ripped it open, kicking at it as I went by, leaping toward the door as the white, choking cloud spread through the room.

Then I made a mistake. I looked back. Even in the confusion, Polk had figured out that he wasn't being shot at and he was on his knees now, right behind me, dragging his arm across his eyes trying to wipe away the soap, the pistol waggling in front of him.

He fired.

I leaped out the door as the gun went off. I don't know what he hit, but it wasn't me.

Where the hell could I go? Where? Down the open beach? Down one of the lanes? He would catch me in the open, or in a corner, catch me someplace, anyplace, catch me with the car. Catch me with a bullet.

The big Ford was parked straight out from the door, next to a low fence that was supposed to keep sand from drifting up against the back of the pavilion. He must have coasted the car in there. I sure as hell never heard him pull up.

I didn't have a choice. I dived under the car and scooted across, coming up on the other side, barely room to move between the car and the fence. I eased back under the car, turning crossways, peeking out behind a tire. Dawn was coming strong now, but so was the rain, the light growing but the clouds thicker, pressing down across the horizon and running hard toward the beach.

The firecrackers had burned out. I could hear Polk coughing and cursing, trying to blow the soap out of his mouth and nose, slamming things against the wall. And then he screamed. It was one of those screams of total anger, total frustration, something deep and primitive, a sound like driving a nail through your mind. He burst through the door and slammed his feet into the sand, twisting, waving his gun around, desperate to do some damage, to hurt someone. He was a snarling ghost, totally white, the soap covering, coating, sticking to every part of him. When he moved, it came off him in puffs, small clouds of cleanliness drifting away from his huge frame like steam from a freight train.

He ran to the corner of the pavilion and slid to a stop, looking. Ran back to the other corner, looking, holding the gun up high now, wanting to bring it down to bear, wanting to use the sights in the growing light, wanting to pull the trigger. He knew somebody was there. It was only a matter of time.

And then he looked at the pier. I wasn't on the beach, I didn't have time to clear one of the lanes, and I was on foot. I had to be on the pier. He stared at the pier for long seconds. There was a sharp 'click' and I knew he had cocked the pistol. He wanted to be completely ready. He moved off toward the pier, directly across the beach, walking steadily, deliberately, the gun out in front of him. An executioner.

He never thought to look for me less than twenty feet from the storage room door.

I watched him go, every part of me wanting to leap and run. But I waited. If he were going to check the pier, I knew he would check every inch of it, all the way out to the end where the benches and tables were. I wanted him to do that, to get his ass way out on the pier, before I made a move.

When he was about halfway out there I crawled from under the car. I wanted to get my bag out of the storage room. It was a risk but, hell, I needed that bag. It was all I had. I stepped inside, grabbed it, and popped out again. He was still working his way along the pier, not looking back, sure he had me trapped out there.

The windows of the Ford were open and I looked inside, thinking there might be something I could use. There was a bunch of stuff, but what really caught my eye was . . . the windows were open.

I dropped the bag, went back inside the storage room and carried out a carton of soap under each arm. I ripped them open and stood just back from the open car windows, then slammed one of the boxes through the front window, one through the back. The inside of the car turned into a solid, white mass, thick clouds of soap boiling up to the roof and out the windows, filtering into every opening, every crack.

The boxes made heavy thumping noises when they burst and maybe he heard me, but it didn't matter. I had a head start.

I grabbed my bag and started away. Then stopped.

His gas cap should have been the locking kind, but it wasn't. It came off in a single twist. I dumped a double handful of the soap into the tank, replaced the cap, and wiped off the extra soap. Maybe he wouldn't notice.

I picked up the bag, vaulted over the low fence, and headed off toward Myrtle.

Before I got out to the highway it started to rain, one of those driving, slanting rains that would probably last all day.

Thirty-Eight

"One of the funniest sights I ever did see," Jason said, laughing, leaning his ass back against the boat. He was using the movie-Negro voice again. He sounded like some black man in an Abbott and Costello film.

"He go past me like a shot, me standing on the side of the road trying to hitch me a ride down to Myrtle, that big old Ford car just *rolling*, the soap coming out the windows, Deputy Pork with his head out the window 'cause he can't see from the inside — everything covered with soap! Put my thumb out but, for some reason, he never stop!"

The other men were listening, some of them grinning, some laughing out loud. But some of them not. I wondered about that.

"And then the whole thing, the car, it just come to a stop, just cough and fart a couple times, maybe a belch in there somewhere, then it just roooollll down to nothing and stay there, *dead*.

"He jump out the car and start screaming, start dancing around in the road, waving his arms. And then he pull out his gun. Don't know what he was going to shoot, but I figure right then I be in the wrong place. I take out through the woods, get the hell out'a that scene!"

We were at a rickety boat dock on a slough somewhere up near Murphy Beach. The boat looked like an overgrown rowboat, longer, heavier. I couldn't tell how long it was, maybe twenty feet, maybe more. It was pulled up on the sand near the dock, the men, all from Homeplace, gathered around holding oars, ready to go to work, ready to go fishing. John Three came down to the boat, listened to Jason for a minute, then started folding up a large fishing net. Usually, it took two or three men to pick up the net, but when John Three was finished, Jason picked up the net by himself and set it in the end of the boat.

When we were in the boat and rowing out of the slough toward the open water, one of the men started singing and we rowed to the cadence of the song, oars dipping in the water in perfect rhythm.

When we got out of the slue, to the beach, a couple of the men jumped out of the boat, grabbed the end of the net and started pulling it out of the boat. It was folded so they could do that, just grab the end and play it out over the end of the boat. We rowed in a large arc out through the surf, curving back toward the beach again, the net running out behind us. When we got back into shallow water we shipped the oars, jumped out of the boat and grabbed the net, the whole crew pulling it in to the beach.

Sometimes the net had fish in it, but usually it was empty. We did that all day. It was one of the hardest jobs I ever did in my life.

Problem was, no one would hire me to do anything. Of course, I couldn't really *do* anything; I wasn't a carpenter, I wasn't a plumber . . . I was just a big hillbilly kid who didn't have the sense to go home — or at least just get out of town — once the summer was over. I was clutter. There was no place for me here.

I spent another day or two in Myrtle, hitch-hiking back to Cherry and sleeping on Rosalind's back porch each night, being careful not to let the neighbors know I was there.

I thought about asking Yvonne to stay at her place, but just couldn't bring myself to do it.

The first fishing boat I saw was just north of Cherry, these black guys rowing, sweating, straining against the sea and the net. Some of the boats had more men in them than others and I figured the crews didn't work regular, just took on whoever came along to work that day. Hell, I thought, I can do that.

No one would hire me. I talked to the men who ran the boats; maybe they owned the boats, maybe they didn't, I don't know. All I know is the crew would point out one guy to talk to and I would talk to him, and he would be white and the crews would be black and the white guy would never be out there in the boat. He would be back on shore somewhere, the white guy, and he wouldn't hire me. The guy wouldn't say why, he would just tell me to go away.

Then one guy said why. It was nigger work, he said. Wouldn't be right for a white boy, even an outsider white boy, to mix in.

And then I remembered what John Three had said about a boat and I found the slough and John Three and the men from Homeplace and John Three hired me. I don't think he really wanted to hire me, but I needed the work and a place to stay and he needed another man in the crew. The other men didn't seem too happy to have me around but no one said anything directly and I went to work.

At the end of the very first day I went home with them to Homeplace.

And that, probably more than anything else, started the end of it all.

Sometimes you just live each day, no particular plan, no particular anything, a quiet process of one day following the next. Little things happening, maybe, but nothing really big. You just . . . go along.

But things never stay like that, at least not for me. It's like . . . stacking small rocks on a flat pane of glass. Seemed like, wherever I was, I kept adding something to the load, always adding another rock to the glass, never thinking about it, about how the weight was building up. And then one day the glass broke from the weight of it and all the rocks and the days and the things that added up went rushing and grinding down through the broken place and my life ended up in a mess of hard pieces and jagged edges on the floor.

It happened on Black Hawk Ridge. It happened in Crum. It happened in Bean Camp. And I knew for sure it happened in those places because, somehow, I *wanted* it to. And it was happening again in Horry County, South Carolina. Only, this time, I didn't want it to happen.

There was a small cabin on the far end of Homeplace, as far from the entry road as you could get, and they let me sleep there. The place was empty but John Three put a bed in there and one of the women brought a pile of quilts she had collected from some of the other families and I was as much at home as I had ever been.

Jason and I were sitting out on the small porch of the cabin, our butts on the floor, our backs against the wall, looking down the center of the village. There had been no fish, none at all, and we had quit work a little early that day.

"You comfortable? Feeling a little tired?" Jason in his real voice. I was looking at the blisters on my hands.

"Yeah. Fine."

"How come you get so comfortable here? Don't you know you aren't supposed to be staying around here, with all these black people?"

"Yeah. I just ain't learned yet that all you people are dangerous. Especially you're grandmama. She's right dangerous, that 'un. Gonna kill me for sure. Gonna kill me with all them pies she bakes."

"Speaking of killing, or at least maiming, you know Polk will forever hang tight on your ass, don't you?"

"Why? He can't prove nothin'. He don't know it was me in the pavilion. Can't prove it was me put the soap in the car."

"You don't understand, Jesse. Polk doesn't have to *prove* anything. Let me add it up for you. First," he held up one finger the size of a sausage, "you are the only one around here, *anywhere* around here, who stands out. Not just because you're a white boy working on a black fishing boat and hanging around the Homeplace. It's not just that. Hell, you'd stand out down in Myrtle. There just aren't that many people, especially northern white boys, who hang around here after the summer people leave.

"Second, Polk has got to blame somebody for what happened to his car. He loved that car, man, really loved it. When he was in that car with his pistol, he was the *man*. He can't let it get around that somebody did that to his car and got away with it. He has *got* to nail somebody. Besides, who the hell else would have a *key* to Banger's storage room? Even Polk can figure that one out.

"Third, Polk does a lot of things sort of unofficially. Uses his badge and gun and car as his power, but he's not really being a sheriff's deputy when he does these things. That means he can do a lot of things, bad shit, as long as people stay scared of his badge. You understand?"

I understood. I remembered Constable Clyde Prince and his gun and his way of doing things, whatever he wanted to do whenever he wanted to do it.

"Fourth, you're an ideal candidate. You're not from around here, got no friends — well, except us, and we don't count, not to Polk — can't do his uncle any political damage. Hell, boy, you're elected, you just haven't been sworn in yet." He said all this calmly, now with four fingers in the air like four small telephone posts leaning in the early evening light.

"Why would he want to bother with me? I'm not anybody. If he'd just let me alone, no one'd even know I was around," I mumbled, almost under my breath.

"He can't do that, Jesse. You are a northern white boy down here fooling around with the blacks. That means you a trouble maker, sure as hell. Must be down here organizing something. And Deputy Pork's uncle and all the others like him, well, they look to the deputy to do his duty. Keep the place safe for all those other folks like them. White folks."

"West Virginia ain't north, goddammit."

"Hell, Jesse, Polk, he don't even like people from *North Carolina!*"

We walked down to Jason's house, strolling through the dappled light and smelling the scent of the pines. Wood smoke drifted in thin cotton layers across the tops of the trees. I thought maybe Evangeline would be there, wondering what I would say to a woman who could stop your heartbeat just by smiling. But she wasn't there.

Jason cooked up a bunch of hotdogs and heated up a pot of hotdog sauce Evangeline had made.

"My favorite meal." He was actually licking his lips as he stuffed hotdogs into buns and ladled the sauce on top. He put on so much sauce he had to put the whole assembly on a plate and eat it with a fork.

"Best damn hotdogs on the beach," I mumbled.

"What?"

"Nothing."

"Here, have some." He shoved a plate toward me. The hotdogs were firm and the sauce was spicier than anything I had ever eaten.

"Got to have some of this, too." He took a huge pitcher from the refrigerator and poured us Mason jars of buttermilk.

Buttermilk. God, I remembered the last time I had buttermilk. I remembered clearly.

Jason ate five or six hotdogs and drank half the pitcher of buttermilk and we didn't turn on any lights, just sitting there with the shadows getting thicker and listening to some wild-voiced insects in the woods getting cranked up for the night. Just sitting there. Two friends.

"Jason," I started, not really sure if I should bring it up.

"You want to know about Evangeline." He said it quietly.

"Well, maybe, sometime," I stumbled, "but . . . I been wondering about something else." I waited, but nothing brilliant came to me, so I just said it out loud.

"I been wondering . . . about how you talk."

He laughed, a sound like soft thunder in a train tunnel.

"You mean, you've been wondering why I sometimes sound like Steppin Fetchit, and sometimes like Eisenhower." He laughed again. "No, wait a minute. Not like Eisenhower. Hell, I sound *lots* better than Eisenhower." He let his laughing tail off to nothing. I waited.

"Went to college, Jesse. Learned a lot. But college wasn't real life . . ." His voice rumbled down into the dark. "Came back here.

"You see that squirrel out there, Jesse?" He pointed out the back door into the near darkness. I didn't see anything.

"Yeah, he too gray be seeing him in the dark." His movie voice. "Camouflage, Jesse boy, cam-o-flage.

"That's the diff-er-ence 'tween Deputy Pork and me, Jesse boy. He *want* to talk like me, like this, but he can't. He can't, don't you see? He got to let you know he smart, he been to coll-ege. Got to make you bee-leeve he not just anotha red neck cracker gonna bust you head. But that what he be, Jesse. Just anotha red neck cracker.

"But I have to do it just the other way, Jesse boy. I can't never let them know I's smart."

He turned to face me, looking me full in the eyes.

"Don't you believe that Steppin Fetchit shit, Jesse. Not for a goddamn minute."

Thirty-Nine

It was like walking down a tunnel, the trees overhanging the narrow road into Homeplace, filtering the thin moonlight.

I had been into Myrtle to see Yvonne. I was worried about going into Wimpo's, so I waited until I was sure Wimpo wasn't there. None of the other regulars seemed to recognize me. A couple of them kept watching Yvonne whenever she talked to me, but there was nothing I could do about that. I sat on a stool, sipping the one beer I could afford, talking to her as she worked the bar, watching her move, watching the light tangle in her hair.

I never saw the car. I was almost on it before its lights came on and it pulled out across the road in front of me. A spotlight blazed and hit me full in the face, little flashes of blue pain dancing in my eyes from the brightness of it. I heard a door open and a man's shape cut into the edge of the light.

"Just stay right there, boy."

Polk.

"What's going on? Am I under arrest, or something?" All I wanted to do was melt backwards into the dark.

"You not under arrest, boy. Nothing official about this here little visit. I'll tell you what else you need to hear, when the time is right."

Jesus. I was getting tired of this southern cop bullshit. I took a step backwards.

"I'd stay right there, boy." And I felt the hard snout of a gun barrel in my back.

Polk drove; me in the back. Wimpo sat in the front seat, turned to face me, the shotgun resting on the seat back, his fat arm dangling over, his goddamn finger on the trigger. No one had said a word since they put me in the car.

We were on a dirt road, back in some part of the county I had never seen. Hell, for that matter, the farthest I had been away from the beach since I had gotten there was Homeplace.

I had never seen *any* of the county; I had no idea where the hell I was.

I figured they were taking me out somewhere to kill me. I really did. How the hell did it come to this? I mean, I was too fucking ignorant to be a threat to anybody.

"How'd you know I was staying at Homeplace?" Might as well be curious. Maybe if I could get them talking . . .

"Yew mean Niggertown?" Wimpo's voice was thin and whiny, like I remembered hearing from that time at the bar. And I thought maybe he was drunk.

"Shut up," Polk muttered. "I'll say what has to be said, when the time comes."

What? A prayer at my graveside, you son-of-a-bitch? I tried to sneak a glance at the door handle and Wimpo caught me looking.

"Go on ahead, make a try for 'er," Wimpo whined, punching the shotgun closer to me. "Shoot you in the ass before you get halfway out."

It took all my concentration not to stare at the muzzle of the shotgun. It was an older model pump gun, a 12-gauge, the barrel almost shiny from use. Long Neck would have liked it.

I looked up at the rearview mirror, trying to see Polk's eyes, but the glass was flat and black.

And suddenly I realized that this wasn't Polk's Ford. This car was long and slim, with leather seats and shiny parts all over the dash. This wasn't a police car at all.

Polk stopped the car. He switched the spotlight on, sweeping it along the side of the road. The light found a rotted wooden sign, its thick post crumbling and broken, leaning against a tree.

"Get out," Polk said, still not looking back at me.

I eased out of the car, Wimpo pushing the shotgun out the window at me.

"Go read the sign," Polk ordered.

"What?"

"Go read the goddamn sign! What's the matter with you, boy? You fucking hillbillies can't read, or what?" Polk was getting angry. Wimpo kept the shotgun pointed at my chest.

I moved off the edge of the road and reached for the sign, a few words painted on a plank nailed to the broken post. Polk adjusted the spotlight.

"It says, 'Horry County Line'."

"That's right, boy. You're standing on the Horry County Line. I just want to make sure you know exactly where it is." His voice sounded angrier. He was building up to something. He got out of the car.

"Now, take off your clothes."

Holy shit. I had thought he was going to shoot me. But maybe he was going to fuck me. I thought I'd rather be shot.

"I can't do that." The hell with him. He could shoot me, but if he wanted to do anything else, it was going to take some effort.

But it didn't really. Take any effort, I mean. He was on me before I could take a breath and I was on the ground, face down in the dirt. He spun me over and grabbed the front of my shirt. I heard the shirt rip away — I didn't really feel it go, it just went and I heard it going, a tattered rag in Polk's hands.

He dragged me onto the road and smashed me across the mouth and I could feel the blood pool up behind my lips. He stood up and stepped back.

"Now, I said, get up and take off your clothes."

I did.

There was a coolness in the air that I hadn't noticed before, but standing naked on a back-country road in the middle of the night had a way of bringing such things to my attention.

Wimpo still held the shotgun. Polk gathered up my clothes and took them to the back of the car. I couldn't see what he did with them.

"Now . . . get up there," Polk said, flicking the shotgun at the car.

"Up . . . where?"

"Up *there*, goddammit! Up on the hood!"

Wimpo began to whine again. "Oh, shit, not up there, not up there on my new car!"

"Shut up! Nothing gonna happen to your car," Polk growled.

On the hood of the car. They wanted my naked ass on the hood of the car! Jesus Christ, just like coming home from a deer hunt! I thought about running, just taking off through the woods, but I didn't know where I was and Wimpo still had the shotgun and I heard Polk get in the car and I knew he was behind the wheel again, waiting.

Wimpo weaved just a little, unsteady from the effort of guarding a dangerous hillbilly, the shotgun wavering slightly, his finger still on the trigger. He raised the gun and pointed it straight at my face. I climbed up on the hood of the car.

I sat there, my ass flat against the cool metal, blood dripping from my chin and dribbling down my chest.

Wimpo got in the car, the shotgun poking out the window. I heard the gears change and Polk started the long car rolling backwards, slowly. Out in front of me the lights pulled back from the sign and it disappeared in the blackness at the edge of the road.

I don't know how long Polk backed down the road. Long seconds went by. I could hear the tires rolling on the crushed red mash that was part of every road I had seen in the South, the sound deadening when layers of pine needles covered the road. I could hear insects in the woods. And the moonlight; I could hear the moonlight, I could feel it, knew the touch of it on my skin.

Polk stopped the car.

"I said, none of this is official, boy, but I do want to get your attention." His voice came out of the window, just loud enough for me to hear over the idling engine.

"What we don't tolerate down here, boy, is outsiders messing with the way we do things, with the way we live. You know what I mean, boy? You hear me?"

He was rushing up on something in his mind and I didn't want to try and stop it. It was his show. I said nothing.

"You come down here from the *North*, you mess around with the niggers, work with 'em . . . hell, that don't matter much, we all work with niggers now and again, when we have to.

"But you, hell, boy, you living with 'em. And that ain't right, boy. That's against the law of God, against everything we know is *right and true*."

The car started to roll forward.

Polk was louder now, almost shouting. "And then, you son-of-a-bitch, you messed with my car . . . !"

The car picked up speed, tearing down the road, trees whipping by, a limb now and then catching me in the face or across the chest. I ran my hands around the hood, trying to find something to hang onto. There was nothing.

"And don't let anybody ever tell you," he screamed, "that I DIDN'T GIVE YOUR ASS A RIDE TO THE COUNTY LINE!"

And he slammed on the brakes, locking the wheels.

There are few times in your life when you are free, truly free, and I was free now, alive and vital and sensitive to the smallest things, the smell of thick rushing air, dust motes brushing my face, the sound a pine needle makes when it hits the forest floor, and I knew all of these things were there, all of them, in my world, in the black of night and the pushing wind against my face and the flailing of my arms and legs in freedom so complete, so pure, as I spun almost lazily through the air.

Freedom is a some-time thing. It seldom lasts forever. It begins, and it ends.

My face kissed the soft padding of the forest junk that covered the road, then kissed it harder, then dug into the junk and found the harder parts underneath and my body caught up with my face and passed it, tumbling and sliding, a huge, soft plow smashing open a furrow in the darkness and the dirt, skidding, twisting, bleeding, scraping. I shot off the road and hit the thick signpost, head on. Until then, I was flying in blackness. But there were lights in my head now, brief and sputtering.

O-fficially, I was out of Horry County.

"You think he's dead?"

The whining voice came through some dense wall of pain around my mind.

"Nah. Don't think so. Look's like he don't even have any broken bones. Got a pretty good head bleeder there, though."

My head moved and I thought he was adjusting it, checking out a scalp wound.

"He had a good trip, sure 'nuff."

"Yeah," I heard Polk say through the wall, "might've we set a record with this one. You think?"

"Maybe so. Went about twenty feet in the air. Better than most. Better than that nigger last month. He hardly get any distance a'tall."

"Too thick. Dense, they are. That's why they can't swim nowhere. Sink, like rocks."

"This 'un hit the sign, too. Head on. That never happen before."

Silence. The sound of breathing. My head was beginning to clear behind the pain, but, for once, I was smart enough to lie there and play dead. Damn near was.

A hand grabbed my arm, almost gently, and waggled it.

"She-it," Wimpo said, "it still in one piece." He dropped my arm. "You 'bout ready for that drink, now?"

"Reckon so," Polk grunted. "Man de-serves a drink after a hard night's work."

Feet moved, shuffling along the road. I heard the noise of someone fooling with the car, metal sounds, a door opening maybe, and then nothing for a while. But I didn't hear the car start. And then I heard them laughing, both of them, and the laughing wasn't too far from me and it didn't move and I knew they were sitting there, just down the road, enjoying. They didn't care that I was there. They had disposed of me like a piece of shit in a brown paper bag thrown from a car window. I was no longer in their lives.

One of them turned on the radio and the music rolled out the open doors and painted sounds across the woods. I'm not sure what the song was.

Seems like it went on for hours, the laughing and talking and the music, off there in the near distance, me hearing it, hating it, while I searched my body in my mind, trying to find the hurt places, the pain places. One at a time and very carefully I moved all my bones, stretching, alert now, eyes open, waiting to move a bone and have it refuse and send a shock to my brain that I wouldn't be able to fend off. But all the bones moved; nothing was broken, just like Polk had said. The son of a bitch.

I had knocked the sign post over and I lay partially on top of it. I slid off the thing and sat up, wanting to scream but clamping my mouth shut. I ran my hands over my body and they came away sticky. I was bleeding from a thousand tiny cuts and scrapes, patches of skin missing, pocks gouged in my chest and face, tiny strips of skin flayed back from the wet meat underneath, dirt and pine needles and forest duff coating my body.

But everything worked. I pulled my legs under me and stood up, careful to hang back in the edge of the trees. The car was there, a few yards down the road, pointed back toward the way we came. They must have turned it around while I was passed out because I never heard the engine. The trunk lid was standing full open and high, blocking my view of the inside. The doors were all open, the interior light on, and I could hear them laughing, hooting, howling, a brotherhood of the Confederacy come to a safe place after the battle.

I knew I was finished there at the beach, at the Homeplace, in Horry County, in South Carolina. I finally got the message. I was standing naked and shivering in the fringe of black woods on a back-county road that led off into country I had never seen or thought about, hearing the howling of men who lived by laws of their own making, laws which did not admit me to the safe places of the earth.

It was ended.

They had won and all the rest of us had lost and that's the way it was going to be down here in the South and I wondered if there were other places in the world as good as this, with the soft air and the warm water and sand that toasted your feet and women who stood next to your chair and let you look down into the tops of their bathing suits. Places as good as this, but without Deputy Pork and Wimpo.

Maybe I should go looking for a place like that.

I moved my shaky legs and stepped quietly out onto the road.

Don't ask me why. I meant to walk away from the car, I really did. I meant to point my blood-seeping naked hulk off toward some other place and just get on with it, be done with it, be away from there. Steal some clothes. Hitchhike. Go.

But it just didn't work out that way. And besides, there really was nothing else for me to do.

Before I realized what I was doing, I was standing directly behind the car, the music of the radio pounding against my head; looking into the open trunk. The shotgun was in there.

I didn't reach down in there and pick it up, I didn't. I looked into the trunk and there it was and then it wasn't . . . it was in my hands, cool and hard, a long shiny thing of grace and beauty, a thing I knew about, a thing that cleared my head and made me calm. It just came up in my hands all by itself.

I wondered if Wimpo had been bluffing, wondered if it were really loaded. I eased the pump back just a little and felt inside the breech with my finger, feeling the hard cylinder, the shell, that was nestled there. Wimpo had not been bluffing.

I didn't know how many shells were in the shotgun. Be damn funny, I thought, if there were only one. But why, why on earth, would any man with balls as small as Wimpo's point a shotgun with only one shell in it. He wouldn't. The gun's long magazine was stuffed full of shells. I could count on it.

I stepped to the side of the car, into the glow of the dome light, back into their lives, trash from the roadside returning to them in oozing and stinking presence. Polk was in the front seat looking at Wimpo in the back, Wimpo with a whiskey bottle raised to his mouth. I pointed the shotgun at Polk's chest. His face froze, his eyes fixed on the muzzle of the shotgun. Out of the corner of my eye I saw Wimpo drop the whiskey bottle. He didn't take it down from his mouth, he just dropped it, whiskey still pouring from the neck, unswallowed whiskey running from his mouth.

"There's something I want to know." I was looking at Polk. Wimpo wasn't moving. "What's your first name?"

Polk thought he hadn't heard me correctly.

"What? My first . . . ?"

"I said, WHAT'S YOUR FIRST NAME, YOU SON-OF-A-BITCH!?"

Polk couldn't get his mouth working.

"Clyde," Wimpo said. "His name's Clyde." Except when Wimpo said it, it came out Clahd.

Jesus H. Christ. Deputy *Clyde* Polk of Horry County, South Carolina. Constable *Clyde* Prince of Wayne County, West

Virginia. I guess when God develops the model for a really good asshole, he doesn't break the mold.

"Goodbye, Clyde," I said softly.

And then the song changed on the radio; the sounds of "Mexico" pumped out into the night.

I couldn't stand it.

There was just time to see their expressions change before I flicked the gun a few inches away from Polk and blew the radio out through the back of the dashboard and into the engine compartment.

When the shotgun went off it was like being trapped inside an oil drum with a thunderclap, in the metal middle of it, all the sound beating around the interior of the car in a rush so hard and painful that I backed up a couple of steps, stunned.

Polk and Wimpo screamed and then I screamed because they did and before the screams died down they both rolled out into the road on the far side of the car, instantly up and running toward the trees. I stepped to the side of the car, worked the slide on the gun, swung it up, pulled the trigger and watched as a streak of flame licked out toward the trees above their heads, the heavy pellets cutting through the woods like tiny leaden bees.

But then I thought, why waste it on the trees? I walked around the shiny car, admiring its detail, its beauty, its craftsmanship. And then I tried to blow it all apart. I blew out the windshield, headlights, radiator and tires, working the slide on the long gun with an efficiency that would have made Long Neck proud.

The gun was empty.

My only mistake was standing back to admire my work.

I heard the bullet go by before I heard the shot, or maybe it was at the same time.

We had argued about that a lot, back in Crum. If someone shot at you, and didn't hit you, would you hear the bullet go by? And when would you hear the shot?

And then another shot, slightly different from the first. Pistols. It was just like those southern fucking rednecks to go around with pistols in their pockets. And they probably were good with them, too, just like those hillbilly fucking rednecks on Black Hawk.

I dropped the empty gun and ran through the woods, heading in what I thought was the general direction of the only place I could go — the ocean.

It took me all night and all the next day to find it.

❧ Forty ❧

I was back at the Homeplace.

The rat wasn't there. Maybe he had gone on to other rat business under another house. The dog wasn't there, either. There were no dogs anywhere. It was almost as though they knew the deputy was there, a hulking mound of menace that shouldn't be messed with. I had dived under the house seconds before his car, the Ford, had rolled into the clearing between the houses, boiling dust up into the late evening air.

I was under the house next to the church again, only this time there was no rat and no dog and no singing. I huddled at the far back where the ground rose slightly to meet the house, my back pushing up against some rotting planks, my face in the fine talcum-like dust, my body jammed and caught, my own personal pool of mud growing under me from the water that ran from my naked body. I had fallen in a creek that I didn't know was there, just at the edge of the village.

I shivered from the dank air, and from fear. And every time I moved the dust roiled up and settled on my wet body, an instant layer of thin, fine mud that seeped into every cut and tear on every part of my body. There was a smell under the house that I hadn't noticed before, an ancient scent of dead and fading things, desiccated things, hurtful lives and pain. I rolled over and braced my bare feet against the floor above and tried to pull inside myself, to control my breathing. Tried not to scream. Every breath seemed to rip down my throat in a gasp that I knew could be heard out in the yard. I pulled my arm up over my mouth and nose and tried to muffle the noise, but it only rasped louder in my ears. My head spun and I knew I was probably going to pass out.

There was a knot of ice behind my stomach, a hard, cold fist that was always there in those times of my life when fear began to overpower my mind. My body always reacted to it, seemed to sweep up the fear and gather it into a cold ball and store it behind my stomach where it froze my bile and rose into the back of my throat, choking me. When those times came,

I would be afraid. But it was more than just being afraid. It was feeling the pure essence of fear, a tangible, cold and sour thing that existed beyond any context of being afraid.

And I felt it now.

I thought if he found me, he would kill me. This time, he would surely kill me.

There was still enough thin light filtering down through the heavy pines and dripping on the ground for me to see legs walking across the dirt yard in front of the house. Two sets of the legs faced each other and I could hear angry voices, one of them John Three's, one of them Polk's. Other feet came across the yard and the noise went up a notch. I was glad there was noise out there to cover the noise I thought I was making, still shivering hard, my feet bumping the floor above me, a soft bass drumbeat in hollow blackness.

When I felt the arms come around me my head snapped upward and I bumped the floor even harder, making a soft booming noise that rolled in my ears like a tired wave against a pier. I twisted to the side, trying to roll away, but the arms held me. It wasn't hard to do. I couldn't even have fought off the rat.

The arms relaxed and fingers began to feel along my body, probing, testing for damage, running gently over the mud and the crusted scrapes. I mumbled something and a hand came up and covered my mouth, softly, not a gag but a signal for silence. The hands kept probing and then rubbing, and in another minute my body was being covered by a soft blanket and a warm sweet-smelling body was on mine, under the blanket, holding me, pressing me into the dirt. The rubbing had spread the mud all over me but the mud felt warm now and the rubbing and the blanket and the hot body against me made me feel secure and gradually my shivering stopped. Lips pressed against my cheek and I could feel the silk of hair against my face. And I could smell magnolias.

Evangeline.

"You got to be still," she whispered. "You got to be still."

She was on top of me, holding, pressing, making tiny movements with her legs and arms and hips, sliding her body into every fitted place, her groin pushing into me, her thin dress hiding nothing.

"He'll be gone in a minute. You got to be still until he goes. Can't let him catch you here. Can't let him catch you anywhere." Her hand was still across my mouth, caressing, fingertips trailing along my lips.

I put my arms around her and slid my hands down her back to the roundness of her hips, so full, so perfect, the hips I had seen at the beach, the hips that worked together under the bathing suit, sliding back and forth until I couldn't look at them anymore. And now they were under my hands and I was gripping them, pulling her tightly against me.

Gradually, I relaxed. I could still hear the angry voices from the yard, could hear John Three's rich baritone rising above the coarse grunts of Deputy Polk. Whatever they were talking about, it didn't matter. If Polk didn't know where I was by now, he wasn't going to find me. I didn't care. I was lying under a house in the darkest corner of the darkest world I had ever known, naked, covered with mud, bleeding from a hundred cuts, with a black woman on top of me, my hands gripped firmly to the cheeks of her ass. I had never felt so safe in my life.

She dripped with sweat, the sweet taste of it running down her face and across my lips. Her body was fired, welded to my stomach. I could feel her all the way to her toes. My fingers began to work at the dress and I pulled it slowly up between us until I could feel her flesh under my hands. I was barely conscious, but I knew I had an erection, and I knew she could feel it.

"I didn't crawl under here for this," she whispered against my face.

"I know," I mumbled, "but I . . . I . . ."

"You think you're a black man? Can fuck me just because you're covered with mud? Mud don't make a black man," she said, but she didn't sound angry. Her whispers came softly, flowing gently. "You think because it's black under here you can get into a black woman? You think we're all alike in the dark, darkies and white women?

"I just came under here to keep you quiet. You making so much racket that deputy bound to . . ."

There was a noise, flatter, thicker. A fist hitting flesh. I heard the shuffling of feet and then the rise of a woman's wail through the dappled sunlight and into the soft sides of the houses. And then the sound again.

Polk. It had to be Polk. He had hit someone, someone who was supposed to know where I was. I twisted my head to the side and saw the two sets of legs still there, still facing each other. But other legs were moving into view. Including the largest set of legs I had ever seen.

God, I didn't want to go out there. I honest to God for Jesus Christ sure didn't to go out there. But it was one thing for me to be chicken shit afraid and hide and shake in the mud and darkness; it was something else to let another man take my whipping. I thought about Long Neck and what he might say. If I didn't go out there, maybe I could never think about Long Neck again.

I pushed against Evangeline, trying to slide out from under her. The harder I pushed, the harder she held on.

"Where you think you going?" Her whisper was harsher now.

"He hit somebody out there. He's looking for me. Can't let him keep hitting somebody . . . " I was trying to whisper but my raspy throat made grunting sounds.

"You don't understand how it works down here. You don't just stand up and fight any old way. You have to pick your time and place."

What the hell was she talking about? There was the deputy out there looking for me, beating up on people, and she was lecturing me on combat tactics.

"If I don't go out there, he won't stop."

"He'll stop. You believe me. He *will* stop. See, for once, this is the time, and this is the place."

"Bullshit." I squirmed some more, twisting beneath her, trying to see out from beneath the house.

She slid her hand down my side, raised her hips and I could feel her fingers probing between my legs, wrapping around me, sending flickers of heat through me, tiny firestorms of sensation that nestled in behind my eyes and gathered in my groin until I thought my balls would explode.

"Now you listen to me, you dumb cracker. You go out there, that deputy know for sure we been hiding you. Right now, he's not sure. Right now, he's just showing off. You go out there, he'll know we made him a fool. He won't forget. We'll pay for it later, harder. And if we going to pay for it, we want to pay for something really good, not just a dumb cracker."

All the time she was talking, her fingers were tightening around me.

"You understand? You go out there, you make us pay down the line, and you won't even be here."

"I . . . okay. Okay. Just tell me what to do."

"For right now, don't do anything. It's going to get fixed, right about now."

And then I heard the train-tunnel rumbling voice of Brother Jason, and the fist-hitting sound again. Except, this time, the sound was even harder, flatter . . . the sound of the largest fist in the world hitting a side of beef. I lay there and watched as one set of legs almost lifted from the ground and then tilted backwards, growing longer until I could see the whole body of Deputy Clyde Polk crash into the ground, flat on his back, his head turned and looking straight under the house at me. Out cold.

I quit trying to squirm out from under her.

We lay absolutely still. The sounds from out in front of the house had stopped. In fact, there were no sounds at all, no shuffling, no footsteps. I turned my head, looking through the dark out into the soft yellow light of the park. There were no legs out there. And Polk was gone.

She moved.

She made a small motion with her hand, a tiny adjustment to the universe, and I was inside her. I tried to push up against her but she held me in place, her hips tight, her legs gripping mine.

"Don't," she whispered. "Just lie still. Just because you can't see anyone out there doesn't mean they gone." She moved her hips. "They be gone soon. Soon." Her hips kept moving.

The dizziness came through from the back of my head again and I fought to control it but I couldn't. I don't know if I passed out or if I just fell asleep. Either way, the darkness became complete.

⚰ Forty-One ⚰

Goddammit, I wasn't a northerner. And from what I had seen, I wasn't a southerner, either; didn't want to be; didn't want any part of it. I didn't know if there were any people called easterners, but it didn't matter. I wasn't going east. I was just another West Virginian stuck in a hate warp that I didn't make but which, sure as hell, would suck me in if I stuck around and let it.

So I was going west.

The old Chevy rolled on toward the edge of the county, Yvonne driving, me hunkered down in the back seat with a blanket pulled up to my neck, ready to hide if a sheriff's car went by. The blanket felt good. There was a hard chill in the air and the Chevy had no heater. But it was a Sunday morning and the roads were quiet and we got all the way to the county line without seeing anything that looked like trouble.

Neither of us had said a word since we left Myrtle Beach.

I watched the gray sky slide by the side window and thought about the sound that coins made when they dropped into the jukebox in the pavilion. Clunking, almost jingling sounds. The minutes of a life counted in the minutes of a song.

Thought about how thick the air was when it drifted in off the ocean and wrapped around my back when I walked across the sand; the softness of the rain and how it tasted when it brushed my face while I was swimming.

Thought about a woman wearing a dress and swimming to England.

Thought about flying off Wimpo's hood and the shotgun going off and bits of chrome splintering from the dash.

Thought about Polk lying there in the dirt, surrounded by all the legs of all the men who lived at Homeplace.

Thought about Evangeline. Thought about being taken to Grandmama's house and how, every day, Evangeline and Grandmama would wash my cuts and gouges, and how I ate an entire cherry pie Grandmama had baked, dipping the pieces into the top of a glass of milk, the heavy cream sticking to the crust.

"You going to stay in Myrtle?"

She never turned her head. "Yes. I like it here, Jesse. Got a job at the college. With any luck, I'll never set foot in Wimpo's again."

She had always been the smart one in Crum and now she had a job in a real college, going to school there, too.

"You think I could do that? Go to college?"

"Sure, if you get rid of that accent." She was grinning, looking at me out of side of her eyes. I didn't know what she was talking about.

Then her voice changed, low and soft and I had trouble hearing her over the noise of the old car. "I don't know, Jesse. I think maybe you could, think you're sure smart enough. But there's something about you, Jesse. Something that just seems to follow you around, something that just seems to . . . stir things up."

"I don't mean to do that. Don't mean to do any of it."

"That's just it, Jesse. You don't do it on purpose — well, not most of it, anyway. But it's always there."

Thought about Jason and John Three sitting on the front porch of the little church. You gonna get out of here, find some place safe? I had asked Jason. Boy, there isn't someplace safe, don't you know that? He had looked over at John Three. Nope, no place safe. I ain't going nowhere, white boy. Guess I'll just stay here and see what happens.

Thought about Evangeline coming into my room in the dark, telling me I couldn't go back to work on John Three's boat, telling me John and Jason had enough trouble without trying to cover my pale ass. Telling me it was her idea, me not going back to work on the boat. And I knew she was right, about everything.

Thought about pulling her against me and her saying we couldn't do it here in Grandmama's house. Wouldn't be right. But we found other places. Lots of them.

Yvonne rolled the Chevy off the side of the road and cut the engine.

"We passed the county line about a mile back. Should be okay for you to start hitch-hiking anywhere along here."

I tried to tell from the sound of her voice how she felt, what was going on in her mind. But I couldn't. I climbed out of the car, dragging the little gym bag that Jason had given me. All I had in it was one extra shirt and a piece of soap in a plastic box. For the first time in my life, I didn't have a book.

Yvonne got out of the car and we stood in front of it, leaning back against the grill.

"I guess you'll be going back, now."

"Yes," she said softly, "guess I will." She wrapped her arms around herself against the chill.

"Look, Vonny, I know there's something I'm supposed to say here. Can't just walk off down the road without saying the right words. But I don't know them words, don't know where they supposed to come from . . . just don't want to say the wrong thing . . . do the wrong thing. Again."

She said nothing, just stood there, her chin down against her chest, her eyes not moving.

"Vonny, there's somethin' I have to ask you . . . back there when I first come across you, back there at Wimpo's, when you hit me. Twice. When you come into the room, there, when I was on the cot, you was a'rubbing . . . a'rubbing . . . yourself. You walk right up on me, still a'rubbing yourself. Why . . . ?"

I shut up. I didn't know where I was going, out here on the road, and I didn't know where I was going, here with this question.

Yvonne stood there for some long minutes, not looking at me. Then, "Jesse, you remember back there in Crum, when we wanted out, when we wanted to make money to get out?"

Oh, God. She was going to make me talk about it.

"Goddamn, Vonny, you know I do. I tried to tell you so many times . . . I didn't mean . . ."

"You remember the five dollars?"

The five dollars. I would remember the five dollars as long as I lived, the five dollars spiked through the door of my sleeping shed. For all I knew, it was still there.

"Vonny, I didn't know what to do, back then. I thought you *wanted* the five dollars . . ."

"No. I never wanted the money. Letting Mule feel me up, out there behind the restaurant . . . I just did that to make you notice me, Jesse. You never really seemed to notice me. But I didn't . . . " she paused, searching around for the right word, then came straight out with it " . . . fuck you for the money, Jesse. I didn't. I didn't fuck you for the money. I just wanted you to notice me. That's why I rubbed myself . . . when you were there, on that cot. I just wanted you to notice me."

"But, hell, Vonny, then you went and whacked me across the face . . . "

I saw the tiny pearls of tears begin to form in the corners of her eyes.

"Yes." She paused, gathering something up. "That's when I got over you, Jesse . . . "

I waited, looking at her, waiting for something more, waiting for some sign to tell me what to do. But nothing came except the tears. I had all I was ever going to get.

She kissed me. It was a very light kiss, not like Evangeline kissed, or Rosalind, or even like Yvonne had kissed me in the past, but a kiss better than all of those, a kiss I can still feel brushing softly across my lips.

And then she got in the Chevy, backed it up, wheeled it around, and was gone.

I stood there at the side of the blacktop, clutching the gym bag, watching the Chevy disappear around a gentle curve in the distance. Somehow, my feet didn't want to move just yet.

Thought about Black Hawk Ridge and Great Uncle Long Neck and Crum and about a motorcycle back there in Homeplace with flowers growing out of its mashed-in gas tank.

I finally turned and faced squarely down the road, away from Myrtle Beach.

Thought about Hugo and jellyfish and young girls with their firm little tits pushing up under the wire frames of their bathing suits.

I started walking, my legs resisting at first, then picking up speed. Within an hour I came to a crumbling old blacktop road, running north and south, that crossed the narrow highway, the intersection not even marked with any signs. I stood in the center of the intersection, battered blacktop running away in the four directions.

I didn't know where I was going.

Thought about the West.

There must be some mountains out there, somewhere. Real mountains. With snow. And rivers bigger than the Tug, rivers that could carry actual boats.

Thought about the best hotdogs on the beach. Jason's hotdogs.

Thought about the only preacher I had ever known, ever even seen, who was a real preacher. Thought about that preacher handing me a dollar. Thought about that preacher with a broom in his hand, sweeping unnoticed around the white feet milling through the pavilion.

I walked west.

The crumbling pavement felt good under my feet, a hard surface that led away to other things. In the far distance I could see what I thought was a rise to the land. Higher country.

I walked faster, working up some heat against the snap of the air.

It was getting colder.

Winter was coming on.

End